WISH YOU WEREN'T HERE

PORTIA MACINTOSH

Boldwod

First published in Great Britain in 2025 by Boldwood Books Ltd.

Copyright © Portia MacIntosh, 2025

Cover Design by Alexandra Allden

Cover Images: Shutterstock

A CIP catalogue record for this book is available from the British Library.

Paperback ISBN 978-1-80426-739-4

Large Print ISBN 978-1-80426-740-0

Hardback ISBN 978-1-80426-741-7

Ebook ISBN 978-1-80426-738-7

Kindle ISBN 978-1-80426-737-0

Audio CD ISBN 978-1-80426-746-2

MP3 CD ISBN 978-1-80426-745-5

Digital audio download ISBN 978-1-80426-744-8

This book is printed on certified sustainable paper. Boldwood Books is dedicated to putting sustainability at the heart of our business. For more information please visit https://www.boldwoodbooks.com/about-us/sustainability/

Boldwood Books Ltd, 23 Bowerdean Street, London, SW6 3TN

www.boldwoodbooks.com

For my wonderful readers

1

14 FEBRUARY 2023

I'm not bossy, I'm the boss!

I examine the pink mug in my hand, smiling at the slogan proudly emblazoned across it, before setting it back down on the desk.

I stretch out in the ergonomic chair, my back arching as I settle into a good spot. I kick off my heel and pop my feet on the desk – perfect.

I notice a Post-it, stuck to my elbow, so I rip it off like it's a plaster.

Nice girls don't get the corner office.

Well, ain't that the truth. I don't know how many corner offices are here (well, I guess I technically do, given that there's, y'know, four per floor) but I'll bet most of those belong to men.

The sun is streaming in through the floor-to-ceiling windows (well, streaming might be a bit OTT, given that we're in February). One of the things I love about Leeds Dock is that it always looks beautiful, no matter what season we're in, and even when the weather isn't a spectacle, there is always something interesting to stare at.

There's always plenty to see around the canal, and the boats that moor there – and I do love to watch the cute little water taxis come and go. It's just such a good spot for people watching and, given that our office looks out at the Royal Armouries Museum, it's not unusual to see a knight or hear a cannon being fired.

There's never dull moment around here. Well, apart from all the very, very dull moments, of course.

I let out a contented sigh, rolling my shoulders back and feeling the tension leave my body. This is the life.

A knock at the door jolts me from my thoughts, and I quickly swing my feet down from the desk, my heart racing as I glance up.

Through a little window in the door, I see a man standing there. Wow. He's hot – like if Josh Hartnett had a younger brother kind of hot. Tall, with that effortlessly tousled dark hair, deep-set hazel eyes, and a jawline that you could cut yourself on.

We lock eyes through the glass for a moment, and as his smile widens, I involuntarily suck in a sharp breath. That was weird.

I shake it off, snapping into professional mode.

'Come,' I say seriously, beckoning him forward with two fingers.

I don't know how else to describe his entrance other than by saying he fills the room. Wow, he really is tall. I suppose I am sitting down but I'm not much taller when I'm standing up. If he's 6' 3" or 6' 4" then he's pushing a foot taller than me and I am into it.

'Hello,' he says. 'Jennifer Carter?'

He glances at the nameplate on the door before his gaze lands back on me.

'I'm a busy woman, what can I do for you?' I cut to the chase, trying to sound as authoritative as possible. Oh, God, what am I doing?

'I'm here to fix the computer,' he says, flashing that smile again.

'Oh, finally,' I reply, leaning back in my chair with a faux-exasperated sigh. 'I'm just so, so busy.'

'Let's see if we can get to the bottom of the problem then,' he says, stepping closer.

He looks at the screen from behind me for a second before placing his hands on the desk, one on either side of me.

As he leans in, his face inches from mine, his chest lightly touching my shoulder, all I can think about is how good he smells. I wonder if there's enough physical contact between us for him to feel my heart beating, because it feels like it's jumping out of my chest like I'm a cartoon character.

'What would you say was wrong with it?' he asks, his voice low and silky smooth.

What would I say was wrong with it?

'Oh, you know computers,' I say, puffing air from my cheeks as I bat my hand. 'It's always something.'

Wow, that was just... awful.

'Let's see then,' he says, moving the mouse around, clicking his way deep into the settings. 'I'm surprised you can't fix your own computer,' he muses, glancing at me out of the corner of his eye. 'I would have thought being in charge of a company that builds apps...'

'Well, why have a dog and bark yourself?' I reply, trying to sound nonchalant, but sounding a little bit like an arsehole. 'If everyone fixed their own computers, you would be out of a job.'

'Fair enough,' he chuckles, clearly amused. 'You know, I think it might just need turning off and on,' he eventually says, snapping me out of my thoughts.

'Seriously?' I blurt.

'Could you do the honours, and flick it on and off at the plug?' he asks, stepping aside just enough for me to squeeze past him.

'Okay,' I say, getting up and leaning over the desk to reach the power bar attached to the back of it.

Just as I'm about to flip the switch, I feel a sharp nip on my bum.

'How dare you?' I say, spinning around to face him, trying to channel all the righteous anger I can muster. 'I'm the boss around here, show me some respect.'

The man just laughs, holding up a bright yellow Post-it.

'This was stuck to your arse,' he tells me.

I blink, as my righteous anger quickly fades into pure embarrassment.

'You almost had an HR nightmare on your hands,' I say, reaching out to take the Post-it from him.

He inadvertently reads it as he hands it over and I notice him stifling a smile.

I cringe when I see the words written on it, claiming:

You are worthy of love.

'A Valentine's Day note to yourself?' he asks, still smiling that infuriatingly perfect smile.

'Oh, well, you know, it's not easy being an important woman in an important job,' I reply, trying to play it cool. 'So many men, so little free time.'

'Is there not a Mr Carter then?' he asks, his tone a mix of curiosity and surprise.

'Mr... oh, no, no, there isn't,' I reply.

'So, no Valentine's Day plans?' he continues.

'No, no plans,' I say, trying to keep my voice steady.

'Would you like some?' he asks, his smile growing cheekier by the second. His dimples are everything – the kind of feature you see on a man and think, you know what, you can ruin my life if you want. 'You're turned on, by the way,' he says.

'What?' I blurt, feeling my face flush. Is he a mind reader as well as an IT whizz?

'Your computer,' he clarifies. 'You're turned on, and everything seems okay.'

Oh, there's no way he didn't just do that on purpose.

'Oh, good,' I reply, trying to regain my composure.

Did he just ask me out? Was he joking? I can't tell, but I definitely, definitely want to know.

'So, Valentine's Day,' he says, leaning in slightly as he gets our conversation back on track. 'Every CEO should have a date on Valentine's Day.'

'COO,' I correct him automatically. 'Erm, yeah, okay.'

He opens his mouth to speak but we're interrupted by the door swinging open, banging against the wall, and then...

'I'm here, I'm here,' Jennifer Carter says as she drops her handbag down on the floor.

The real Jennifer Carter, that is.

My heart sinks as she marches straight to the desk, dropping into her chair with a huff. Then she turns her attention to the man and a smile slowly spreads across her lips.

'Oh, you're here,' she says to the man – no doubt changing her tune now that she can see what a hottie he is. 'Can I get you a coffee?'

'Sure,' he replies, glancing at me with a mischievous twinkle in his eye.

'Pemberton, can you get us two coffees?' Jennifer barks at me, her tone sharp.

Shit. I wasn't even supposed to be in here, in her actual office, never mind cosplaying as her to pass the time. If this guy says anything to her about this, I'm dead.

'Pemberton,' Jennifer says slowly and loudly, trying to get through to me. 'Honestly, you can't get the staff, can you?' Jennifer mutters as she turns back to the man. 'My assistant is off, again – she's always bloody off.'

'Annual leave?' the man asks, clearly unsure what else to say.

'Annual bloody maternity leave,' Jennifer replies, rolling her eyes. 'Honestly, that girl is like a log flume. She's a bloody good assistant, when she's here – but you can't fire them for getting pregnant again and again, can you?'

'I don't suppose you can,' he says, looking as uncomfortable as I feel.

'You can't, I've checked,' Jennifer confirms, oblivious to the awkwardness in the room. 'So I've got Pemberton here, from downstairs, who I told to sit *outside* my office and answer my phone...'

'I was just, er—' I start, but the man cuts me off.

'She was just showing me in,' he says smoothly, throwing me a lifeline.

'Oh, well, that's something,' Jennifer says dismissively. 'Come on then, Pemberton, two coffees. I'll take mine black – I'm cutting out milk.'

'Just milk for me,' the man says, turning to me again. 'I'm sweet enough.'

I scurry out of the room, my heart pounding as I head to the small kitchenette next door.

I chew my lip as I make their drinks. He can't have ratted me out yet, because if he had Jennifer would be in here with more steam coming out of her ears than the kettle is currently pushing out, and if he hasn't done it yet then perhaps he isn't going to? I mean, he did just lie for me, so that's something.

I return with their coffees, trying to steady the tray with my shaking hands.

'Just put them down there, Pemberton,' Jennifer says, barely looking up. 'And I'm going to need you to stay up here a bit longer, until the temp arrives. Hold all my calls.'

'Okay, sure,' I say, placing the drinks on the desk before retreating back to the desk outside the office, where I'm supposed to be.

I fidget in my chair, twirling it from side to side, trying to listen in to their conversation but I'm getting nothing through the wall.

After what feels like an eternity, the man finally emerges from Jennifer's office. He closes the door quietly behind him and then saunters over to where I'm sitting, a grin spreading across his face as he approaches.

'Pemberton?' he says, pointing at me.

'That's my last name,' I reply quickly, feeling a little flustered. 'I'm Lana.'

'Ethan,' he says, extending his hand. Now that he's holding me, I don't want him to let go.

'You're not an IT technician, are you, Ethan?' I say, narrowing my eyes at him.

'And you're not Jennifer Carter or a COO,' he replies, making my heart sink. 'I would still like to take you out for Valentine's Day, though.'

Holy shit. Did he just—?

'Er, yeah, okay,' I say, trying not to sound too eager.

'Here's my number,' he says, grabbing a pen from the desk and scribbling on the back of another one of Jennifer's motivational Post-it notes that he must have lifted from her office. This one says:

Your intuition knows her shit.

'Send me a message, so I've got your number, we'll make a plan,' he says with a smile.

'Okay,' I reply, my heart racing – somehow getting faster, I really thought I was at my maximum bpm when Jennifer walked in and almost caught me pretending to be her.

'See you later,' he says, his smile lingering as he turns to leave.

'Yeah, see you later,' I echo.

And just like that, he's gone as quickly as he appeared.

As soon as the door closes behind him, I can't help but kick my legs with glee under the desk. To think, I thought I was going to be spending Valentine's Day alone – not that I cared, because Valentine's Day is shit – but, well, perhaps this one might not be quite as shit as usual.

2

I don't feel well. I'm kind of warm, my heart is beating really fast, my breathing isn't right, and I've got this overwhelming feeling of... oh, God. I'm nervous. I'm not ill, I'm fucking nervous. About a boy. What is going on with me? I don't get nervous before a date and yet here I am, in the ladies' loos, checking my outfit, my hair, my make-up – everything, like he didn't see me at work earlier. The dim lighting in here is more forgiving than the fluorescent lights at the office, and I've spent a couple of hours trying to look my best, but I'm still scrutinising every detail.

My blonde hair falls in soft waves, framing my face in a way that almost hides the nerves – or at least I tell myself it does, because I can sort of hide behind it. I move a strand, ensuring it's perfectly in place.

I'm wearing a black off-the-shoulder minidress that hopefully hugs my curves in all the right places. The idea of a little black dress is a cliché but that doesn't mean it's a bad call. It's the kind of outfit that looks sleek and effortless, without looking like you tried too hard, and it just gives off a cool, confident vibe that you don't really get from anything else. You can wear it to any occasion (even a funeral although, granted, I would probably go for one that covered both shoulders, and probably my knees, but you take my point) and it's almost unreadable. Was it four digits from Prada or two digits from Zara? Do you know who can't answer that question? The kind of guys who go on dates with me (FYI, though, it's the latter).

My red heels add a few inches to my height, making me feel a bit more powerful, even if they're not the most comfortable shoes in the world, and my bright red lipstick goes a long way toward that too.

Finally, I smooth down the fabric of my dress one last time and take a deep breath. Why am I so rattled? I'm no stranger to going on dates – I've been on more than I would have liked – but there's something about Ethan that rattles me.

I sent him my number earlier, and he replied almost right away. That never happens. Boys usually keep you waiting, right? Or maybe it's just the ones I've been seeing. But not Ethan. He told me to meet him at Thin Aire, a rooftop bar in the city centre (something else I'm no stranger to). So here I am, nerves and all, to see if seeing him again gives me that funny feeling in the pit of my stomach.

I step out of the bathroom and make my way through the crowd. It's Valentine's Day, so the place is packed with couples, groups of single women sipping cocktails, and men who are out with their mates – no one wants to spend Valentine's Day alone, do they?

It's a good atmosphere. If anyone is desperate, no one is letting on. Everyone looks like they're having a great time laughing, dancing and drinking – well, those who can actually get to the crowded bar are drinking, anyway.

And then I see him. Ethan. He's standing by the entrance, right on time. Not fashionably late, not even a little bit, just... there. And shit, he looks even better than he did earlier.

He's wearing a sharp dark blazer over a fitted white shirt, the top few buttons casually undone in that way that makes you want to undo the rest – with your teeth. His trousers are slim and stylish, matching his blazer perfectly. There's something about the way the dim lighting of the bar catches his dark eyes that makes them smoulder even more intensely. Christ, do you think he'd marry me?

'Hello,' he says, a warm smile spreading across his face as he steps forward and greets me with a kiss on the cheek. His lips brush against my skin just lightly enough to send a shiver through my body. 'Good to see you again, Jennifer.'

'Har-har,' I say, shaking my head. 'And you, IT support guy. So, what were—'

Before I can finish, the young blonde hostess standing nearby interrupts us.

'It's standing room only, unfortunately,' she tells us with a pout.

'That's okay,' Ethan replies smoothly. He turns to me with a playful look in his eyes. 'Shall we see if we can get to the bar?'

'Okay,' I agree, trying to match his easy confidence and optimism.

We weave through the packed bar. It's boiling in here, prob-ably from all the people, to the point where I want to pretend I smoke just so that I can step out for (ironically) some air. It's not exactly romantic, but I imagine the genuinely loved-up couples have gone somewhere more intimate – although it feels quite inti-mate in here, given how close some people are pressing their bodies against mine as they squeeze past me.

As we reach the bar, I notice a few couples scattered among the crowd, but mostly it's groups of friends, presumably of single people, who don't have dates and refuse to stay in alone, even if it is a Monday.

'So, what were you actually doing at the office?' I ask, curious about how he ended up there in the first place.

It's loud in here so my sentence increases in volume with each word.

'I was there for a job,' he replies, leaning in a little so I can hear him better.

'Wow, we really are short-staffed if Jennifer is the one interviewing you,' I say, half-joking. 'How did it go?'

He shrugs, but there's a hopeful something in his eyes.

'I'm not sure. I guess we'll see.'

'Oh, you're not one of those optimists, are you?' I reply. I can't help but smile at his sunny outlook. 'You must be, to think you can give a girl a good date on Valentine's Day at the last minute. Surely everywhere good is booked up, and everywhere else is rammed?'

'That's where you're wrong,' he replies. Oh, I can see the mischief all over his face. 'Did you ever see that movie, *Yes Man*?'

'No,' I admit, though I can't help but smile at the irony.

'Well, that's what we're going to do tonight,' he explains. 'Anything anyone asks us, offers us – anything – we're going to say yes.'

I narrow my eyes at him, trying to figure out his angle.

'Is this some kind of loophole to get me into bed?' I check. 'You ask and I have to say yes?'

He chuckles, shaking his head.

'It isn't. In fact, let's say that's the only question where we can say "no" to each other,' he clarifies. 'And it goes both ways – don't think I haven't seen you undressing me with your eyes.'

I burst out laughing.

'Okay, let's do it.'

As we finally reach the front of the bar, Ethan drums with his hands on the bar top enthusiastically.

'What do you recommend?' Ethan asks him. 'Whatever it is, we want two of them.'

The barman rubs his chin.

'You two look like you can drink,' he points out. 'Is that right?'

'Yes,' Ethan replies, kicking things off.

I can, so that's fine.

'How about a couple of our Zombies?' the barman replies. 'Strongest in the city, here.'

'Yes,' Ethan says. 'We'll take two.'

'What, two each?' the barman replies.

I don't think that's what Ethan meant but he looks to me with a smile.

'Yes,' I say, my voice a little unsure.

'Yes,' Ethan says, echoing me.

'Yes!' I say again, laughing this time.

The barman raises an eyebrow, but he doesn't question it. He sets about mixing our drinks, and I can't help but watch Ethan out of the corner of my eye. There's something about him – his confidence, the way he carries himself – that's different from the other guys I've been out on dates with. It's like he knows exactly who he is and what he wants, and he's not afraid to go after it.

'Okay, we need somewhere to sit, if we're drinking two of these,' Ethan says, scanning the crowded bar.

As if on cue, a man standing nearby overhears us and leans in.

'We're just popping out for a smoke,' he says, nodding toward the group of guys he's with. 'You can have our table while we're gone, if you want. Save it for us, what do you reckon?'

'Yes,' Ethan replies without hesitation, and just like that, we've got ourselves a table.

We settle in, our Zombie cocktails in hand (well, hands technically), and I take a sip. It's strong, but surprisingly good. The alcohol hits me right away, warming me from the inside out, making me kind of dizzy. Yeah, okay, wow, these are strong.

'Oh, boy,' Ethan says. 'You could clean the bar with this stuff.'

'Where are you from?' I ask, noticing a hint of an accent that isn't local.

'London,' he replies. 'But I'm up here for work. I'm living with my parents at the moment and they're on my case about when I'm going to get my life together, so that's fun.'

I feel a pang of sympathy.

'I get that,' I tell him. 'My parents – well, my dad and my stepmum – are exactly the same. They're always banging on at me about getting a real job – whatever that is – settling down, getting married, having kids – and I only turned twenty-eight a couple of weeks ago.'

'I just turned thirty,' he tells me, widening his eyes for effect. 'As far as my parents are concerned, the best years of my life are over.'

'And how old are they?' I ask, stating the obvious.

'A thousand,' he replies dramatically.

I laugh, relieved to find someone who understands.

'Mine think I'm some kind of wild child, because I don't want to settle down yet,' I tell him. 'And of fucking course I have a perfect little sister who is doing everything they want. But I just like to have a good time, and honestly, I'm happy with my job right now – well, in theory. I'm not exactly loving working for Jennifer. I'm tempted to get on maternity leave just to avoid her.'

Ethan chuckles, shaking his head.

'It's fine to be a wild child, and it's fine not to want to settle down yet – or ever,' he reassures me.

'Yeah, except they think I'm smoking crack and having orgies every night,' I tell him. 'When in reality I only do that every other night – I'd be shattered.'

Ethan laughs at my joke, which gives me the flutters, but before I can continue my stand-up set I notice one of the men has returned to the table. He looks back and forth between us, clearly trying to figure something out.

'You two together?' he asks bluntly.

Ethan hesitates only for a second before replying, 'Yes.'

Ah, the game. Of course. Silly me.

The man's eyebrows shoot up in surprise.

'You in an open relationship then?' he asks. 'Just, with the, er, the orgies...'

Again, Ethan nods.

'Yes.'

The man smirks, leaning in closer.

'Fancy a third person joining you tonight?' he suggests. 'Me, I mean, obviously. I've always wanted to try something like that.'

Oh, boy. I'm about to politely decline his offer when I catch Ethan's look – a subtle reminder of the game we're playing. I roll my eyes but play along.

'Yes?' I tell him, my voice shooting up at the end of the word, like my lips can't quite believe I'm making them say it.

'Fucking ace,' the man says, slurring his words a little. 'I'm going to get another drink – can I get you guys another?'

'Yes,' Ethan replies without missing a beat.

'Are they Zombies?' the man checks, noticing the drinks in front of us – he doesn't even acknowledge that they're not empty. 'Two more Zombies?'

'Yes,' I say, laughing at the absurdity of it all.

Our new friend – and potential threesome partner (I know we're playing the yes game, but we're not doing that) – greets two of his friends at the bar. He talks to them, waving his arms around, performing some kind of charade... oh, it's shagging. Then he points at us.

One of his friends strolls over, looking amused.

'He's bragging about going home with you two,' he says, glancing between us. 'He says you're going to let him have a go on your bird.'

He's looking at Ethan who – of course – says yes.

'Him?' the man says in disbelief. He obviously thinks his friend is punching – and he definitely is, in this respect. If I was going to roll the dice on bringing another man into the mix (multitasking isn't my strong suit – I've never been able to pat my head and rub my tummy) then it would have to be someone seriously worth it, like Jake Gyllenhaal or Tom Hardy. Oh, the audacity. Even thinking about the two of them jumping into bed with me feels pretty bold of me, given that they're movie stars, and I'm me.

'He's paying you, right?' the man checks. 'He must be.'

Ethan smirks.

'Yes.'

The friend laughs, shaking his head in disbelief.

'Wait, are you two... are you two... do you like, charge for sex and that?'

I stifle a laugh, nodding.

'Yes.'

The friend widens his eyes and then walks away, all of his questions clearly answered.

'Does this game ever end in tears?' I ask, turning to face Ethan.

He just shrugs and smiles.

'I don't know. I've never played it before,' he tells me.

I raise an eyebrow at him.

'You should have said yes, according to the rules of the game,' I point out.

Ethan grins, leaning in closer.

'I can't imagine this night ending in tears.'

Before I can respond, the blonde hostess reappears with two doormen in tow. She looks at us sternly, hands on her hips.

'I'm going to have to ask you to leave – for soliciting.'

'What? Really?' Ethan asks, feigning surprise.

The hostess narrows her eyes.

'*Were* you soliciting?' she asks.

Ethan looks at me, then back at her, a slow smile spreading across his face.

'Yes.'

He turns to me, extending his hand.

'Shall we take this party somewhere else?' he asks.

I smile, taking his hand.

'Yes.'

And for the first time all night, I really, really mean it.

3

The night air is crisp, maybe a bit too crisp for my liking as I lean against the wall in one of the tunnels under the bridge by the train station. It's late, but the road is still busy with cars, and the pavement is still busy with people walking past us.

I'm leaning to steady myself because, after a night of saying yes to every drink I was offered, I'm feeling a little unsteady on my feet.

I'm the nice kind of drunk though, where everything's just a little bit funnier and the world just looks and feels softer. Life's all right sometimes, isn't it?

The lights overhead cast a warm glow on the wet pavement, and while I know that I'm cold, I don't seem to be feeling it in the same way I would if I were sober.

Ethan's standing next to me, leaning against the wall like a cool guy, smiling contentedly.

Tonight has genuinely been nothing short of amazing – I can't stop smiling either. The only thing that is missing is a soundtrack, for me to pretend I'm in a quirky, romantic indie movie.

'Well, thanks for an awesome Valentine's Day, Lana,' he says, his voice loaded with that warm, easy charm that seems to come naturally to him. 'You saved me from a night of solo activities... so to speak.'

I giggle, a sound I would usually hate coming from my own mouth, but tonight it feels just right.

'Thank you for making mine so... different,' I say.

'Different isn't always good,' he replies, his tone teasing but with a hint of something deeper.

I tilt my head, meeting his gaze, and wait for a second for the world to stop spinning.

'That's true, but this time, it is.'

All at once, it feels like the entire world fades away. The noise of the city disappears, the lights blur into the background, and it's just us, locked in this perfect moment. I don't want it to end.

Then, suddenly, it's like everything clicks into place. Ethan leans in, closing the distance between us, and my heart feels like it's going to beat its way through my chest. When our lips meet, it's electric – literally, it's almost like he gives me a static shock that shoots through every nerve in my body. I've never felt anything like it before. I'm kissing him back before I even realise it, my arms wrapping around his neck, pulling him closer, deeper, needing more.

I lock my arms around his neck as he cups my arse in his hands, steadying me as the world spins just a little faster. We're completely lost in each other, like nothing else matters.

Well, apart from breathing, I guess. As Ethan pulls back to take a breath, I have to physically stop myself from chasing his lips. My tongue tingles, still craving his touch, as I catch my breath.

'Before I ask you this,' Ethan says, his voice soft and serious, 'I just want to make it clear that you no longer have to say yes to everything.'

He pauses, biting his lip in a way that makes me want to throw all caution to the wind.

'I'm staying at a hotel, just along The Calls. Do you want to come back with me?'

The question hangs in the air between us, and for a moment, my mind races. I do. Here it is, the moment where I have to decide if I'm going to be the girl who says yes to everything, or if I'm going to do something different for once. Because, yes, I really, really want to go back to his hotel with him – of course I do, he's the hottest man I've ever met. But at the same time, I can't shake this feeling that Ethan isn't just another hot guy, maybe he could be something more, and maybe rushing things would be a mistake. This doesn't feel like just another one-night stand, and that scares me as much as it excites me. Maybe this time, I should do the thing I never do – take it slow.

My lips part, ready to say something, anything, but the words get stuck somewhere between my brain and my mouth. Thankfully, Ethan seems to get the message.

'Can I walk you home instead?' he offers, his voice gentle and understanding.

'I live in Headingley,' I tell him, feeling a pang of regret already. 'I'll have to get a taxi.'

I know I should say something to let him know I'm not turning him down because I'm not interested (because I am, I really am), but before I can figure out how to phrase that, my phone buzzes in my bag. I pull it out and see my dad's name on the screen.

'Oh, God, it's my dad,' I say, half laughing, half worried. 'I'd better answer. It's late; it could be an emergency.'

I hit the answer button, and my dad's voice comes through, clear as day.

'Dad? Is everything okay?' I ask.

'Lana? Everything's fine,' he replies.

'I worried, when I realised how late you were calling,' I point out.

'Oh, we're in Australia,' he says, as if that explains everything. 'It's morning here. I didn't think about the time difference.'

'You're in Australia?' I repeat, stunned.

Ethan, ever the gentleman, leans in and whispers: 'I'll go to the taxi rank over the road and book your lift home.'

I nod, appreciating him keeping his voice quiet enough that my dad doesn't hear it.

'Yeah, we're in Australia,' Dad continues, his voice echoing a bit.

'Hurry up, Walter,' I hear my stepmum in the background.

My parents split up when I was really young and even though Dad stayed in our nice family home, I wanted to live with my mum. We lived in a tiny house, on the outskirts of Leeds – but to be honest, I was much happier living in a small house without warring parents than I was living in a big house trying to avoid their arguments. Mum met someone, a few years back, and moved to Connecticut to live with him and his family – and she really does seem so happy. Dad met someone else too – Beatrix – very soon after the split, and had another daughter with her, so I have a half-sister called Persephone who is my polar opposite in almost every way. Dad was a banker (although I've heard Mum pronounce it differently) but it was only after he and Mum split that he hit the big time at work (and rolling in it will always be the easiest way to get a new wife, especially a snooty one like Beatrix). Dad has been retired for a while now – he's one of those already old-money men who got even more rich off the back of, I don't know, stocks, and financial crashes. Basically, if you can't afford a house right now, it's probably because of something my dad did years ago.

I guess you could say, in this divorce, I'm the only one who didn't land on her feet. In case you were wondering, no, the family wealth does not trickle down – not to me, at least. It's more like it's funnelled to his new family. Aside from offering to pay for our schooling (boarding school though, which I obviously declined as a kid), Dad and Beatrix very much believe that kids should not be bankrolled by their wealthy parents into adulthood. I would be surprised if they were funding Persephone's Paris Hilton circa-2004 lifestyle but it doesn't really matter because Persephone has a boyfriend who is happy to keep her in the lifestyle she's accustomed to. How would I describe Chester's level of wealth? Stinking rich, old money. The man plays polo with royals – that rich.

'We have news,' Dad continues. 'You're on speaker. I'll let your sister tell you... Seph, lean in so Lana can hear you.'

Oh, wow, they're all there.

'Lana? Can you hear me?' my sister says, her voice getting louder as she gets closer to the phone.

'Yep, Seph, I can hear you,' I reply. 'So, you're all in Australia, eh?'

'Yep, the gang's all here,' she says – confirmation I'm not in 'the gang'.

'Are you out?' Chester's voice cuts in, and I can practically see the smug grin on his face. 'Are you out partying, Lana?'

I grit my teeth.

'No,' I lie, not wanting to give him the satisfaction.

I can see a group of lads in fancy dress approaching me, on their way to their next drinking spot, so I try to step out of their way.

'I'm so wasted,' a bloke dressed as a prisoner screams. He stops in his tracks as I catch his eye. 'Hey, baby, you ever had a convict go down on you?'

He couldn't have timed that any worse if he tried.

'I'm watching TV,' I tell my family, who you can bet heard that, as I wave the drunk man away.

'You sound like you're on to a promise there, girl,' Chester chuckles.

I detest the way Chester talks to women, almost like we're horses.

'Anyway,' Seph continues, clearly done with small talk, 'we have news. We're engaged!'

And just like that, the world stops turning again, but not in the fun, romantic way it did with Ethan. No, this is more like the kind of world-stopping where you're not sure if you want to scream or cry or laugh hysterically.

It's not that I begrudge my sister getting married, or that I'm jealous, and please don't think I'm making this all about myself, but I'm terrified of what this means for me. My baby sister is getting married – she's lapping me – and at this point it goes beyond how I feel about it, it's more about how other people are going to make me feel about it, like it's a competition and I'm losing... despite not actually competing. Then again, I might be wrong.

'She's speechless,' Chester points out.

'She's jealous,' Beatrix adds, with that perfect blend of condescension and faux concern that only she – my literal wicked stepmother – can pull off.

'Yeah, sorry I'm beating you to it, sis,' Seph says, not sounding the least bit sorry.

'What? Don't be daft,' I say quickly, forcing a laugh that

sounds more convincing in my head. 'Sorry, the line isn't great, but I think I heard you right. Wow, congratulations, guys!'

'This is us letting you know we've set a date too,' Seph continues. 'And it's going to be a destination wedding, so just keep February free, okay?'

'This February?' I ask, feeling like I've missed a step.

Beatrix scoffs.

'You're such a silly goose,' Seph tells me, laughing, and it's a sound that grates on my nerves. I hate it when she calls me a 'silly goose' – what is it with some people who think they can insult you so long as they call you 'silly goose' instead of a 'dumb bitch'? Obviously I know what she means. 'You clearly have no idea how long dream weddings take to plan,' Seph points out.

I would have thought that would be obvious.

'Right, okay, next year,' I say, trying to keep up.

'Lana, honestly,' Seph replies, like I'm being an even sillier goose now. 'February 2025. These things take time to plan – especially if we're doing it out here.'

'You're getting married in Australia?' I repeat.

'Yep, Sydney. Keep up,' Seph says.

'My rentals live out here now, they've got a beaut place,' Chester adds.

Rentals is posh for parents, in his world, apparently. I don't think Chester has ever rented a thing in his life.

'So, February, after my birthday?' I check.

'She's making it about her,' Beatrix whispers, like she doesn't know how speakerphone works. Then again, this is Beatrix, so she probably does.

'To be honest, we hadn't thought about that,' Seph says, and I can practically hear her rolling her eyes. 'There might be some crossover with dates, but it's not exactly an awful place to celebrate, is it?'

I can feel my blood beginning to boil. Not only is no one acknowledging that her wedding is probably going to overshadow my thirtieth birthday, but they're all acting like this isn't a big deal that one might get in the way of the other. Well, if something (or someone) has to give, you know it will be me.

'I can't... you're... I... can yo—' I say, then fake some static in my voice to make it seem like the line is bad.

'She can't hear us,' my dad says.

'Hopefully we stopped whatever poor decision she was about to make,' Beatrix adds.

'Oh, we know Lana, she'll find someone to carry on through the night with,' Seph adds.

Right, that's enough of that. I hang up before I hear what else they have to say, because the urge to say something back is overwhelming.

I finally let out the breath I didn't realise I was holding as Ethan joins me again.

He gives me a look, like he's concerned, and somehow it only makes him hotter.

'Seemed like a long call, so I held off on your taxi,' he says. 'How are things down under?'

He says this in a spot-on Aussie accent that makes me laugh despite everything.

'Wow, you're great at the accent,' I tell him. 'Are you actually Australian?'

That might be the only thing that could make him even sexier still.

'My dad's from New Zealand,' he says. 'And I know, that doesn't explain it, but my mum was from here and they talked about living somewhere between the two places. Anyway my dad won and we lived in Australia – or over the ditch as he called it –

for a few years when I was a kid. It made me cool, over there when I went, and over here when I came back.'

I smile as his easy conversation melts away some of the tension that has built up in my shoulders. Being around him is like being on something. Whatever he's putting out, I'm breathing it in, and it's giving me a high.

'Oh, I bet,' I reply. 'You would be too powerful if you had that going for you now. An Aussie accent and I might've said yes to going back to your hotel...'

'Oh, really?' he replies.

I don't want to say that interacting with my family has egged me on – like, if they think I'm out having fun then I may as well be – but it did give me a moment to pause and rethink my decision. When something worth grabbing is on offer do I want to be the kind of person who plays it safe, or do I want to be the kind of person who says yes?

'Yes.'

'Fair dinkum,' he says with a grin, as he slips back into the accent. 'Let's stop carrying on like a couple of pork chops and head off.'

I should probably find this ridiculous, but I don't. I'm way into it. In fact, his silly, jokey accent is the reason I practically throw myself at him, our lips meeting again with a force that leaves me breathless.

'The Calls, you say?' I check between kisses, my heart racing.

'Yeah,' he replies, taking my hand.

'That's not far,' I say, dragging him in the right direction. 'This way.'

It's only supposed to be a short walk, but it feels like a marathon when we keep stopping to kiss every few steps – under the train arches, in the courtyard outside the Marriott. At one point, a group of friendly drag queens even cheers us on as Ethan presses me against the wall of Viaduct Showbar, the heat between us building with every touch.

With the hotel almost in our sights, we manage to tear ourselves apart for long enough to make it there, and I'm even more relieved when he leads me to his ground-floor room, because the thought of being inside a small lift (even for less than a minute) with him feels like it might be too much to take.

Ethan unlocks his room and leads me inside. Bizarrely, now that we're in here together with the door locked and no audience, there's a bit of distance between us. I'm almost enjoying it, the anticipation, the wondering about what's going to happen next...

Ethan approaches me slowly and drops to his knees in front of me. Wondering what he's going to do makes my knees feel weak – like, literally weak, like I need to sit down, and with his face being just inches from my body there are no prizes for guessing what I have in mind.

He doesn't touch me though, he reaches behind me, into the minibar. Eventually he returns to eye level with a bottle of champagne in his hand.

'Drink?' he suggests.

'Sounds great,' I reply.

I watch him as he fusses with the bottle for a second. Yes, I want a drink, but I want him even more.

I throw myself at him again, the two of us snapping together magnetically, knocking the (thankfully unopened) bottle from his hand. We kiss, only for a few seconds, before parting again.

Ethan picks up the bottle and goes to remove the cork. I want to tell him to stop but my drunken reflexes aren't up to it. The words don't come out in time and as he pulls the cork away the champagne erupts from the bottle, spraying us both.

'Bathroom,' I tell him quickly, noticing the open door behind him.

Ethan runs into the bathroom and steps into the large shower. The champagne is showing no signs of stopping so Ethan just holds it helplessly, laughing wildly at the ridiculousness of it all.

I'm soaking wet so I step into the shower with him. I lean over the bottle and drink from it, like it's a garden hose on a hot day.

This just makes Ethan laugh even harder.

'No point wasting it,' I point out.

'Fair enough,' he replies, but as he goes to drink from the fountain it quickly dies down to nothing.

'Ah, tough luck,' I say with a pout. 'It really does taste better, from anything but a glass.'

Ethan licks his lips. I would imagine they're like mine – and the rest of my body – which is seriously sticky.

'Oh, well, I can think of a way to test that,' he says.

He leans forward and starts kissing my neck, slowly working his way down until he's practically licking the champagne from my chest.

'Mmm, you might be right,' he tells me.

'We should probably get this off, before we go back through there,' I point out. 'We don't want to make a mess.'

'Fair enough,' he replies.

In one swift movement, Ethan reaches out and turns on the large shower head that hovers above us. As the initially freezing cold water crashes down over us I squeal.

Of course, the second Ethan peels off his shirt and drops his trousers, revealing his muscular, underwear-model-type body, I forget how cold I am. He reaches forward to help me remove my dress so I turn around, so he can undo my zip.

He lets my dress fall away before pressing his body up against my back, pinning me to the cool tiles.

I know, I know, I'm rushing into things, but I just keep thinking about Jennifer's motivational Post-it that Ethan wrote his number on.

Your intuition knows her shit.

Tonight I'm going with my intuition, not my common sense, and maybe it's a recipe for disaster but tonight... maybe I don't care?

4

The shrill sound of my alarm practically punches me awake, dragging me out of a dream that I've already forgotten. Ugh. It feels way too early for this, and my head is pounding.

I fumble around for my phone, to silence the alarm, to try to stop the high-pitched tone vibrating through my skull. When it finally stops I let out a groan, because if my alarm is going off, that means it's a workday.

I rub my eyes, trying to get them to accept the fact that they have to open, and that's when it hits me. Oh my God. My eyes snap open as I suddenly realise where I am and what I've done. I'm in a hotel room – Ethan's hotel room. And not just in his room. I'm in his bed.

I stare up at the wall in front of me, given that I'm lying on my side, and it's like there is a projector showing scenes from last night on the blank space as the flashbacks come in thick and fast, in all their horny glory. Bloody hell, no wonder I feel like I barely slept – I don't recall spending much time on my back. I feel exhausted, but... in a good way?

Just as I'm wondering how to navigate things this morning,

there's a soft knock at the door. I freeze, my heart leaping into my throat. Ethan shifts beside me, and I feel the bed dip as he gets up to answer it.

There's a murmur of voices, Ethan's low and soothing, the other person's too soft to make out. I take a deep breath and slowly roll over, the throbbing in my head intensifying with the movement.

When I open my eyes again, Ethan is walking back toward the bed, pushing a large room-service trolley loaded with all sorts of things. He looks unfairly good for this hour – hair tousled in that sexy, effortless way and a grin that's just too charming for my poor sleep-deprived brain to handle.

'Breakfast,' he says. 'I thought you might appreciate something to eat, before work.'

'How are you perfect in the morning too?' I blurt.

'Thanks,' he says with a smile as he pours two cups of coffee.

'It's definitely a compliment but I think I need an answer,' I reply, laughing softly to myself.

Is he real? This godlike man standing in front of me, with nothing but a towel wrapped around his waist, pouring me a cup of coffee.

He sits down on the bed next to me, handing me my cup. I take a sip and, ugh, it's heaven.

'That's so good, thank you,' I tell him, setting it down on the bedside table. 'This place is... wow, it's really nice. So fancy.'

'Yeah, it's all right, isn't it?' he replies. 'It's so hi-tech though. Look.'

Ethan dumps no less than four remote controls down on the bed.

'Beyond the TV one, I have no idea,' he admits.

'I wonder if one makes the bed do something,' I say, picking one up to examine it. 'The only thing I'm missing is a massage.'

'Is that a hint?' he asks.

'It wasn't, but...'

Ethan moves over, so that he's sitting behind me, with one leg on either side of me. He starts working on my shoulders with his thumbs and, wow, that's incredible.

'Oh my God, you angel,' I practically groan. 'Mmm.'

'Don't make noises like that, you're giving me flashbacks,' he jokes.

'Would a little memory refresh be such a bad thing?' I reply.

Taking the hint, Ethan leans forward and starts kissing my neck. I lean back into it, letting him wrap his arms around my body, holding me close.

'Your breakfast will go cold,' he whispers into my ear.

'I'll get over it,' I reply.

I drop forwards, onto my elbows, as Ethan takes my hips in his hands.

Obviously I'm a little distracted, but I am vaguely aware of a quiet but strange noise coming from somewhere in the room. It's only when I open my eyes that I realise the room is suddenly much lighter, and the blinds are open, and we're on the ground floor and, oh God, we're starting to catch the attention of people walking by on their way to work.

'Oh my God,' I blurt.

'The blinds!' Ethan says.

He grabs the duvet from under us and quickly pulls it down over us, leaving us hiding in a sort of bed den.

'What happened?' I ask him. 'And what are we going to do? People are looking – how do we close them?'

Ethan just laughs.

'I think you leaned on a remote,' he tells me. 'I think this one might be for the blinds.'

He pushes a button and sure enough we hear that sound again.

I dare to peep out from under the covers and sure enough the room is in near darkness again.

'I wonder if everything we do will be chaotic,' I say, seeing the funny side. Well, you have to see the funny side, don't you, when you accidentally commit an indecent act in front of an audience?

'I hope so,' he replies. 'I'd really like to see you again. Tonight, maybe? While I'm still in Leeds?'

'I'd really like that,' I say, trying to keep my cool, even though I can feel a smile yanking at my lips.

'Great,' he says. 'I'll message you the details later.'

I nod, already thinking about what I'm going to wear, wondering where we'll go, wishing that I didn't have to go to work – shit, work!

'I should probably get ready for work,' I say reluctantly, grabbing my coffee for another sip. 'Actually, I really need to get a move on if I'm going to have time to apply the emergency make-up I keep in my desk.'

Ethan chuckles, shaking his head slightly.

'You look beautiful as you are,' he says, and I almost believe him, but a quick glance in the mirror tells me otherwise. Bed hair and smudged mascara from the champagne-explosion-shower combination will definitely get people at work talking. I keep a simple white blouse in my drawer too, just in case I ever end up pulling an all-nighter, and don't have time to go home. A plain white shirt over any dress makes it look instantly businesslike.

'Thanks,' I reply, blushing just a little. 'But you know what Jennifer is like.'

I slide out of bed, gather my clothes, and head toward the bathroom with a smile that almost makes my face ache.

'Looking forward to later,' Ethan calls after me, and there's something in his tone that makes me think he actually means it.

'Me too,' I call back, before shutting the bathroom door behind me. Yep, privacy, for the girl who showered champagne from her boobs in front of him.

As I turn on the tap and splash my face with cold water, I catch a glimpse of myself in the mirror. There's a sparkle in my eyes, one that I haven't seen in a long time, and a lightness in my chest that makes everything feel... possible? Oh my God, what am I saying? That's so cringe but... I don't know, I guess it's been a long time since I've felt this happy, and hopeful and, for the first time in ages, I'm actually going on a second date. I know, it's hardly wedding bells like my sister, but it's a start, right?

5

I'm sitting at my desk, I'm tapping away on my keyboard, and I am working but everything I'm doing today is very much on autopilot because all I can think about is last night – and when I'm not thinking about what happened last night, I'm thinking about what might happen tonight.

I keep smiling to myself, like a crazy person, but it's that image of him – the last thing I saw before I left him this morning – the look on his face, like I was the only person in the world.

At the desks across from me, Faye and Molly are deep in conversation, and if they were talking about work then it would be something to do with... data? Honestly, I've never been entirely sure. Something to do with algorithms or analytics – I assume they're different things? This place is techy beyond my GCSE IT qualification. My role here is more to do with admin and managing the general office chaos, and sometimes I can't shake the feeling that they look down on me for not speaking their techy language. They're besties, with their own secret code and in-jokes that always make me feel a bit like an outsider. One time, when they did bring me into their conversation, they both agreed that I wasn't a 'girl's girl', whatever that is, but apparently there's no greater crime when it comes to girl code.

'Mark texted me this morning, so he obviously enjoyed last night,' Molly says, her tone making it clear that something happened between them. 'He wants to see me again tonight.'

'Already?' Faye raises an eyebrow, clearly impressed. 'What did you say?'

'I haven't replied yet,' Molly says, leaning back in her chair with a satisfied smile. 'And I'm not going to, at least not for a while.'

'Good idea,' Faye agrees, nodding. 'You don't want to seem too available.'

'Why?' I ask.

I can't help it. The question just slips out before I can stop myself.

Both heads swivel toward me. Molly gives me a look like she's not sure if I'm serious or just clueless.

'You can't give them everything they want right away,' Molly explains, her tone dripping with that condescending edge that gets my back up. 'You've got to hold back a bit, make him work for it.'

I raise an eyebrow, genuinely confused.

'But if you've already slept with him, isn't that giving him what he wants? I mean, if you asked most guys if they'd prefer a night together or a text, they'd probably choose the night together,' I point out. 'So... you're making him wait for a text?'

Molly thinks for a moment, questioning if I may be on to something.

Faye rolls her eyes, leaning forward as if she's about to put me in my place.

'That just shows the kind of guys you've been hanging out with, Lana. It's important to get the upper hand from the start.'

I resist the urge to roll my eyes right back at her.

'I don't know,' I reply. 'I just don't think men are that complicated. If you don't reply to their messages, they're not going to think you're playing hard to get. They'll think you're not interested.'

Molly shakes her head like I'm some naïve child who just doesn't get it.

'And that's why you're single,' she tells me.

I decide not to say anything back, deciding it's not worth getting into with the two of them. If this is what it means to be a 'girl's girl', then I'm fine sticking to my own rules.

I turn back to my screen, focusing on the email in front of me, because the sooner I crack on with work, the sooner it will be time for my date.

'Hi, Lana,' a familiar voice says, and I look up to see Steve sitting on the edge of my desk.

Steve is exactly the sort of guy you would imagine working in a place like this. I feel like you would just know he wrote code, even if he didn't tell you – even if you didn't even really know what that meant. He's got sandy brown hair that's perpetually tousled, like he's just run his fingers through it, and brown eyes that are kind and unassuming.

He comes and sits on my desk most days, for a quick chat, while he's going to and/or from the coffee machine. I don't feel like I know him all that well but he's nice enough – and he's never accused me of breaking girl code, which is a plus. Wow, perhaps I really am a guy's girl.

'Hey, Steve,' I say, forcing a bit of cheer into my voice. 'How's your day going?'

He shrugs, a lopsided grin on his face.

'Not bad, just can't believe it's only Tuesday,' he replies.

'I know what you mean, I feel like I've been here all week,' I joke. 'It will be the weekend before you know it.'

'Let's hope so,' he says, and there's a pause, like he's gearing up to say something else. He scratches the back of his neck, looking almost shy. 'Hey, I was wondering... do you fancy grabbing a drink sometime?'

'Oh,' I say, caught off guard.

'Like a date?' Molly chimes in, giving away that she's been listening this whole time.

Faye's head snaps up so fast I'm surprised she doesn't get whiplash.

'Well, yeah,' Steve says, glancing at her before looking back at me. 'What do you reckon, Lana?'

Oh, boy. Steve and I have always got along, and sure, he's been a bit flirty now and then, but I never thought he'd actually ask me out. It's typical, isn't it? As soon as I find someone I really like, someone else comes knocking.

'Thanks for asking, Steve,' I say, giving him a soft smile. 'Ordinarily, I'd love to, but... I'm sort of seeing someone.'

His expression shifts for a moment, disappointment flashing across his face before he quickly covers it up with a smile.

'No harm done,' he says, waving a hand dismissively. 'I totally get it. My problem has always been missing my window while I build up the courage.'

He stands up, his easy-going grin back in place.

'Anyway, I'd better get back to work. Catch you later?' he says.

'Yeah, catch you later,' I reply, watching as he walks away, cringing to myself because I do feel bad.

'Wow, savage,' Faye says.

'What?' I ask, turning to her, a little defensive.

'There's you, telling me off for not texting a guy back, and then you go and treat Steve super mean when he's already keen,' she says, shaking her head like I'm some kind of hypocrite.

'I really am seeing someone,' I insist, not liking the way she's looking at me.

'Well, you weren't yesterday,' Molly chimes in. 'Everyone in the meeting was talking about their Valentine's Day plans, and you kept your head down.'

I pause, realising she's right, but yesterday I didn't have a date at that point.

'It's early days,' I tell them, my voice firm. They're both looking at me like they don't believe a word I'm saying, but I don't care. Let them think what they want. I would rather it was true and they didn't believe me, than have them be super jealous about something I had made up.

I'm really looking forward to tonight and that's all that matters. I know that Ethan is real – unless I'm imagining him. Imagine if I've just conjured him up, desperately, in an attempt to feel like I've got the perfect guy. That would be a new low.

That's the thing though, he is perfect. He really is.

And now I'm excited again.

6

———————

Turning up for my date with my heart fluttering in that nervous-excited way is not something that I'm used to. Sure, sometimes I get first-date anxiety, but this is different. This is the kind of feeling that you only get before a second date, and only when the first date was really fucking good.

Ethan's already there, waiting for me, leaning casually against a lamp post. He looks effortlessly handsome in dark jeans and a white shirt. His smile widens when he spots me, and I feel this warm, happy glow spread through me. It's weird because even though I'm nervous, I'm so relaxed too – like just being around him makes everything better.

Honestly, I can hear myself, and I'm stunned. This isn't me talking. I don't say things like this.

'Hey,' he says, stepping forward to greet me, giving me a peck on the lips. 'You look amazing.'

'So do you,' I reply, feeling almost shy to be in his eyeline, but also loving every second of it.

We start walking together, and I notice he's leading me away from the usual bars and restaurants.

'Where are we going?' I ask, glancing up at him.

'You'll see,' he says with a smile. 'I thought you might appreciate something different.'

We round a corner, and I see a sign that reads 'Dying to Escape'. I can't help but smile to myself. He's brought me to an escape room? That's the kind of dorky date that you go on with someone when you're comfortable with them.

So he isn't just looking to get me drunk and take me back to his room again – which is what I would expect of any man, to be honest – he's actually put thought into this.

'I love it,' I say, genuinely impressed.

'I'm glad you think so,' he replies, holding the door open for me. 'Because we're about to be locked into it.'

Inside, the place has a sort of eerie yet exciting vibe. Dim lighting, mysterious music playing softly in the background, and a front desk cluttered with old books, items of evidence, and plastic severed limbs.

The host, a middle-aged man with a friendly smile, greets us and explains the rules.

'It's a murder-mystery escape room,' he says, adjusting his glasses. 'I'll be watching you on cameras, and I can give you hints if you get stuck. Don't worry, you're not actually locked in, but the goal is to follow the clues and escape within an hour. Think you're up for the challenge?'

Ethan and I exchange a look. I've never done an escape room before but I'm actually really excited.

'Let's do it,' I say, sounding confident but actually having little faith in my ability to escape. Ethan laughs – his voice so low, sexy – it sends a shiver down my spine. Hopefully it just seems like I'm really into the murder mystery.

We're led into the room and it's like stepping into a video game. The walls are lined with bookshelves, there's an old-fashioned desk in one corner, a fireplace in another, and various items scattered around – a typewriter, an ornate box with a combination lock, and a large, ominous-looking painting hanging above the mantelpiece. Oh, and then there is the serial-killer-style wall of photos, letters, receipts and even a lock of hair.

I take a breath, taking it all in.

'Wow,' I blurt.

'Okay, I'll leave you to it,' the host says. 'Your hour starts now.'

And then it's just us.

'I don't even know where to begin,' I say, twirling around on the spot.

Ethan chuckles, moving closer to me as we start to look around.

'I know where to start: by telling you that I haven't been able to stop thinking about you since last night,' he says, his voice just loud enough for me to hear. 'It was amazing. You're amazing. I've had that image of you in my shower all day, the way you felt – I feel like I can still taste you on my lips...'

His words make me feel dizzy.

'I—'

Before I can say anything more, a voice crackles over the speaker, awkwardly interrupting. 'Uh, just a reminder – I can hear you as well as see you,' the host tells us.

Ethan and I burst out laughing, the tension breaking for a moment.

'Good to know now,' Ethan says, grinning at the camera, giving the host the thumbs up. 'Wish I'd known earlier.'

I laugh as we get back to searching for clues, but the sexual tension between us is almost overwhelming. It's like we're in the build-up, seeing how long we can last before giving in to the pull that's constantly drawing us together. It makes everything so much more difficult but we do what we came here to do, and look for clues, opening lock after lock, piecing it all together.

Ethan brushes past me, his body pressing briefly against the back of mine as he reaches for a locked box on the sideboard. The familiar physical contact sends a jolt of electricity through me, and I have to bite my lip to keep from reacting too visibly.

'I'm in,' he says, triumphantly entering the numbers we've been collecting into the combination lock. It clicks open, revealing a handle – the final piece we need to escape the room.

'Good work, detective,' I tell him.

'Thanks,' he replies. 'Fancy grabbing a drink with a genuine hero?'

'Sure,' I say as I watch him fuss with the door we're supposed to leave through.

He has the handle in place but it doesn't budge.

Ethan frowns, trying the handle again, but it's definitely stuck.

'Let's just go out of the door we came in through,' he says. 'We know we did it.'

Would you believe it, that door is stuck too – what the hell is going on? We exchange puzzled looks for a moment before Ethan tries something else.

'Erm, I think we've got a problem,' Ethan says, looking up at the camera. 'Both doors are stuck.'

'I'll sort it out. Don't panic,' the host says, his voice calm – but it's oddly hard to keep calm when someone says 'don't panic'.

While we're waiting, Ethan silently takes my hand, his grip firm yet gentle, and pulls me to one side. Before I know it, I'm pressed up against the wall, his body close to mine, his lips hovering near my ear.

'This is a CCTV blind spot,' he whispers, his voice sending shivers all through my body.

I barely have time to process his words before he's kissing me, slow and deep, like he's savouring every second. My hands slide up to his shoulders, pulling him closer, and for a moment, I forget about everything else – including the host who is currently trying to barge his way through one of the jammed doors. I don't care, the world outside the escape room doesn't exist – all I'm interested in is him, here, now.

You know what, I don't care if these doors stay locked all night (ideally if they turn the cameras off, but if they can't be turned off I still don't think I could promise I would behave myself). I'm perfectly happy where I am.

7

Ethan and I practically fall out of Thin Aire, the two of us laughing like drunk maniacs.

The city is freezing tonight but my cheeks feel like they're on fire.

Ethan pulls me close, kissing me, wrapping his arms around my waist.

'Do you want to go back to your hotel room?' I ask him between kisses.

'About that,' he says, laughing to himself. 'I got kicked out.'

'What?' I reply, pulling away to look at him. 'What happened?'

'Well, Lana, we went full Amsterdam in the window this morning,' he reminds me. 'They didn't like that.'

'I did,' I dare to joke.

'Some people are just funny about public displays of affection,' he adds with a laugh. 'We could go back to yours?'

'We can't,' I say. 'My flatmate has her sister and her kids to say, so I said I would sleep on the sofa.'

'Okay, so definitely no to that,' he replies.

'What were you going to do tonight?' I ask.

He shrugs his shoulders.

'Stay out all night,' he says casually. 'My things are in my car.'

'Where's that?' I ask, in my sexiest voice, because I clearly really am desperate now.

'Trinity multistorey car park,' he replies, 'and I'm pretty sure they don't let you sleep in there.'

'I wasn't talking about sleep,' I reply. 'A different hotel?'

'I don't think anyone's going to check in two very drunk, very horny people at this hour without thinking it's something seedy,' he replies with a smile.

I bite my lip, laughing.

'What can we do? What can we do?'

'We can always call it a night,' he tells me. 'I need to head back to London tomorrow so...'

I don't want to say goodbye, not yet. I can't just let him leave. Plus, I want him so bad.

'We could go to the office,' I suggest in a whisper. 'It's just a PIN code to get in, and people often work late there, so no one will think anything of us coming and going.'

Ethan raises his eyebrows.

'Wow,' he says. 'That's so... hot.'

'We could go to Jennifer's office,' I tell him.

'Well, I would love to meet the original Jennifer again,' he says. 'Because I think she's got a computer that needs some very intensive, very deep repairs.'

'Yes, I do,' I say seriously. 'But... I can't afford to pay you...'

I smile at my own silly role-play voice.

'We'll think of something,' he says. 'I've got a floppy disk that needs transferring to a hard drive.'

I snort with laughter.

'Okay, even I know enough about tech to get that one,' I reply.

Ethan picks me up in his arms and kisses me slowly and deeply.

Yep, I'm too weak to back out now.

'Let's go,' he says.

We make the short journey to the dock, where the office is.

'You're a bad girl, aren't you?' Ethan teases as we approach the door.

'You're the one leading me astray,' I tell him.

He rests his hands on my hips as I type in the code.

'Maybe…' he replies.

It's hard to say who is the ringleader, really, I think we're as bad as each other. Either way, it feels right.

8

Lying in Jennifer's office, on her sofa – well, technically Ethan is on her sofa and I'm on him – I can't help but smile.

We're tangled together like we've been doing this for years. I've got my head on his chest, his heartbeat a steady rhythm beneath my ear, while my hand traces the contours of his abs.

The room is dark, the only light coming from the well-lit dock outside. It's a dreamy, glowing light – perfect for a dreamy situation. I can't believe I'm here – in more ways than one.

'That was fun,' Ethan says, his voice vibrating through his chest.

'It really was,' I reply, letting out a deep, contented sigh. The kind of sigh that only comes after a night like this, where everything just clicks into place. 'Are you always so much fun?' I ask, tilting my head up to look at him, a playful smile on my lips.

He laughs.

'Life is short,' he replies simply. 'Are you always so much fun?'

'I thought I was, but when I'm with you, I don't know, it's something else,' I admit, my voice softer now. 'Obviously, I liked the look of you when we first met, but... I don't know... it's different.'

'I've never flirted with a woman who was pretending to be someone else,' he says, a teasing edge to his voice. 'I knew you weren't Jennifer, by the way. That's why I pretended to be IT support.'

I laugh.

'Work can be pretty boring, so I have to figure out ways to get through the day without losing my mind,' I tell him. 'But something about you made me want to cause more trouble than usual.'

'Well, we've certainly done that in our short time together,' he points out. 'It's nice to meet someone who matches my energy.'

I smile to myself. It does feel like we're trying to match each other – if not one-up each other. I mean, obviously, because I've never brought a guy back to the office before.

'You seem like someone I could dance all night with,' I say, letting my drunk brain take the wheel. 'But you also seem like the kind of guy it would be nice to just chill with – I bet nothing is boring with you.'

'Thanks,' he replies, a hint of a smile in his voice. 'Although we don't call this dancing all night down south.'

'You know what I mean,' I say with a laugh, lightly batting his stomach. 'I don't think I would say this if I wasn't a little bit drunk – or if I wasn't surrounded by Jennifer's motivational Post-it notes – but why do I feel like I've known you my whole life? Ugh, I never say shit like this, how have you got me saying shit like this?'

'Sorry,' he says with a soft laugh, his fingers gently brushing through my hair. 'I'm having to figure it out myself, why, when I first clapped eyes on you, everything else seemed to stop, nothing else seemed to matter.'

His words crash over me like a wave, and suddenly, I'm overwhelmed by this intense connection I feel with him. My whole life, I've been criticised, overlooked and written off as a good-time girl who doesn't want anything serious out of life. But with Ethan, it feels different. It feels real. Like he sees me, really sees me, and he likes what he sees exactly as it is. Not because of anything, or in spite of anything – just because.

'I feel like I'm on fire when I'm around you,' he tells me. 'But at the same time, I feel like I can be myself around you. No bravado, no brave faces, no worrying about what you'll think of me.'

The alcohol is definitely pulling the strings now, making me say things I would never dare to otherwise. But it's like I can't stop myself.

'Do you believe in love at first sight?' I ask him, the words tumbling out before I can second-guess them.

'I'd like to,' he replies. 'But if you're not sure, I could walk by again?'

I burst out laughing, pushing myself up so that I can sit on top of him.

'It's not that late, you know,' I point out, hoping the night isn't going to end anytime soon.

'Then let's keep this party going,' he says, his smile as contagious as ever. 'It's a shame we didn't bring anything to drink.'

'Oh, we have a booze fridge for entertaining clients,' I tell him, feeling a wicked grin spread across my face. 'Shall we raid that? I'm sure I can replace it, before anyone notices – it's only stuff from the Tesco Express downstairs.'

'I thought you'd never ask,' he says, his eyes lighting up as he takes my face in his hands and pulls me down for a kiss.

I can't believe this is real. Here I am, in my office after hours, sitting on a man who is not only drop-dead gorgeous but who also seems to genuinely like me. The thought makes me feel a little sick, a little dizzy, but mostly... amazing.

I need to pinch myself – or maybe I just need to find that booze.

9

10 JANUARY 2025 – ALMOST TWO YEARS LATER...

I stifle a yawn.

I'm sitting in the back of the meeting room, desperately trying to keep up with taking meeting notes for Jennifer. Yes, her assistant is on maternity leave, again, so it's down to me to fill in. And, yes, I am entirely convinced she's getting pregnant just so that she doesn't have to work for Jennifer. I can't even blame her.

Jennifer's at the front of the room, talking about the Redflags app – one of the apps the company has developed, and one I actually care about because it's all about keeping women safe.

'We have to be extremely careful with the personal information we collect and share,' she says, her tone sharp and focused. 'We're dealing with sensitive data, and potential accusations...'

The app contains a message board where women can post about the men they have dated, who have given them serious red flags – like if they turned out to be married, if they were unpleasant to be around, or if they were potentially dangerous. It's a great idea, it really is. The dating game is a seriously scary one to play.

Kelsey, who always has a knack for pushing the boundaries, leans forward.

'We can get away with more on the message board,' he says. 'As long as people know they're sharing information at their own risk.'

I scribble down his words, my handwriting becoming something that even I don't recognise. Well, this isn't part of my job, I haven't had to write quickly since my A-level exams.

'But the client wants something more,' Jennifer insists. 'Something that can be used in real time.'

'Like what?' Ariana asks.

I try to keep up, my pen racing across the page. I know this isn't why I'm in the room but I do have an idea – a good one, actually, if I do say so myself. I've had it for a while, and it would fit perfectly within the Redflags app. But I'm not sure if now's the time.

'Perhaps we could add in a quick search?' Steve suggests. 'A dedicated page where people can drop in information in real time, about the people they're out with, and see if anything flags.'

'Quick-flags,' Jennifer says, suggesting a name. 'I like it.'

I hesitate, but the idea is bubbling up inside me, and if I don't say it now then when will I get the chance?

I clear my throat.

'I know that when I'm on dates, and I'm not feeling safe, I would feel better if I had a quick tool to use,' I say.

'Well, no one has been on more dates than Lana,' Molly jokes – probably wanting to get everyone laughing at me, not with me.

I shoot her a glance, then turn to Steve, who is frowning – so that's two people I'm probably not going to have on my side.

'What women really need is a quick and easy way to get out of situations,' I continue, undeterred.

'Okay, Lana, thanks,' Kelsey says, already dismissing me.

But Jennifer, surprisingly, seems intrigued.

'No, it's okay, let her finish,' she says.

I swallow hard, feeling the eyes of the room on me.

'Sometimes you just get a bad feeling, or you know you need to get out of there, or you're just not feeling the date,' I explain. 'And in situations like that, what you need is an out. Making a big fuss, saying you want to leave – it doesn't always feel like an option, and sometimes it doesn't feel safe to say you're not interested. But a quick, easy, non-confrontational out is perfect. It gets you out of a situation without putting yourself at risk.'

Jennifer tilts her head curiously.

'So, what's that?' she asks.

'A shortcut button, that looks like something else – like a cycle-tracking app or something – on the home screen that you can press,' I explain. 'After a short countdown, it will give you an automated text or a fake call, to look like it's from your mum or whoever you want, saying there's been an emergency and you need to come quick.'

Jennifer's eyes narrow slightly.

'And you would utilise something like that?' she checks.

'Oh, absolutely,' I reply, my voice firm. 'I would use it to get out of all sorts.'

She pauses for a moment, and I feel a flicker of hope – until her mouth twists into a smirk.

'Well, as ideas go, that's the dumbest thing I've ever heard,' she tells me. 'So I would stick to taking notes if I were you.'

My face burns, and I sink into my seat, focusing on the notepad in front of me. The rest of the meeting blurs together as I mechanically jot down notes, alternating between feeling furious that she dismissed me and embarrassed that I tried to get out of my lane.

When the meeting finally ends, I shuffle out, planning to take an early lunch so I can go and seethe somewhere. But of course, Steve calls after me.

'Lana, Lana!'

I turn around to see what he wants.

'Yeah?' I reply.

'I meant to ask you earlier – did you empty the dryer?' he asks, his tone casual.

'Erm, I think so,' I reply, my mind still half in the meeting room.

'Getting in late is a killer on the old memory,' Steve says with a chuckle. 'I'm making a shepherd's pie for dinner tonight.'

'Lovely,' I reply. Well, there's not much else you can say to that, is there?

'I was thinking shepherd's pie, a movie, a bottle of wine...'

'God, you two are like an old married couple,' Molly quips as she breezes past us.

'I'm going out tonight, actually,' I tell him, hoping to nip any ideas he has in the bud.

Steve's expression changes, narrowing.

'You're seeing him, aren't you?'

'Steve...'

'You are, I can tell,' he says, his annoyance clear. 'Why, Lana, why?'

I sigh, because this has come up before. Honestly, you'd think I was cheating on him. 'Steve, we've talked about this,' I remind him.

In hindsight, I should have known it was too good to be true when Steve, my ex, offered to let me move in with him. My old flatmate moved away, and I couldn't afford to live there on my own, so it seemed like a lifeline at the time. We weren't together that long, and it was last year when we were a thing, so I didn't think it would be a big deal. He was very clear when he said he was helping me as a friend, with no strings attached. But now, it's painfully obvious that he thought this would be the thing to get us back together.

It was subtle at first but now he just can't hide it. Like, it was weird when he showed me to my room and it had a single bed in a spot that definitely looked like it had a double there until recently, but now he doesn't even try to hide his jealousy. The sooner I can get enough money together to get my own place, the better. I need to get out as soon as possible.

'I'm just seeing a friend tonight,' I lie, hoping to defuse the situation.

He looks visibly relieved which makes me feel so awkward.

'I'll save you some dinner then, yeah?' he says, his tone softening.

'You don't have to,' I reply, trying to keep things light. 'I'll probably eat while I'm out.'

'It's all good, I'll save you some,' he reassures me. 'And I'll wait up for you.'

And this is why I can't tell him that I have a date, because he's intense and he's weird, and if I ever felt inclined to use the Redflags app he would be the first person I added – or maybe the second.

Ah well, enough about exes, enough about the past, I need to focus on the future. Here's hoping tonight goes well – and if he turns out to be a property developer with houses to spare then even better. But I'm not usually that lucky.

10

I'm sitting in a bar that's trying very hard to be trendy, sipping on a cocktail, doing my best to enjoy my date – and not think about my ex waiting at home for me with a shepherd's pie. I can just imagine him there, sitting by the door, fish slice in hand as the food goes cold, staring into space, waiting for me...

The man sitting across from me is Oliver, who has explained – twice now – that he's a quantity surveyor (so sadly not a property magnate who is going to put me up in a penthouse) and no, I still don't really understand what that is, but he didn't explain it in an especially exciting way, so I figured we could just leave it at that.

I take a sip of my cocktail, which is as silly-looking as they come, but I'm into it. It's bright pink, with an old-school umbrella, a slice of pineapple, and a cherry that's impaled on a tiny plastic sword. It's called a Big Retro and it's certainly living up to its name – it's delicious too.

Oliver, on the other hand, is sipping on a tonic water. When he first told me he didn't drink, I'd assumed – because I'm a ridiculous person who maybe drinks too much – that it was because he'd had a problem in the past. But nope, he's just not a fan of drinking. There's obviously nothing wrong with that, but I'm starting to realise that I might be a bit too fond of hanging out in bars and being silly for the two of us to hit it off.

Oliver has just been telling me about his hobbies and the top of the list appears to be playing *Final Fantasy* video games, because he's been telling me about them for, oh, I don't know, (what feels like) six hours now.

'...that's why I thought I'd replay them all, in order,' he continues. 'Original consoles, obviously, unless there's been a remake or a remaster, in which case I play it on the more current gen.'

'Yeah, absolutely,' I say, unsure what exactly I'm agreeing to.

'The early games, especially, have this raw quality to them,' he continues. 'You can't really replicate that feeling with modern technology. However, the remasters – well, some of them are good, but they lose the charm of the originals, even if the revamped textures and mechanics are far superior. It's all too polished now. Except for *Final Fantasy VII*, of course. But even then, I still like to go back to the original.'

'Yeah, totally,' I reply, still none the wiser, still no idea what a chocobo is – but he really seems to like them, so...

The conversation isn't exactly flowing. I need to do something, to liven things up.

'I know, let's play a game,' I suggest.

Oliver raises an eyebrow.

'A video game?' he replies.

'No, like, a real-life one,' I say. 'Like a party game.'

'Such as?'

'Truth or dare,' I say, because why not?

'I've never played, but isn't it kind of dumb to pick dare?' he replies, clearly missing the point.

I can't help but laugh. I suppose he has a point.

'Okay, fine. We'll stick to truth. But if you don't want to answer a question, you have to drink.'

I glance down at his tonic water, realising how silly that sounds.

'Well, yeah, it's fine, just… let's just see how it goes,' I say.

He shrugs.

'All right, fine. You first,' he says, not sounding all that into it.

I tap my finger on my chin, pretending to think hard.

'What's the craziest thing you've ever done?' I ask – more than anything, I just want to know, to get a sense of what I'm dealing with here.

He takes a moment, clearly digging deep for something wild.

'Well, I was visiting a site for work, and I heard they had this, well, this really tall tree, growing in the woodland nearby. We're talking really tall – you've never seen a tree so tall, or so old. So, I crossed the train tracks to go have a look.'

'Oh, wow,' I say, not meaning it in the way he takes it.

'They were clearly disused tracks,' he reassures me, 'but I'd stated in my health and safety report that I wouldn't be going near them.'

He gives me a look that makes me feel like he thinks he's Jason Statham right now.

'Oh, you bad boy,' I say flatly, barely managing to keep a straight face.

'Right?' He grins, clearly thinking he's nailed it. Then he thinks for a moment. 'Worst date you've been on?'

Oh, is he joking?

'And the best,' he adds quickly. 'Tell me both.'

I take a sip of my cocktail, stalling.

'You know what, they might actually be the same date,' I confess.

'How so?' he asks.

I bite my lip, as I try to carefully let just some of the memories come to the forefront of my brain.

'I had an absolute dream date with this really cool guy,' I tell him. 'Everything was going perfectly. But then... things started going wrong, really wrong. I'm talking disaster movie, criminal-damage levels of wrong. It was like whatever we had between us was so powerful that when we got together, there was, like, a fallout zone – a blast radius of carnage around us. You know what I mean?'

He sighs, clearly unimpressed.

'And I'm supposed to compete with nuclear fallout?' he replies.

'Well, no, because it was awful, and we swore we would never see each other again,' I explain. 'And, well, he's taking that promise very seriously. I haven't heard from him since.'

I say that like *he* ghosted me when really it was a joint decision to part ways, for the good of all mankind, but even so... it really did feel like I lost something.

'Lucky for me, I guess,' Oliver says, with just a hint of sarcasm in his voice. 'And you – it sounds like you had a lucky escape.'

'Oh, yeah, definitely,' I reply. Ugh, I need to get him out of my head. Focus, Lana, you're on a date. Forget about *him*.

'Okay, your question... shag, marry, kill—'

'I don't do that,' Oliver interrupts.

'You don't do what?' I reply.

'I don't shag, marry, or kill people,' he says, dead serious.

I burst out laughing, but he just stares at me, unamused.

'I mean, I don't play that game,' he clarifies. 'It's demeaning to women.'

'I could give you three men,' I suggest, but he's even less taken with that idea.

Right, maybe not then.

This date is officially a stinker. Marginally better than staying home to eat shepherd's pie with my ex... but only just.

11

I turn the key in the lock as slowly and quietly as I can manage, the door creaking open with an uncooperative groan.

Well, tonight's date was officially another dud, and for some reason I'm feeling more demoralised about it than usual. Normally, I'd brush it off – just another mildly annoying waste of time and perfectly shaved legs. But tonight, something feels different, and I think it might be my thirtieth birthday, looming in the not-so-distant future, creeping up on me and whispering all sorts of nonsense into my ear.

I never thought I'd care about turning thirty. I've always been pretty happy with my life – free and single, working a simple job, and living with no commitments. Who needs a career, a mortgage or a husband to be happy, right? As though they are things on a tick list that needs checking off to be living life.

But lately, I've noticed the way people look at me shifting, and the way they talk to me. Everyone has always thought of me as a bit of a wild child, someone who doesn't want responsibility, who just wants to have fun, and even if they didn't agree with me, it was like it was fine because I was in my twenties.

Apparently it's not cute any more though. It's like they're all judging me now, as if my choices are suddenly tragic once they're stacked up against my age. Oh, she's single because she can't get a man. She's in a dead-end job and she will be until she dies. She's living with her ex because she's got nowhere else to go. When you put it like that... wow, it does sound kind of tragic.

But I'm not one to wallow. I'm not going to throw myself a pity party just because society has decided thirty is the magical number where you're supposed to have your life together. Maybe it's time I did grow up a little though, and turning thirty could be the perfect push into a new era. A boyfriend wouldn't be the worst thing in the world, and I've got all these ideas at work – maybe I just need to find a way to implement them. And as for finding a place of my own, well, if I could just earn a bit more, I could even start thinking about a mortgage. Having my own space would be a dream come true.

The more I think about it, the more excited I get. It's time to take charge, to really go for it. I bet no one ever thought they would hear me say that, least of all me, but here I am, on the brink of a breakthrough. With less than a month until the big day, that gives me plenty of time to be proactive. And hey, maybe I'll even throw a party to say goodbye to my twenties. I'll be in Australia for the wedding, but what better place to throw a big party and go out with a bang? My family, for better or worse, loves a good party, and my cousin Tiggy will be there. Tiggy's a blast – a good-time girl like me, but with a more refined edge, thanks to her boarding-school upbringing. One big party to usher in my grown-up era – that's exactly what I need, and I'm not just saying that because I'm a bit drunk.

Finally, I make it through the door and start creeping along the dark hallway, hoping to sneak into my room unnoticed.

'There you are.' Steve's voice interrupts the silence, making me jump out of my skin.

He's sitting in the dark on the sofa, facing the door, like an absolute psycho.

'Shit, Steve! You scared the hell out of me,' I say, my hand flying to my chest to try and steady my heart.

'You're home late,' he points out, his tone as flat as a teacher having a go at a pupil for not doing their homework.

'We got chatting, you know how girls are,' I reply, trying to keep my tone light. But Steve's clearly not having it.

'Chatting?' he repeats back to me. 'It's nearly midnight, Lana.'

I sigh, rolling my eyes.

'I'm a grown woman, Steve, not a teenager sneaking in past my curfew,' I remind him. 'And you're not my dad.'

Although he absolutely feels like it. Well, like a dad generally, not my dad, who has always taken the hands-off approach (at least that's what we'll kindly call it).

He gives me that look, the one that makes me feel about fifteen years old.

'You should have let me know you'd be late,' he says. 'I was worried.'

'Worried?' I reply. 'I was only on Call Lane, it's hardly the Wild West.'

I suppose it is Friday, so that's not unheard of, but it's still a bit early for the usual chaos.

'So, out with a friend,' he says, his eyes narrowing. 'Did you have a nice time?'

'Yeah, it was nice to see him,' I say automatically, and then immediately realise my mistake.

'Him?' Steve's eyes are widening and narrowing like a camera lens trying to focus. 'Him?'

Shit. I've messed up.

'Yes, Him,' I say, trying to sound casual. 'My friend Him. Have I never mentioned Him before? Lovely girl, she talked way too much about video games, though.'

'Right,' he says slowly, like he's filing away this new piece of information for future interrogation – I need to remember that I said that. 'Do you want some food?'

I fake a yawn, stretching my arms over my head.

'No, I'm exhausted,' I reply. 'I think I'm just going to head to bed.'

Without waiting for a response, I head for my room, shutting the door behind me. The single bed stares back at me, a constant reminder of Steve's not-so-subtle attempts to keep me from bringing anyone else home. The faint marks on the floor where the double bed used to be are still visible, so it's not even like he's done a sneak job of it. Unless he wants me to see them, to remind me...

Well, the joke's on him, because I manage in a single bed just fine, when I get the chance, or his double bed if he's ever away for the night.

I flop down onto the bed, staring up at the ceiling. God, I really do need to get out of here. But I feel good about my plan, to grow up a little – to naturally evolve, but because I want to, not because people think I should.

Now, I just need to figure out how to make it happen.

12

I stare down the long driveway leading to my dad's house like it's the barrel of a gun – well, 'house' is a bit of an understatement (gun, however, is not). This house is a Grade II-listed Georgian manor, always simply referred to as 'the manor' by the family. It's a grand place, rich in history, in a small village just outside York.

It's beautiful, of course it is, but it's also intimidatingly big. It's made of solid stone that looks like it could withstand a siege – so obviously I've ruled that out, for when they're annoying me.

The grounds stretch out on either side of the driveway – formal terracing, perfectly manicured lawns and a walled garden that requires a small army to maintain.

There's parkland beyond that, with managed woodland framing a wildlife lake. It's all so meticulously organised, and managed, that the place runs like a well-oiled machine. You would think a big house like this would feel lonely but, honestly, every piece of it feels alive.

I should feel more at home here, I suppose, since this is technically where I would have grown up if I'd stayed with Dad instead of going with Mum (although I don't have any memories of living here). But every time I come back, I'm reminded how different our worlds are. This place is gorgeous, but it's also the kind of beautiful that makes you feel small. I guess that's why they have staff, because who could possibly manage this all on their own? Still, the idea of having people hanging around all the time, doing things for me, makes my skin crawl. I wouldn't want that.

It's been a while since I was last here. I never come willingly – usually, I'm summoned, like today, for a pre-wedding gathering ahead of the big day (that's actually a big week, because why settle for a day when you can drag it out?). And of course it's going to be a catered lunch, because nothing's ever as simple as just popping over for a cup of tea and a chat in this family.

The invite – yes, an actual invitation to lunch with my family – said 'smart casual', which to me means black skinny jeans, a silk blouse and a leather jacket. But to the people inside this house, it probably means ceremonial robes and their second-fanciest tiaras.

I hate arriving through the front door because you don't just walk in; you're greeted by Alec, the house manager, who will lead you through the labyrinth of rooms to wherever you're supposed to be.

Life hack though, if you're ever here and something is going on, it's easy enough to slink in through the side door with the caterers, so that's what I'm going to do today.

As I turn the corner, I spot a van parked near the side entrance, with a team of people unloading things. There's a man leaning against the stone wall, smoking a cigarette. He's got that bad-boy vibe – tall, with dark hair that looks like he just rolled out of bed, a leather jacket slung over his broad shoulders, and the kind of stubble that's too perfectly maintained to be accidental (honestly, even with stubble, I wouldn't be surprised if Bea dismissed him on the spot).

'Are you with the caterers?' I ask as I approach him, pausing by the door.

He takes a drag of his cigarette and shakes his head.

'Waitstaff,' he replies, his voice deep and rough.

'Have you met any of the family yet?' I ask, wondering what kind of mood they're in.

'Oh, yeah,' he says, widening his eyes for effect. 'It's a special kind of awful in there. They're a bit *Saltburn*, honestly. Actually, they make the *Saltburn* family seem normal.'

'They're my family,' I reply, without missing a beat.

His eyes widen in horror.

'Shit, I'm sorry, I didn't mean – not shit, sorry for swearing, I just—'

'Don't worry.' I cut him off with a smile. 'I'm sort of the family outcast, and you're not wrong about them.'

He relaxes, the tension easing from his shoulders.

'Is it some kind of special occasion?' he asks curiously.

'It's a lunch to talk about my sister's upcoming wedding,' I explain, rolling my eyes.

He lets out a low whistle.

'All this for a lunch? That's crazy,' he says.

'I know,' I say with a sigh. 'I'm jealous that you're here to serve it, instead of having to attend it.'

He flicks his cigarette to the ground and crushes it with his boot.

'I'm Tyler, by the way,' he says, his tone vaguely flirtatious.

'Lana,' I reply.

'I guess I'll see you in there,' he says, nodding toward the door.

'If you see me looking like I need rescuing, make up an excuse for me to step outside,' I joke. See, this is why my app idea is great, because it could be perfect for situations like this too.

'Deal,' he says with a laugh.

With no other ways to put off the inevitable, I finally head inside. The rear hallway is just as I remember – elegant and imposing, with polished floors that reflect the light from the chandeliers overhead. The walls are lined with oil paintings of people I'm probably related to but wouldn't recognise if I bumped into them in the next room (although the fact they were ghosts might tip me off). The air smells faintly of polish and something floral, like the manor's trying to convince you it's a welcoming cosy home and not a stone-cold museum of a place.

I make my way to the drawing room, where everyone usually gathers before moving on to the dining room. If you like rich fabrics and antique furniture, with massive fireplaces and old charm (aka creaking floors and drafts) then you'll love it here. As mansions go (as if I would ever have a choice) I would much prefer something cool and contemporary.

As I walk in, everyone looks at me like I've just crashed their party, which, I suppose, I have in a roundabout way.

The thing you need to remember is that this isn't my world. I was out of it before I was old enough to understand what it meant to live here. My upbringing was far more typical – in Mum's tiny house, just us, living a modest life. This place was something I visited from time to time, like a theme park attraction (specifically, the haunted house), not somewhere to live. I never learned the (usually pointless) etiquette they all swear by, or shared their taste, or hobbies.

Naturally, as I grew older, I spent less and less time around Dad and his new family. I really am only summoned here for special occasions or formalities.

'Here she is!' Seph exclaims, jumping to her feet and rushing over to give me a hug. Seph is all brunette waves and designer clothes, with a perfect figure (nothing is too big or too small and, if it was, she's had it quietly tweaked). She's flanked by her bestie,

Eleanor, who stands close by but you can tell she's trying to keep herself out of hugging distance – as if I would, it would be like hugging a hornet nest.

'Hello,' I say, forcing a smile. 'Sorry I'm a little late.'

It's only a few minutes, because I was chatting to Tyler, but I'm starting as I mean to go on – polite, enthusiastic and present.

'That's okay, we know what you're like, so we gave you the wrong time,' Bea says with a tight smile.

'Hi, Bea,' I say, offering her a smile.

She leans in and gives me a kiss on both cheeks, managing to radiate her resentment for having to be polite in a way that I can feel. My body stiffens up in response.

Beatrix 'Bea' Pemberton is in her fifties, with a face that's been lifted just enough to look perpetually surprised, and hair that's always perfectly coiffed – uptight, like her. She's got that posh 'horse-girl' look – probably used to do dressage in some kind of professional capacity. I've never been all that into horses myself – unlike Seph, who has been known to get horses for her birthdays.

'My soon-to-be big sister, bring it in,' Chester says, bounding over with his usual enthusiasm. He wraps me in a tight hug, squeezing just a little too hard. Chester is tall, with sandy blonde hair and a boyish charm that makes him look younger than he is – and also like Boris Johnson could be his dad. He's always been a huggy, tactile kind of guy, and this is not a huggy, tactile kind of family beyond the phoney greetings.

Finally, Dad stands up to greet me. Walter, in his sixties now, dresses like an extra from *The Crown* – probably because Bea tells him to. His suit is tailored to perfection, and his shoes are polished to a mirror-like shine. I have his eyes, which is ironic because we see the world in very different ways. Proudly, though, I didn't inherit his heart or his brain. Really, the only thing I could imagine wanting to inherit from him is probably his bank balance.

'Lana,' he says, kissing me on the cheek. His tone is warm but distant, like he's trying to connect but doesn't know how.

'Hi, Dad,' I reply, matching his tone.

Dad isn't one for small talk – or talk talk, sometimes – and today is no different.

'Shall we get comfortable in the dining room?' he suggests, already heading for the door. 'Get this show on the road, as they say.'

'Let's,' Bea replies.

I feel a hand on my arm, stopping me in my tracks, holding me back.

'Lana, can I have a moment?' Bea says, and it doesn't sound optional.

'What's up?' I reply.

'I was just going through the gift registry, for the wedding, and I've noticed that we don't have you down for anything,' she explains, with the tone of a waiter in a snooty restaurant letting you know that your card has been declined. 'I did send you this list, well in advance, and as you know we're quite late in the day now...'

'Oh, that's okay, I have a present for them,' I tell her.

'But on the registry...'

'I just bought them something,' I say simply.

'What do you mean?' she replies.

'Like, I went to a shop, I picked something out, I paid for it, wrapped it – that sort of thing.'

Okay, so I haven't wrapped it yet, I'm not that organised, but it feels like a needed detail to make her understand.

'You're supposed to buy them something that they want,' she says, horrified. 'From the registry.'

'I thought it was supposed to be a gift, so I bought them something I thought they would like, ages ago,' I explain. 'I saw, on Seph's Instagram, that she'd had a new pantry fitted in her kitchen, and I noticed all of the copper in her kitchen, so when I saw these fancy mason jars with copper instead of silver, I thought they would love them.'

Bea looks unwell.

'Do you really think Persephone uses her kitchen?' she says in disbelief.

'She does on Instagram,' I point out.

'Perhaps she pretends to,' she corrects me.

'Then she can pretend to use these – what's the big deal?'

Bea must hit her limit with me because it's at this point she abandons the conversation.

We all filter through to the dining room, where the large, round table is perfectly set.

I take my seat, feeling like I've just walked on to the set of *The Traitors*, except here, you know everyone's a traitor, and I'm the faithful they probably all want to murder. I'm glad I'm not staying here tonight.

Tyler enters the room to take drinks orders. We exchange secret smiles, but it's the kind of smile that makes Bea, who never misses a thing, look between us with a slight narrowing of his eyes. When her gaze finally locks on Tyler she clicks her tongue. It's the stubble, I'm telling you.

'Whisky on the rocks,' Dad orders, his voice firm.

'Alcohol this early? You'll be tight before we hit the golf course, Walt,' Chester teases, his grin wide enough to fit the table in.

'Well, you know what they say...' Dad starts.

'That it's 5 p.m. somewhere?' Chester interrupts with a smirk.

'No, that it's my bloody house,' Dad corrects him.

'Daddy, don't be beastly,' Seph playfully ticks him off.

'Bit early for me. I'll stick with wine,' Chester says, and I genuinely don't think he's joking.

'Wine for me too,' Seph adds, and Eleanor quickly echoes, 'And me,' because of course they're having the same thing.

'Yes, wine for me,' Bea says.

I glance at Tyler, who's standing nearby, jotting all this down.

'Tyler, do you reckon you could make me a cocktail?' I ask him. 'I don't mind what kind, you can surprise me.'

He smiles.

'I'll see what I can whip up for you.'

'Tyler?' Bea repeats, looking and sounding like the name tastes bad in her mouth.

'You know that boy?' Dad asks, and I have to suppress a laugh at him calling a man who's clearly in his thirties 'boy'.

'I met him outside,' I explain. 'He seems nice.'

'Oh, Lana banana, flirting with the staff,' Seph snorts, as though I've just committed the ultimate faux pas.

Before I can respond, Bea jumps in.

'Shall we get down to business? After all, that's why we're all here, to get ready for the biggest society wedding since Wills and Kate.'

You know Bea is going to be the kind of woman who acts like she knows them personally and obviously overlooks Harry and Meghan's nuptials.

Seph clears her throat, drawing everyone's attention back to her.

'Right, yes, so,' she begins, each word gathering speed. 'The wedding will be here before we know it, and we'll be jetting off to Oz even sooner, so this is really just about making sure everyone is up to speed with details.'

I feel like I'm in a school assembly, fighting to concentrate, my brain trying to check out when I know I'm supposed to be singing 'Give Me Oil in My Lamp'.

'So, the dress code,' Seph continues. 'This is a black-tie event, very exclusive, so a very strict dress code. Tuxedos for the gents – no button-down collars, please. This is a wedding, not a high-school prom, I want to see wingtip only. And for the ladies, it's black silk gowns. Gowns should be to the floor, please, and we kindly request that anyone above a C cup thinks carefully about their neckline.'

I blink as my ears prick up.

'What?' I ask, just to make sure I didn't imagine that.

'Anyone above a C cup needs to consider their neckline,' Seph repeats, her tone as matter-of-fact as if she's announcing the weather. 'A plunge looks great, on the right body, but the more a lady has up top, the less ladylike she looks in a lower neckline.'

Wow, that's offensive generally but especially seeing as though I have 'more up top'.

I catch Bea's eye as she looks at me pointedly.

'I assume you're buying a dress that is appropriate?' she asks, her tone layered with the kind of condescension that makes me want to throw my swan-shaped napkin at her.

'I've bought a dress,' I reply simply. I don't mention that it's one I've had for ages, but it's perfect for a wedding, so why waste money on a new one?

'Do you need help?' Bea says, her voice dripping with faux concern. 'I know you're not used to events like these, and that it might be difficult for you to find a suitable dress...'

Bea is the kind of woman who can always home in on your insecurities and, if you don't have any, she can easily point some out for you.

'Events like these? Weddings?' I ask, sarcasm oozing from every word. 'I've been to weddings before.'

'Of course you have,' Seph says, as if she's trying to calm a feral cat. 'I think Mummy just means that this is a nice wedding.'

Oh, boy.

'The next point of order is wedding companions,' Seph continues, clearly oblivious to how irked I am right now. 'Everyone has, of course, received an invitation that also accommodates a wedding companion. I think it's important that we discuss this, as we only want a certain calibre of person at the wedding, so...'

Why is everyone looking at me? I make a big point of turning to Eleanor.

'Are you bringing a plus-one?' I ask her.

Eleanor stiffens like I've asked her to take her top off to prove she isn't trying to smuggle an unsavoury C cup into the wedding.

'I will be attending the wedding alone,' she says primly. 'My sole focus is to be on the bride and groom, and celebrating their special day.' She glances at Seph and smiles. 'It's all part of my role as principal bridesmaid.'

Of course. I've long since realised that Eleanor's role in this wedding is less about helping Seph and more about making sure I know that she didn't pick me, which is crazy, because I really don't care. Being a bridesmaid sounds like a nightmare – having all eyes on you, wearing what you're told, and having jobs to do. Who wants to do jobs at a wedding? Weddings are for getting drunk and flirting with hot groomsmen.

'Lana,' Bea prompts me, dragging me back to reality.

'Yeah?' I reply.

'Are you bringing a companion to the wedding?' she asks.

Chester smirks.

'She's bringing the waiter,' he says just as Tyler returns with our drinks.

'Don't be silly,' Seph jumps in, but by the end of her sentence, she actually sounds worried. 'She isn't – are you, Lana?'

Does she really expect me to dignify that with a response?

'Look, Lana is a big girl, let's not beat about the bush,' Dad interrupts, clearly at the end of his patience. 'Lana, some people are worried about how you might behave at the wedding, and so this lunch is just to make sure that you're up to speed on the dress code, that you don't bring a companion who may make things unpleasant or embarrass you, and that you behave in a way that is befitting of this family. Obviously, we would all love for you to be there, and we're looking forward to spending time with you.'

Yikes. That's not just a shit sandwich; it's a shit buffet. I don't know if I'm in a state of pure disbelief or furious anger. Did they really invite me here just to make sure I don't embarrass them at the wedding?

'Sorry, what?' I say, keeping my cool. 'This whole thing is to tell me to behave?'

'Somewhat,' Seph says carefully.

'Yes,' Bea says at the same time, without flinching.

I can't decide what's worse: that they think so little of me, that they're so comfortable saying it to my face, or the fact that this entire thing is an intervention for me – a fucking catered one. What do they think I'm going to do? What have I ever done that was so wrong, other than be what they consider common?

'What makes you think I'm not just going to, you know, turn up, be a guest, and have a nice time?' I ask.

'I'll take this one,' Chester says with a smirk. 'We all know what you're like, and we love you for it, but you're known for your antics. Remember when there was that spot of something, out on the lawn, and you went on a dating website to find us a greenkeeper?'

I frown. 'It was a dating app, not a website, and I didn't go on there to find him, he just happened to be someone I was talking to when you were talking to Dad about the grass problem – I was trying to help,' I remind him.

'Did he see to your turf?' Chester jokes.

'Don't be an ass,' Dad ticks him off.

'Sorry, Walt,' Chester replies before turning back to me. 'There was also that time we caught you in flagrante delicto at the New Year's Eve party...'

'With the pianist,' Bea adds – again, horrified I would fraternise with the help.

'I was hugging him because he was crying,' I reply. 'Someone had upset him.'

And that someone was Bea, because she was incredibly rude to him – I know, that may be hard to believe. *Not.*

Wow, is this really what everyone thinks of me? That I don't know how to behave at a wedding, how to dress, and that I would probably bring a plus-one who would lower the tone? Is that really, really what they think? Honestly, I know what this lot can be like, but this is just the worst. They really think so, so little of me. I'm in two minds not to go to the stupid thing.

'Look, this is getting a little messy,' Seph says, her voice the epitome of faux diplomacy. 'Dad is being silly, and so is Chester. That isn't the issue. You are... you're fine. This is just about making sure that you feel like you fit in. And, yes, okay, that the first of February is the best day of my life.'

For a second it feels like my breath gets caught in my neck somewhere.

The first of February? As in, my birthday? My thirtieth fucking birthday?

'It's on the Saturday?' I check, my voice unnaturally calm.

'I know, a Saturday, how tacky, right?' Seph says with a laugh. 'We wanted to have the wedding on the Sunday, but Chester's grandmother is incredibly superstitious, and it's their family tradition that a couple's... consummation is not on a Sunday.'

'Nanny is religious,' Chester says, like it's a reasonable request. 'Thankfully, we were able to shift the day, relatively last minute.'

They're getting married on my thirtieth fucking birthday because Chester's gran doesn't want them shagging on a Sunday? And it's so dumb, because most weddings go on until at least midnight, so it will probably be a Sunday when they 'consummate' (even thinking it gives me the ick) regardless.

I can't believe they're taking over my birthday like this. They really do think so, so little of me. My God, my blood is really boiling now.

You know what? Fine. If that's the kind of girl they think I am then maybe that's the kind of girl I should be. I should go out and buy a new dress (one that breaks the C cup rule), I should still go to the wedding and have an absolute blast of a time (they're paying for everything, after all), and I should take a plus-one with me... the absolute worst plus-one I can find.

13

I'm officially back on the apps.

It's a tale as old as time: girl meets app, girl swipes right, girl gets disillusioned by the endless stream of underwhelming men and deletes the app in a fit of frustration. But this time, it's different. This time, I'm not searching for true love, mind-blowing sex or (the most likely option of the three) someone to underwhelm me into swearing off men for life. This time I am a woman on a mission.

Matcher is always the app at the top of the app store. Everyone uses it; it's as usual to see on a single person's phone as Instagram is. All the cool kids are on Matcher (and most of them are single).

It's funny when you think about how movies from a decade ago painted online dating as the last refuge of the desperate – introverts, weirdos, serial killers (and, if you were really unlucky, all of the above). Now, it's just what you do when you're single and/or bored. But instead of swiping through the sea of disappointing options with the vague hope of finding something decent, I'm using it with a specific purpose in mind. I'm looking for a grade-A wanker. Matcher's finest export.

I fill out my profile with a bemused smile, adding a line that I'm sure will raise a few eyebrows:

Love getting into trouble and causing chaos? Want a free holiday to Australia? Drop me a message.

Then I start swiping right. On everyone.

It doesn't take long for my phone to light up like a Christmas tree. Notifications are coming in faster than I can read them, my phone getting hot from the sheer volume of replies. I expected to get some interest, sure, but this is ridiculous.

Wow, I can't believe that so many people are actually messaging me, and I have a sneaking suspicion it has less to do with my profile pic and more to do with me offering a free holiday in a cost-of-living crisis.

I start scrolling through the messages, but it's overwhelming. How am I supposed to sift through all of this? I don't exactly have time to vet them all, and I definitely don't want to wade through the typical 'hey beautiful' or 'what's up' messages. I need someone who stands out, who screams, 'I'm the absolute worst, pick me!'

And then, one message catches my eye. It's from a guy named Joseph. His profile picture shows a cute enough guy – blonde, with his hair long and floppy on top and short on the sides, who wears round-rim glasses that give him a kind of nerdy charm. But it's the message that hooks me:

I'll bet you're getting a lot of messages from a lot of freaks. But I'm the freak you should choose.

I laugh out loud. He might be a freak, but at least he's a funny one. And that's more than I can say for most of these guys.

Normally, I'd take my time, maybe chat to him for a few days, before arranging to meet up. But I'm on a schedule, and if I'm going to pull this off, I need to move fast. Besides, the worse he is, the better it is for me, right?

I type out a reply:

> You've got my attention, Joseph. What makes you the freak I should choose?

It doesn't take long for him to reply:

> Because I'm the kind of guy who sees 'free holiday' and thinks, 'there must be a catch'. And I'm not afraid to find out.

Another laugh escapes me. He's definitely intriguing, I'll give him that. I hesitate for only a moment before firing back:

> How about we discuss it over a drink? Tonight.

He agrees without hesitation, suggesting a bar in town.

Joseph seems like the right balance, between wild and normal, the kind I can work with. After all, I want someone who can cause trouble, but not someone who will cut me up into a million little pieces.

On Matcher, you just never know if you're going to meet Magic Mike or Michael Myers.

14

I'm not sure how much a girl can expect to get out of a date with a man who is only in it for a free holiday... and yet here I am. I suppose, usually on dates, everyone is desperate for something. At least we're being 'cards on the table' honest about our motives, and maybe that's a good start? Who knows? Like I said, I'm here.

And so is Joseph, which is the first good sign. The second is that he looks exactly like his photos. He's cute, with messy blonde hair, and he's as tall as his pictures made him look which is rarer than you might think. It always baffles me, when men actively trick you into thinking they're much taller than they are, because the rationale is clearly something along the lines of: if they can just get you through the door, they can sell you anything.

The only thing I am not expecting is his outfit. Specifically his Spider-Man shirt. I mean, it's fun, I guess, in a geeky way. It's very loud and bright, like something an eight-year-old might wear to go to a restaurant with their parents. Child formal – and yet adult-sized.

'Lana, hello,' he says excitedly, offering me a hand to shake.

Interesting choice. Not many men start a date with a handshake.

All I can do is go with it so I reach out my hand, only for him to quickly whip his away, put his thumb to his nose, and wiggle his fingers.

'Ayy, I got you,' he says with a laugh.

'Erm, yeah, you did,' I say with a polite laugh, wondering if I'm in some sort of *Big* situation, because seriously?

This is going to be a long night.

We find a table for two and take a seat. I can't help but notice that Joseph seems to be looking around for something.

'Is everything okay?' I ask.

'Yeah – you're going to like this,' he says, leaning in slightly. 'I told them it's your birthday.'

'You did?' I reply.

'Yeah, but not just that,' he continues. 'I told them you were eighty.'

'You...?'

'They're bringing you a cake,' he tells me, pleased with himself.

I don't even know what to say right now.

'Well, who doesn't love cake?' I eventually reply.

'You're welcome,' he replies with a wink. 'And I ordered us a couple of cocktails. They're on their way.'

Joseph seems like... I don't know. Like there's a lot going on, but it all just feels off. I can't put my finger on it.

Sure enough, a waiter arrives and places two cocktails down in front of us.

'Oh, wow,' I blurt as I stare at the two glasses, one filled with a bright blue liquid and one that is green. There is something fancy going on with the glasses – I think they must have an LED in the bottom, that makes the drinks glow.

'What flavour are they?' I ask Joseph.

'Blue and green,' he tells me vaguely. 'Enjoy.'

It is the blue one that has been placed down in front of me so I take a sip. Oh, boy, that is sweet and sour and it tastes of absolutely nothing specific, as though the flavour truly is just blue.

Joseph pulls a face at his green drink.

'Actually, no, this isn't what I want,' he says. 'Can we swap?'

'Can we swap drinks?' I reply, like I may have misheard him.

He nods, holding out his hand.

'Erm... sure,' I say, because I don't really know what else to say.

I slide my drink his way and he pushes his back to me.

He takes a sip and pulls a face.

'I know – why don't we see if the table next to us wants to swap drinks,' he suggests, his eyes wide.

'Wait, what?' I reply.

I'm not sure I can go with the flow for much longer because, seriously, something is up.

'Actually, why don't we order every drink on the menu,' he continues. 'We could keep sending them back. I saw this prank video, on YouTube...'

Joseph throws his arms out wildly and accidentally hits a woman walking past us.

'Oh, my goodness, miss, I'm terribly sorry,' he tells her. 'My sincerest apologies.'

'That's okay,' she tells him.

'Anyway, as I was saying, there's this guy on YouTube, who does pranks...'

As he continues, something occurs to me. Oh my God – he's faking it. Joseph isn't a bad boy at all. He's doing this for the free holiday!

Oh, suddenly it all makes sense. The odd behaviour, the ugly shirt – telling people it's my eightieth birthday.

I narrow my eyes at him.

'Is this all an act?' I ask him.

'What do you mean?' he says, clearly feigning innocence.

'Are you faking?' I reply. 'Are you pretending to be undateable?'

'No,' he insists. 'Of course not!'

'Oh, you are such a terrible liar,' I reply – it's hard not to find this amusing.

Joseph exhales heavily.

'Okay, yeah, fine, I am… exaggerating, shall we say, just a little – but there's a free holiday on the line,' he reminds me – as though I could forget.

'I appreciate the effort,' I reply. 'I'm guessing you went out and bought that ugly shirt for the occasion?'

As Joseph winces, I realise I've just put my foot in it.

'No… no, I already owned this,' he admits.

Oops.

'Here's the thing,' he begins, leaning in. 'Look what a great job I'm doing, of faking it. You don't want to take someone who is actually a nightmare, you want someone who is willing to act like it. And I can do it, I really can. I'm prepared to go full-on crazy, just say the word.'

I can't help but smile. Joseph is clearly a good guy but his version of pretending to be crazy is just actually kind of crazy. It's too much.

'I don't think this is going to work,' I tell him. 'Sorry. It's my fault, it was my own silly idea. I appreciate you trying.'

'Give me one last chance?' he suggests.

'Sorry,' I say again, shaking my head.

Joseph sighs.

'I'm going to the bathroom,' he tells me, pulling himself to his feet.

Alone for a moment, I laugh to myself as I sip my drink. Why on earth did I think this would work? Whether Joseph is actually crazy or just acting that way, he's in it for himself, for the free holiday, and if I stick myself on a dating site like Matcher and tell everyone there is a free holiday up for grabs, well, that's a sure-fire way to isolate the worst of an already generally pretty bad bunch. Now that I think about it, I'm lucky that Joseph was putting it on, because things could have got seriously out of hand otherwise.

The loud, high-pitched scream of the fire alarm snaps me from my thoughts. I instinctively place my hands over my ears and glance around – yes, because ignoring it is exactly what you're supposed to do.

The music cuts out and staff spring to action, trying to calmly usher everyone towards their closest exit, until we're safely outside in the chilly night air.

As we stand in the street, I hug myself to keep warm. Everyone looks as confused as I feel – no one seems to know what's going on, and I have no idea if Joseph has made it out okay.

It's amazing how reassuringly quickly the fire brigade arrives on the scene, and they spring to action in an instant. I notice one flustered-looking member of staff pointing inside, showing them where to go, before they run in. I'll always be in awe of people who run towards danger instead of away from it. Okay, sure, I'm a bit like that myself, but not actual danger – it's more like I run into stupidity.

'Oh my gosh, Joseph,' I blurt as he finds me in the crowd. 'Are you okay? Did you see a fire or anything?'

'No,' he replies, tucking his hands into his pockets to keep them warm. 'Just the chaos.'

I watch as more firefighters run into the building.

'I wonder what's going on,' I think out loud.

I turn to Joseph who is glancing around, looking left to right, making sure no one can hear us.

'I did it,' he blurts, his expression wildly darting between guilt and pride.

'What?' I whisper back, my jaw on the floor.

'I pulled the fire alarm,' he tells me. 'I told you I could be crazy.'

There's crazy and then there is just plain stupid.

'Are you serious?' I reply.

'Yeah,' he says. 'I just wanted to show you that I can be what you need me to be. I'm not all talk – I'm willing to do what it takes, to cause trouble.'

If there is one thing I am certain of, it's that I do not want to take someone to the wedding who is going to ruin it. Joseph is really taking things too far.

Before I can say anything, a member of staff approaches us.

'Hi, I'm just making sure that everyone is okay, and seeing if anyone has left any belongings inside,' she checks. 'Obviously, no one is going back in tonight.'

I shake my head.

'No, nothing,' Joseph tells her, his cheeks flushing.

'That's great,' the staff member replies. 'We apologise for the inconvenience, but we want to reassure you that no one got hurt – everyone involved is okay.'

'What do you mean?' I can't help but ask.

'The fire,' she says, looking at me like I'm stupid. 'One of our new employees was being careless, trying to light a birthday cake with eighty candles, and he started a fire. Luckily someone pulled the fire alarm right away and we were able to get it under control, or it could have been a lot worse.'

Joseph just stares at her blankly. I manage to wait until she's gone before I allow myself a smile.

Poor Joseph. Even when he's trying to be a bad boy, he still winds up doing good. Either way, I definitely shouldn't take him to the wedding with me. I'm just going to have to think of something – anything – else.

15

So, the date last night didn't go to plan. Honestly, it's a dark day on earth when you can't even rely on Matcher for a genuinely bad date.

The irony, in all of this, is that Joseph actually seems like he might be a nice, cool guy – when he's not pretending to be a psychopath to bag himself a free holiday.

I'm sitting at my desk, trying to work, but all I can think about is my next move. Anyone who dares to say I have no drive or motivation has obviously never seen me when I'm angry, because spite and pettiness light a fire under me like nothing else.

I really thought mentioning what I was doing on my Matcher profile might only attract the weirdos I needed but it turns out everyone is willing to go a long way (you can't get further than Australia, can you?) to get a free holiday, and I'm getting so many messages that my phone might quite literally blow up from the heat it gives off every time I use the app for too long.

'Honestly, it was the worst date I have ever been on,' Molly tells Faye.

That catches my attention. I turn my attention from my computer screen and focus on Molly and Faye's conversation.

'Oh, no! What happened?' Faye asks.

'Oh, where do I even start?' Molly sighs, leaning back in her chair. 'First of all, he was late. Not just a little late – like, an hour late. And when he finally shows up, he doesn't even apologise. Just walks in like he owns the place, sits down, and immediately starts talking shit about his ex, and not just to me, he even started telling the waiter.'

'Wow,' Faye says with a wince. 'How long did that go on for?'

'The entire evening,' Molly says, rolling her eyes. 'I know more about his ex now than I know about my own exes. Apparently, she was the love of his life, and no one will ever measure up to her, but she was also a "hoe-bag" who slept with his brothers – plural.'

I don't think I've ever seen Faye lost for words, so that's kind of cool to witness.

'And then...' Molly continues – there's more? '...he orders the most expensive thing on the menu without even looking at it. When I mentioned that it seemed a bit over the top, he gave me this smug smile and said, "Don't worry, I've got money coming out of my arse."'

Faye's mouth drops open in disbelief.

'Please tell me you made him pay for everything,' she replies.

'Of course I did,' Molly says, laughing. 'Even if I could have afforded it, I wasn't going to waste my money on that. But the best part? After all of that, he insists on walking me home – like he's some kind of gentleman – and when we get to my door, he offered me a fist bump.'

'No!' Faye gasps, laughing. 'Please tell me you're joking.'

'I wish I was,' Molly says. 'He fist-bumps everyone and calls them "matey". Even women. Like, who does that? And, then he asked if he could come in...'

Wow, he sounds like a nightmare. And a great bad date for a wedding.

'Can I get his number?' I ask with a laugh, maybe only half-joking.

'Why the hell would you want a bad date?' Faye asks, raising an eyebrow. 'You overheard all of that and thought he sounded like a catch?'

Faye and Molly exchange glances, clearly confused, but not looking all that surprised if I'm being honest.

I hesitate, wondering if I should just tell them. It could be good, to be honest with someone about what's going on, and to talk to some girl's girls about the issue. Maybe they'll talk me out of it? Sure, I'm still raging with anger, but maybe I'm overreacting... maybe? I need a second (and third) opinion.

'My sister, Seph, is getting married, in Australia – that's why I'm taking time off,' I explain.

'Okay,' Faye says, waiting for it to make sense.

'Except it's become clear that it's not exactly the type of wedding where I'll be welcomed with open arms. It's going to be this snooty, old-money, over-the-top wedding. Seph grew up rich, with my dad, and uses "summer" as a verb. I grew up in a normal house, with my mum, and I use summer as an opportunity to buy my winter wardrobe for 80 per cent off.'

'Oh,' Faye says plainly.

'And you might think I'm paranoid, or insecure about not being part of the elite like they are, but the other day, my family staged this... well, it was basically an intervention,' I continue, feeling the anger bubbling away inside me as I recall all of the details. 'They called me over for lunch, so we could all "talk" about the wedding, but really, it was just an excuse to warn me – *only me* – not to embarrass them.'

'Are you serious?' Molly asks, her expression mirroring Faye's outrage.

'Yep,' I say, nodding. '"Lana, make sure you behave, make sure you dress modestly, don't bring a date who will embarrass you and this family" – like they're expecting me to show up in ripped jeans with a guy who just got out of prison. Apparently anything above and including a C cup isn't classy – breasts aren't classy – so they want me to, I don't know, keep them covered? Absolutely not awkward at all, sitting at the dining table with my family, talking about my tits. And if that's not all bad enough, at the very last minute, they have moved their wedding day to my thirtieth birthday, because the groom's gran is superstitious, that's the only reason, and they didn't even mention that the date was my birthday.'

'That's so messed up,' Faye says. 'I'm fuming for you!'

'Me too,' Molly chimes in. 'That's just... awful. Who does that to their own sister?'

'Right?' I say, feeling a strange mix of validation and fury. 'And the thing is, I'm not like them, so I can't prove them wrong, so part of me really wants to prove them right. I want to show up with someone who'll really shake things up, just to make a point. But then again, maybe I should just not go at all.'

Faye shakes her head emphatically.

'Absolutely not. You should go. And you should cause as much trouble as you possibly can. Show them they can't treat you like that,' she tells me.

'Exactly,' Molly agrees. 'And you need to look incredible while doing it. Go out and buy the hottest, most jaw-dropping "fuck you" dress you can find.'

'A "fuck you/fuck me" dress,' Faye adds, grinning.

I laugh, the idea of strutting into that wedding in a killer dress and wreaking a little havoc sounding better and better.

'I like the way you both think,' I tell them. 'I was worried I might be overreacting…'

'Not at all,' Faye says. 'Show them that they can't mess with you. Go in there, living your best "worst" life and show them how happy and comfortable with yourself you are.'

I do like the sound of that…

Molly nods.

'I could give you the number of that guy I went out with, but honestly, he was just kind of sad. Not the kind of guy who's going to make a scene,' she tells me.

'Yeah, I think I need someone who is going to be more… impactful,' I reply. 'Not someone who is going to make people simply feel sorry for me. I need a certain sort of date… a real piece of work. Someone who'll drive them absolutely insane.'

Faye's eyes light up as her mouth twists into the kind of grin that makes me think she's on to something.

'I know just where you can find the perfect man,' she says, clapping her hands excitedly. 'My brother is the doorman at Eros, and he can let you in, so that you can find a rich arsehole to take, to compete with the other rich arseholes – your family – no offence. That's exactly what you need.'

None taken, she's not wrong.

My eyes widen in surprise. I've heard of Eros – everyone has. It's the most exclusive club in Leeds, where the rich and famous go to play. The place with the notoriously strict dress code, where people have been turned away for having blue nails, or not seeming happy enough, or seeming too happy, or having a phone that wasn't an iPhone. Of course, it's where Seph used to go for nights out, before she settled down with Chester, because apparently it's fine and sophisticated to enjoy a night out if it's at an exclusive venue, but if you spend your night dancing at somewhere like Saturn until 4 a.m., drinking alcopops, surrounded by dry-humping students, it makes you some kind of loser. Hmm, okay, perhaps that wasn't the best example.

'Can you really get me in?' I ask, feeling a spark of excitement, not just at the idea of finding someone to take to the wedding to cause a stink, but because I'm getting to go to Eros!

'Of course,' Faye assures me. 'He does it for me all the time. I'll let him know.'

Oh, this is exactly what I need. I need to fight fire with fire, and Eros is just the place to do that.

16

On top of being a commoner, a pauper and the owner of an extra-tacky pair of D cups, I am an eternal pessimist, so I wasn't expecting to get through the door at Eros tonight.

So it was no shock to me when the bouncer's eyes narrowed as I approached the entrance. Even with Faye's assurances that her brother would let me in, I still wasn't expecting to make it past the velvet rope.

And yet here I am, walking through the club, surrounded by beautiful people who look like they've been picked straight off their busy Instagram grids. It's a weird feeling, like I've somehow wandered on to the set of a movie, but I'm trying my best to blend in.

To play it safe, I opted for an outfit that screams 'I totally belong here, honest'. A sleek black jumpsuit with a plunging neckline (I know, not demure, not mindful at all...) paired with a tailored leather jacket that's warm enough to survive the chilly January weather outside. My boots are designer knock-offs, but they're the best ones you can get without actually being designer, and my hair is styled in loose waves that I'm hoping read as effortlessly cool and chic. It is just hair, though, so who knows if I'm pulling it off.

You don't have to look far to spot a famous face – and while it could be a good idea to take a famous person to the wedding (assuming I could talk one into it – doubtful) because they could totally overshadow the whole thing, it's also possible that Seph and Chester might think it's cool, like it would give them street cred, even as a novelty, so that might backfire. I need someone more like them, some old-money A-hole. Someone well off, someone full of it, someone who will compete with them and annoy them and make them feel bad about themselves so that they can see how it feels. I don't know how I'm going to find someone like that, but I'm going to try.

I make my way to the bar, feeling a little out of place as I order a drink.

'One porno martini, please,' I say, reading the edgy name from the menu.

The barman looks at me like he's sizing me up, but then nods and gets to work.

A moment later, he slides the drink over and says, 'That'll be £32.'

It's funny, that it's called a porno, because I really feel like I'm getting fucked. £32 for one drink? Wild.

I take a sip (it's nice, but £32, come on!) as I wander around the club, trying to look like I belong here. But as I weave through the crowd, it quickly becomes apparent that I'm invisible. No one makes eye contact, no one smiles or nods in my direction. It's like they can all sense that I'm not one of them, like rich people have some kind of sixth sense for spotting impostors. Which is ironic, really, because I feel like a ghost right now.

As I'm wondering how the hell I'm going to pick someone out

and actually get them to talk to me – and that's before I convince them to be my wedding date – I feel a hand on my arm.

'Hey, you,' a voice says, and I spin around, my heart leaping at the possibility of a man approaching me. But then I realise it's someone I know.

'Oh my gosh, Fergus, hello,' I say, trying not to sound too disappointed.

Fergus leans in and gives me a kiss on the cheek.

'It's been forever, Lana. How are you?' he asks.

I smile, a little awkwardly.

'I'm doing great. How about you?' I ask.

'I'm good, I'm good,' he says, nodding. 'Well, apart from a knee injury that put an end to the old ruggers career. Now I just play for fun, but I'm doing all right. It's so good to see you. Can I buy you another drink when you're finished with that one?'

I glance at my half-empty glass (ha! I told you I was a pessimist), and I know that I can't really afford to keep up with the drink prices here. 'Sure, thanks. That would be great.'

It's worth pointing out, at this point, how I know Fergus, because it explains why I'm feeling slightly awkward. Fergus is Seph's ex-boyfriend.

'Let's grab a seat, catch up a bit,' Fergus suggests, and I follow him to a quiet corner where we can talk.

We settle into a plush, dimly lit booth.

'How's the family?' he asks.

'They're all fine,' I reply, not really wanting to dive into that particular topic.

'Good, good,' he says, nodding again. There's a pause, and then he looks at me with a smile. 'You're looking good, Lana. I always really liked you, you know? You were different from the rest of your family.'

I laugh, though there's an edge to it.

'I know I'm different. But people who know my family don't usually think that's a good thing,' I point out.

Fergus shakes his head, his expression softening.

'No, I mean it as a compliment. You're... normal,' he tells me. Erm, is that a compliment? 'And in our circle, that's rare. Most of the people we grew up with are a bit mental, honestly.'

I can't help but laugh at that.

'Yeah, I guess they are,' I reply.

We chat for a while longer, exchanging the usual pleasantries and carefully reminiscing about the old days, but avoiding the topic of my sister, of course. Fergus is easy to talk to, and it feels good to be around someone from that world who actually seems to like me for who I am, not despite it.

Eventually, Fergus points out that my drink is empty and offers to get me another one. I thank him as he heads back to the bar, watching him for a moment. He's a typical rugby union player – tall, broad-shouldered, with that rugged, slightly scruffy look that comes from years of playing a sport where getting roughed up is par for the course. He's good-looking in that boy-next-door way – if you live next door to Buckingham Palace, that is.

He returns with another drink, setting it down in front of me.

'Come on then, let's get it over with,' he says. 'How's Seph?'

I hesitate, not sure how much to share, but then decide to be honest.

'She's doing well. Really well, actually,' I reply.

'Yeah, I heard she's getting married,' he says, and there's a flicker of something – maybe hurt, maybe bitterness – in his eyes. 'It broke my heart when she dumped me for Chet.'

Chet is what Chester's friends call him.

I ignore the latter half of his statement.

'Yes, she's getting married in Australia. Really soon, actually,' I tell him.

'Are you going?' he asks curiously.

'Yeah, I am,' I say, feeling a bit of the old resentment bubble up. 'I told them I'm bringing a plus-one, but... well, I haven't quite figured out who that is yet.'

Fergus looks thoughtful for a moment.

'I know it might be a bit awkward, but... you could take me,' he suggests.

'You?' I reply – did he really just say that?

He reaches out, taking my face gently in his hand, and I can't help but freeze.

'Lana, I've always thought you were interesting. Beautiful, too. It would be an honour to be your date,' he tells me.

I think for a moment. Showing up to Seph's wedding with her ex-boyfriend would certainly send a message. It would rattle them all, maybe even distract everyone on the big day. But is that really me? Am I the kind of girl who would do something like that? Even for revenge? That's never been my style. Sure, I want to turn up with someone to annoy them all, but I don't want to actually ruin it, or hurt anyone on a personal level.

Before I can answer, Fergus leans in a little closer, his voice taking on a persuasive tone. 'Plus, it would make Seph sick with jealousy. Her sister and her ex, getting sloppy at her wedding – it would absolutely fuck the day.'

There's a flash of something almost evil in his eyes, a look I only catch for a second before he leans in for a kiss. Oh my God, is he serious right now?

I pull back, my heart racing.

'Erm, that's probably not a good idea,' I point out, oddly politely, given the circumstances.

He stares at me, a mix of disbelief and frustration on his face.

'Are you crazy? Your sister never had a nice word to say about you, and if I were you, I'd burn her wedding to the ground,' he tells me.

I know Seph isn't my biggest fan, so I'm not surprised to hear that, but even so, there's a line I can't cross. Staying true to myself is important, and while my family may think I'm a disappointment, I don't want to let myself down.

'I appreciate the offer,' I say softly, 'but I'll figure something else out.'

Fergus looks at me for a long moment, then sighs, leaning back in his seat.

'You're too nice, Lana. That's your problem,' he tells me. 'I know, they're your family, but you're their family too. Think about that.'

I mean, he's not wrong about that last part, but I know that taking him would be a big mistake. I'll find someone to go with. Someone I can have a laugh with, someone who will piss them all off, and cause chaos with me, but the fun kind.

He must be out there somewhere...

17

'Come on then, spill the beans,' Faye says, her voice echoing slightly in the fitting room area. She and Molly are lounging on a bench just outside the dressing room, where I'm currently trying on what feels like the millionth dress of the day.

'Not great,' I call back from behind the curtain. 'Honestly, it actually went worse than I was expecting it to.'

'You got in though, right?' Faye checks.

'You didn't get turned away for not having a gold-plated handbag or something?' Molly jokes.

'Oh, yeah, I got in,' I reply. 'That wasn't the issue at all. I wasn't expecting much, I had managed expectations. I was just hoping to find someone obnoxious enough to take to Seph's wedding, who would out-rich them and out-posh them and make me feel better about the whole thing.'

'So, what happened?' Molly asks, almost excitedly.

'I was wandering around the club, feeling like a complete ghost because no one was even looking at me. I went to the bar, I ordered a drink – it cost £32.'

'Daylight robbery,' Molly replies.

'I nearly spat it back out, in shock, but it was too expensive to waste,' I joke. 'Anyway, I'm standing there, trying to figure out how I'm going to talk to anyone, when this guy approaches me.'

'Finally!' Molly says. 'Who was he? Was he hot?'

'Well, that's the thing,' I say, pausing for dramatic effect. 'It wasn't just some random guy. It was Fergus... my sister's ex-boyfriend.'

'No!' Faye shrieks.

'Yep,' I confirm. 'He comes over, all smiles, and starts chatting like we're old friends. Offers to buy me a drink, which I obviously accepted because there was no way I was paying for another one of those overpriced cocktails.'

'What happened next?' Molly asks – honestly, she's enjoying this way too much.

'We sat down, had a little chat, and then out of nowhere, he tells me he's always thought I was "interesting" and "beautiful". And then he offered to be my date to the wedding.'

'No way!' Faye exclaims. 'That is unhinged.'

'I know, right? I mean, on the one hand, turning up with Seph's ex would definitely make a statement. But on the other hand, it just felt... wrong, you know? Like, I want to piss them off, but I don't want to actually hurt anyone. That's not me,' I explain.

'You're right,' Molly says. 'But seriously, what was he thinking? That sounds so awkward.'

'I know,' I say, laughing a little. 'And to make things worse, he tried to kiss me.'

'The audacity of men,' Faye says.

'I had to pull back and tell him that was definitely not happening,' I continue. 'He told me I was crazy and that if he were me, he'd burn Seph's wedding to the ground.'

'Oh my God,' Molly says with a gasp. 'That's intense.'

'Yeah, I could have really used that fake phone-call app

everyone at work thinks is so stupid,' I joke. 'It would've been perfect for that moment.'

Faye snorts.

'Forget the phone call, you needed an ex-orcist,' she quips.

We all burst out laughing at that.

'So, it's back to the drawing board, I guess,' I tell them with a sigh, smoothing out the dress, almost ready to step out and show them.

'Maybe you're not out of options just yet,' Molly says. 'What about Redflags?'

'What do you mean?' I ask, frowning slightly.

'Well, some of the guys posted on there are total creeps, sure, but some of them are just really shitty dates,' she tells me. 'You could use the app to find those guys and go on dates with them, see if any of them might be right for the wedding.'

Use Redflags for bad instead of good?

'That's... actually kind of brilliant. Crazy, sure, but so crazy that it might work,' I reply.

'You should definitely give it a go,' Faye says. 'Even if it's a stupid idea, it might be a fun exercise, and good feedback for the app.'

'Maybe I will,' I say as I step out of the changing room.

The dress I'm wearing is... well, it's something else. It's black and tight, stopping about halfway down my thigh, clinging to my curves in all the right ways. The neckline is high, but the middle of the dress features a panel of see-through black mesh that plunges almost down to my belly button. The hips have mesh panels too, giving the whole thing an edgy, daring look. It's the kind of dress that meets the dress code with the high neck but definitely pushes the boundaries with the mesh panels. Seph never said anything about mesh, though, so technically, I'm in the clear.

'Oh my God, perfect,' Molly says, practically squealing.

'Are you kidding me? I'd fuck you in that thing,' Faye adds, giving me a quiet round of applause.

I bite my lip, turning slightly to get a better view of the back in the mirror.

'Are you sure?' I ask.

'You might have to buy me dinner first,' Faye jokes, making us all laugh again.

'No, I mean about wearing it to the wedding,' I clarify, still feeling a little unsure.

'Absolutely,' Faye says, nodding emphatically.

'Honestly, it's so nice,' Molly adds. 'You look so comfortable, and so yourself in it.'

'I feel it,' I reply, feeling a smile tug at the sides of my lips. 'I feel really good in it, really confident.'

'Then buy it,' Faye commands me.

I smile to myself, looking at my reflection one more time. The dress is so me, and it does technically fit the dress code. My family might hate it, but that's kind of the point, isn't it? They already think I'm beneath them, so why not show up in something that's completely and unapologetically me?

'Okay,' I say finally. 'I'll take it.'

And everyone else can deal with it.

18

—————

I walk through the front door, juggling my keys, my shopping bags and the cheap bottle of white wine I bought myself for my busy night in.

The smell of something cooking hits me immediately, and my stomach drops. Oh God, please don't tell me Steve's cooked for me again. Why did I believe him, when he said I could live with him 'no strings attached' – all I have done is made myself available for unsubtle persuading to give things another go, 24/7. It's going to take more than a lasagne, or whatever it is he has cooked – even if it does actually smell pretty great.

As I turn the corner into the living room, ready to launch into some half-hearted excuse, I stop dead in my tracks. Steve is sitting at the dining table, but he's not alone. Is he on a date? Oh, awkward...

Then I notice the woman next to him. She's in her early twenties, with lilac hair, and a nose piercing.

Steve jumps up as if I've just caught him in bed with her.

'Oh, Lana, you're home early,' he blurts out, his face flushing.

I glance at the clock on the wall. If anything, I'm late.

Oh, this is sad. So, so sad. I see what he's trying to do, and it's tragic.

'It's okay, I've got stuff to do. I'll just head to my room,' I say with a smile.

Steve's relief is theatrical.

'That might be best,' he says, his voice a little too eager.

As I walk away, I can't help but laugh to myself. What is he doing? Trying to make me jealous? Because as attempts go, this one is seriously pathetic.

In the relative safety and privacy of my room, I plonk myself down on the bed with a heavy sigh.

Déjà vu hits me like a tonne of bricks. Here I am, back on the apps – again. After swearing off Matcher only a matter of days ago, I'm now downloading Redflags.

I guess Redflags isn't technically a dating app, but I'm about to misuse it as one, so same difference, right?

I sign up, and as soon as I'm in, I start scanning the message threads. Curiosity gets the better of me, and the first thing I do is dive into the posts marked with the biggest red flags. Wow. Some men are such creeps. I'm actually really glad this app exists, and I feel a twinge of guilt for making a mockery of it by using it this way, but it's doing its job because I'm definitely steering clear of these guys.

Instead, I shift to the section with minor flags, where people seem to be having more of a laugh about the dumb things some men are doing on dates. I need someone my family won't like, but not someone actually bad.

One post catches my eye: *Rude with a twist*. Intrigued, I click on it. The thread describes a Matcher user named Mike – username BigMikey69, he sounds perfect already – who is apparently mildly rude to everyone. Not great, but the use of 'mildly' makes it sound like it could be subtle enough to be funny, in a 'laughing at him not with him' kind of way? Maybe? I don't know, I've never picked out a man for his bad qualities, although my dating history might suggest otherwise.

The really interesting fun fact is the 'twist' though: the woman who posted about Mike says that he has a bulge in his trousers – a long, hard one that stretches down his thigh, and he not only enhances it with seriously tight trousers but he also likes to sit in a way that showcases it. She says it's so monstrous, and so emphasised, that she is 100 per cent convinced it's a cucumber, that there is no way it's real.

The comments are funny, with lots of people saying they're going to look him up on Matcher, but everyone generally agreeing that it's too bizarre and they wouldn't want to go on a date with him.

Ding, ding, ding (or should that be dong, dong, dong?) – just my type on paper.

BigMikey69 would definitely catch some eyes at the wedding – probably quite literally. The idea of my family trying to work out what to do with their faces, figuring out where to look, and what to say, while I parade around with Mr Cucumber on my arm seems so funny to me – plus, the kind of guy to stuff his trousers is definitely going to be the kind of guy to cause trouble with me.

But to look him up, I'll have to download Matcher again.

'This is the last time,' I tell myself out loud as I reluctantly start downloading the app. I've definitely said that before, though.

There's a knock on my door.

'Yeah?' I call out, half-distracted by my phone.

Steve walks in, looking awkward.

'Sorry if that was uncomfortable for you,' he says, rubbing the back of his neck.

I stifle a laugh.

'Steve, it's fine,' I assure him.

He hesitates for a second, as though he's working out what to say next, to get a reaction out of me.

'I'm ready to move on, and you need to accept that,' he adds.

I nod, trying to keep a straight face.

'I have, Steve. Really,' I insist. 'I promise.'

He turns to leave but then stops in his tracks. After a moment, he turns back around, looking almost pained.

'Why don't you seem remotely bothered that I'm having dinner with another woman?' he asks, frustrated that his little stunt hasn't worked.

'Do you really want to know?' I ask him.

'Yes,' he says, clearly very keen to know where he's going wrong.

'It's because I know that's your cousin, Steve,' I say plainly. 'I remember seeing her in your Facebook photos.'

Steve's face goes beet red. He stares at me for a second, looking both embarrassed and annoyed, before storming off without another word.

I lie back on my bed, laughing to myself now that I'm alone again. Did he really think that was going to achieve anything? The whole thing is so pathetic, I almost feel bad for him. Almost.

19

There are two things I am grateful for, on my date with BigMikey69 right now. One is that this place is dimly lit and the other is that we are sitting at a table, because if 'the thing' was in my eyeline, I don't think I would be able to concentrate.

It has to be a cucumber – it has to be. There's just no way that thing is real, and it's low-key disturbing that he thinks it's going to help him pick up women. He really does accentuate it, in tight trousers, and he almost brandishes it as he moves around.

'Okay, Lana,' Mike says with a grin. 'You know the drill. Tell me about yourself.'

'Well, I work for a company that builds lifestyle apps,' I begin.

'Lifestyle apps?' he repeats my words back to me.

Oh, God, don't ask me which.

'Yeah, just little things, to make day-to-day life easier for people,' I explain.

'Yeah, people are idiots,' he replies. 'If you can convince them they need apps, to function, why not milk it?'

I nod, not sure how to respond to that. I see what the person who added him to Redflags meant, when she said he was kind of rude.

'What about you? What do you do?' I ask.

'I'm in property development,' he says, leaning forward slightly. 'I've got a monster development right now.'

I can see that.

'Basically, I buy semi-detached houses in shit areas, do them up, knock them through into one – you wouldn't believe the crap people are willing to pay for, if it gives them more space.'

'Sounds... enterprising,' I reply.

'Yeah, if you ever need a big semi, you know who to call,' he tells me.

Oh my God, is he joking?

'Enough about work, what do you do for fun?' he asks. 'Please don't say yoga or some other basic chick thing.'

Yikes.

'I like going out,' I tell him. 'Watching movies, going out for meals, bars – basic person stuff.'

'Okay but there's going out for meals and there's going out for meals,' he replies. 'A McDonald's isn't a meal.'

I mean, it's definitely a meal I eat at least once a week...

'There's nothing wrong with fast food,' I reply. 'Some items on the menu are healthier than what you'd order in a fancy restaurant.'

Honestly, my family fucking love any food with another food inside it, and I'm not just talking like truffle-stuffed chicken, I mean they'll eat like a rabbit, in a duck, in a turkey, in a calf. Ergh, it's putting me off the chicken nuggets I'm going to get on the way home.

'Healthier is just another word for bland,' he says with a shrug. 'But hey, if that's your thing. Just don't ask me to eat any of it.'

'Noted,' I reply. 'So, what about you? Any hobbies?'

'I like sports,' he says, stretching his arms out like he's showing off. Ha, and he accused me of having basic 'female' hobbies. 'Football, rugby, whatever. I'm a man of simple pleasures. I usually prefer pubs to bars like this though.'

'Yeah, these places can get a bit crowded, and loud,' I reply. 'They're less laid-back.'

'Full of posers,' he corrects me. 'It's like, come on, you're not impressing anyone by trying to flaunt what you've got.'

My thoughts exactly.

The waiter arrives with our drinks. As Mike takes his whisky he nods at the waiter. 'Thanks, man. Hopefully this one isn't as watered down as the last one.'

Yeah, he's definitely rude. So rude my family might actually quite like him.

Mike suddenly stretches his back, standing up from his chair. He places his hands on his hips and pushes his crotch in my direction, making the bulge in his trousers even more noticeable.

'I'm just a bit stiff,' he tells me.

I purse my lips, trying desperately not to laugh – or look.

'So I, erm, I'm going to Australia next week,' I tell him.

'Oh yeah?' he replies. 'I've never been, not sure it's my thing.'

Funny, because he looks like he's got the didgeridoo for it.

'It's my first time going there,' I reply. 'My sister is getting married. The wedding is going to be huge, and fancy, and I stupidly lied about having a plus-one to take with me, to save face, and now I don't have one, so it's going to be so embarrassing...'

Mike raises his eyebrows.

'So, you need someone to go with you?' he says. 'Someone impressive.'

'Yeah, but I have no idea where I'll find someone last minute,' I reply. 'I know it's a free holiday, free booze, free food – but it probably sounds too good to be true.'

He leans back in his chair, the cogs in his brain clearly turning.

'You're telling me all the drinks will be free?' he checks.

'Yep, all night long,' I say with a heavy sigh.

Mike's eyes light up, like he thinks he's just won the lottery.

'I could come with you,' he tells me.

'You could?' I reply, like the thought hadn't even crossed my mind.

'What's the deal though?' he says. 'Do I get to share a bed with you?'

I almost choke on my drink.

'It's more of a friends thing,' I say plainly – I don't think there would be room in a bed for the three of us anyway.

He nods, seeming to consider this.

'Yeah, if I'm being honest, I'd rather have the free holiday than a night with you – no offence.'

I can't help but laugh.

'None taken,' I assure him.

Now I'm more convinced than ever that he's packing a cucumber, because for all the work he's doing to shove it in my face, he isn't all that keen to actually show me it. Not that I mind, I hasten to add.

Mike reaches under the table and visibly adjusts himself. It's almost like he's daring me to comment on it.

'Well, I may be willing to help you out,' he says with a smile. 'I just need to pop outside and make a quick call first.'

'Okay,' I say, watching as he takes his phone from his pocket and walks away.

Hmm. Is Mike really the right guy to take with me? I mean, I don't actually want a date-date – I just need someone to send a message. They can have their own hotel room, do their own thing, but show up for the wedding events, show their face... or their cucumber, in Mike's case.

This isn't a stupid idea, is it? I know I'm upset, acting on pure emotion rather than logic, but Faye and Molly think I should go for it, and Fergus thought I should be going even harder... although I'm not sure *this* was quite what he meant by that.

'Lana,' Mike's voice interrupts my thoughts.

I look up at him and smile.

'Yeah?'

'Sorry,' he says with a big sigh. 'I can't come. My wife says no.'

His wife?

I blink, trying to process what he's just said.

'That's okay,' I manage to reply, and it really, really is. He's married? And on Matcher? I'm shocked right now, although not surprised generally – there are always plenty of married men on Matcher.

As Mike sits back down, looking almost apologetic, I decide it's definitely time to end this weird date. If only there was an app for that...

It's silly, but it's true, that despite the fact he just told me he was married, being a woman it still feels so scary, to knock someone back. You never know how a person will react, no matter how justified you are.

I would rather be embarrassed than unsafe.

'Oh my God, I'm so sorry, I need to go,' I tell him.

'What, really?' he replies. 'Is it because I'm married, because we—'

'Oh, no, nothing like that,' I insist. 'Just... period stuff. Like, it's come on thick and fast. I mean, I'm relieved, because I'd been checking my calendar in a bit of a panic, if you know what I mean but, yeah, I need to go sort it.'

He looks genuinely violated at the mention of that word.

'Yeah, right, you should go,' he tells me.

I stand up, grabbing my coat and bag – more than happy to be leaving.

As I walk out of the restaurant, I can't help but laugh to myself. This guy was more of a walking red flag than I expected – literally. Which reminds me, on the bus home, I should probably go on Redflags, and update the thread about Mike. Because being married is a way bigger deal than smuggling salad in his pants.

20

What is it they say about getting back on the horse?

Unwilling to be put off by my bizarre date with Tragic Mike, and with time running out before the wedding, I've already dived back into the murky waters of Redflags. This time, I've found another potential wedding date – a guy who works at a bar in town, and honestly, he sounds like he could be perfect. Or at least, perfect enough for my current needs.

I pick up the pace as I try to dodge a slow-moving group of schoolkids, clearly on their way to the Armouries, all suitably hyped to go and look at old weaponry.

I glance at my watch, swearing under my breath when I see the time. I'm here, at the bloody dock, it's just like trying to walk through quicksand, getting to the office door.

Late again – that's what Jennifer will say. She is going to have a field day if she catches me strolling in after 9 a.m. I really hate working for her. It's always supposed to be temporary, just until she finds a decent temp or her real assistant stops having babies to avoid her, but it never seems to end fast enough.

I finally make it to the office, a little breathless, and slide into my chair, trying to appear as though I've been there for ages.

'Morning,' I mouth to Faye and Molly.

Faye is on the phone, so she gives me a wave. Molly whispers good morning back.

Now that we're friendly, they don't judge me for things like being late, which is nice. Actually, no, we're not friendly, we're friends – and I really appreciate having them onside. Most of my friends are strictly night-out buddies, the kind of people you rarely see in the daylight. But with Faye and Molly, I have someone to talk to during the day, someone to hang out with, who I can tell all about my stupid problems – and they actually want to help me fix them, not just drink with me to forget them.

I mean, yeah, it does feel like they're egging me on with this whole wedding date thing, but isn't that what friends are for? To back you up when you're on a mission, no matter how ridiculous that mission might be?

I glance around the room again, praying Jennifer is in her office, or too busy to notice I've just come in. And then I spot her – thankfully deep in conversation in the meeting room. I let out a breath I didn't realise I was holding. It looks like I've got away with it, so maybe I can even grab a coffee before I start, as I didn't get the chance to make one before I left the flat.

'Coffee, anyone?' I mouth at Faye and Molly, already halfway out of my chair.

Faye smiles and nods.

'Please,' Molly adds.

I head toward the kitchen area, my mind already drifting to my plan for tonight – for my date. Well, my sort of date.

I hover in the kitchen area, and as I wait for the coffee machine to warm up, I aimlessly glance toward the meeting room, just to be nosy really.

Ugh, Steve is talking. Just the sight of him gives me the ick in every way imaginable these days. The harder he tries to get me to like him again, the less I'm interested.

We weren't even really a couple; we just dated for... what, a few weeks, max? It didn't last long enough for me to recall exactly how long it went on. But when I needed a place to stay, he swooped in with an offer, acting like it was no big deal, just a friend helping out a friend. We'd been over for ages by then, and he made it seem so innocent, and I really was grateful.

Now, though, it annoys me. The whole thing was a trap. He thought he could lure me back in, save the day, and win me over. To be honest, one of the reasons I'm still there is probably because of the fact that he only did it to manipulate me – it serves him right. I'm saving up, to get my own place – which is easier when you live rent-free – but once I have enough, I'm out of there.

I'm about to get back to making the coffee when something catches my eye in the meeting room. The back of a man's head – broad shoulders, familiar hair... No, it can't be. But that neck, that body language, even the way he's tilting his head slightly. I suddenly feel like I can smell his aftershave, which is impossible, right? I mean, even if it was *him* – which it most likely isn't – there's no way I'd be able to smell him through the bloody wall. Still, I can't stop staring, not because I think it's him, but because I really, really wish it was.

I often think about him, about how amazing things were when we were together. No one has measured up to him since. Sure, it was for the best that we parted ways when he went back to London, but the best thing generally isn't always the best thing for you personally, is it?

The meeting looks like it's coming to an end. People start standing up, gathering their things, and I keep one eye on the door, stirring my coffee more than it really needs. And then the man turns around, and my breath catches in my throat. It is him. It's Ethan, and he's heading this way.

Panic literally jolts through me, and before I can steady myself, I knock over a mug, sending it crashing to the floor. The noise is loud enough to make everyone around me turn their heads to see what it was. Great, Lana. Just great. Ten out of ten, as usual.

But at least the awkwardness is out of the way now. He's seen me. I've seen him. And now he's coming over to say hello, and...

'Hi,' I say, probably a little too brightly.

He laughs and it feels like a punch to the stomach.

'Hello, still causing trouble, I see,' he replies.

'You know it,' I reply, smiling back at him. 'Still trying to work here, I see...'

He laughs again. God, I've missed that laugh.

'I think I'm finally getting somewhere,' he says with a grin. 'You're looking good.'

'Thanks,' I reply, trying to keep my tone casual. 'You too.'

He isn't just looking good; he's looking phenomenal. Better than he did two years ago, if that's even possible. It's somehow both wonderful and devastating to see him again. Of course, I want him more than ever, but seeing him here, in this office of all places, reminds me of why we parted ways. We were nothing but trouble together, a dangerous mixture of chemicals that was always going to explode.

'How have you been?'

'So, how are you?'

Our questions collide in mid-air, overlapping in a way that makes us both laugh. There's this strange mix of familiarity and awkwardness between us, like we're trying to pick up from where we left off, but we can't quite do it.

Before either of us can say anything more, Steve rocks up alongside us, clearly muscling his way in to see what's going on.

'Hello,' he says – how did I ever tolerate his voice because lately it just makes me mad?

Oh, God, not right now, Steve.

'Lana,' he continues, not waiting for a reply – and louder now, like he's making an announcement. 'Can you get us some toilet roll on the way home, please? You wiped the last one out this morning.'

My eyes widen in horror, and I feel my face flush. That absolutely did not happen, and I can see exactly what he's doing. He's trying to embarrass me in front of Ethan, mark his territory, point out that we live together in the hope it puts him off. But I know better than to let him rattle me.

'Okay, Steve, sure, I'll do that,' I say, forcing a smile. My voice is calm, even though I want to throw the coffee in his face. 'Can you give us a minute, please?'

Oh, he's not happy with that. I can see it in the way his smile falters, but he slinks away, thankfully.

'Wow, you two are living together?' Ethan asks, unable to mask his surprise.

'No,' I blurt out quickly, maybe too quickly. 'I mean, yes, technically, we are living in the same flat, but we're not living together. I'm in his spare room while I find a new place. Are you still living in London?'

'Yeah,' he says with a smile that doesn't quite reach his eyes. 'Some things never change. So, you're still single?'

His question hangs in the air, and it only takes me a second or two to mentally dissect every word of it. 'Some things never change.' Does that mean some things have changed for him? And by asking if I'm still single, is there some kind of tone there? A hint? Does that mean he isn't still single? Or am I just over-thinking it? But then again, why wouldn't I overthink it?

I must already seem like a total loser, because nothing has changed since he saw me last, except now he knows I'm living with Steve out of desperation. I need to say something to make me look good, like I've got things going on too.

'Well, I'm actually going on a date tonight,' I say, the words slipping out of my mouth before I can think them through.

'Oh, that's great,' Ethan replies, his voice steady, and his expression annoyingly unreadable. 'Anywhere nice?'

'There's a new-ish bar I've never been to in town, called 24bar,' I reply, trying to sound casual. 'Should be good.'

It's not technically a date, though. I saw this guy, Pat, on Redflags, and his profile screenshot showed that he's the manager at 24bar. His main red flag was that he's a serial flirt with all women, even when he's on dates. But his other red flag... well, I need to see that one to believe it.

'Great,' Ethan says again, although his enthusiasm seems to be dropping off. 'Sort of a shame really, because I'm only here for one night, and I was going to see if... ah, it doesn't matter. Anyway, Jennifer wants to talk in her office. It was good to see you again though. Take care, yeah?'

And with that, he's gone, and I'm just standing there, watching the back of his head until he disappears.

Shit, maybe I'm clutching, but he didn't seem happy at the idea of me having a date (even though it's not a date), did he? And now I'm beating myself up, wondering why on earth I said it. But I can't look back, I suppose, I have to look forward.

Unfortunately...

21

I like a good time, and a wild night out, but even for me 24bar seems like a bit much. It's the sort of place where you would go if you wanted to party all night (and all day too), and while it isn't quite open twenty-four hours a day, it seems as though it stays open as long as it is allowed as far as licence rules go.

It's trying a bit too hard, if you ask me. The neon lights, the chaotic strobe, the loud thumping music that you can feel rumbling through your body – the kind that feels like it could stop your heart, if you stood on the spot for too long.

Walking up to the bar, to order a drink, I hope that Pat is working this evening.

Oh, and there he is. It doesn't take me long to spot him, because he matches his Redflags description exactly. Ironically, one of his red flags is that his online dating profile photos doesn't quite paint a full picture of Pat, but it's not that he's shorter than he says, or not as physically fit, or that he's airbrushed impercep-tions or anything like that... it turns out that Pat has a tattoo that he keeps hidden in his photos. Standing here in front of him, I can see why.

'Oh, hey, can I get a drink, please?' I ask him.

'I'm just finishing for the evening,' he tells me. 'But Rory will serve...'

His voice trails off as he turns around to look at me. All I can look at is his tattoo.

'Hi,' he says with a cheeky grin.

'Hi,' I reply.

'My eyes are up here,' he jokes.

'Sorry,' I say with a laugh, averting my gaze, forcing myself to keep contact with his bright blue eyes instead. 'It's not every day you see a man with a tattoo of a... a... erm...'

'That's okay,' he says with a laugh. 'Do you like it?'

'Oh, it's great,' I reply – well, it's great to piss people off at a wedding, anyway.

My family hate tattoos. All of them, with no exceptions. They think they are idiotic, and tacky, and a very easy way to tell if someone is bad news. I have a few small ones, in places that are generally hidden, and I genuinely think they would disinherit me (if they haven't already) if they saw them – not that I care.

So, sure, if it's true that Pat flirts with every woman he meets, then it might be kind of funny to take him to the wedding, to see him flirting with Bea, or Seph – imagine him flirting with the bride – but I think it's the tattoo that's going to really piss them off. I don't think they would be happy about the tattoo – which takes up most of his neck – no matter what it was of, but what it is... oh, what it is... I'm laughing, just thinking about the looks that will be on their faces. Pat has what I can only describe as a medical diagram of the female genitalia – a worm's eye view, if you will – complete with labelled parts and artistic pubic hair.

My God, it's so hard not to just stare into the thing. The detail is just... wow. I have one, and even I feel like I'm learning things, seeing it from a whole new perspective.

'Can I make you a drink?' Pat asks.

'I'd love one,' I reply. 'What are we having?'

'Let's find out,' he replies.

Pat places bottles down on the bar before stepping out from behind it and walking around to sit next to me.

I feel weirdly excited, as I watch him get to work, pouring various ingredients into a shaker before mixing them up (with that level of flair only the pros have), and pouring the finished drink between glasses.

It's thick and bright red, almost like blood, but it smells so fruity and light.

Pat accidentally knocks the cocktail mixer on the floor, as he quickly extends his arms to reveal two straws hiding in his sleeve. Okay, so maybe he doesn't quite have the routine nailed, but the drinks look good at least.

'Shit,' he says with an awkward laugh. 'Almost cool, eh? Can you grab that for me?'

'I didn't see a thing,' I reassure him as I bend down to pick it up.

It takes me a few seconds to locate it, on the dark floor, but as a disco light homes in on it, the flash of light on the silver metal catches my eye. Got it.

I have no idea what is happening but all of a sudden I see something hurtling towards me. A man – a drunk, probably – crashes into us. He knocks Pat, then the stool I was sitting on, sending it crashing to the floor.

'Watch where you're going or I'll kick you out, you moron,' Pat yells at him.

'Sorry, sorry,' the drunk man replies.

'Here, let me help you,' Pat says, crouching down on the floor. 'Are you okay?'

'Oh, yeah, I'm fine, he didn't get me,' I tell him. 'Are you okay?'

'Yeah, took a bit of a bump, but all good – and the stool isn't broken, no harm done,' he says. 'It's sort of an occupational hazard.'

I bet.

'Are the drinks okay?' I ask him. 'That's the real question.'

Pat laughs, helping me to my feet.

'Yeah, they're all good,' he replies. 'That one is yours, right there.'

I get back on my stool, pick up my glass and take a sip.

'Oh, wow, that's amazing,' I tell him.

I try to say it to his face but it's so hard, trying not to stare at his neck tattoo, so I find myself averting my gaze again.

That's when I see him, the man that bumped into us, walking away with a smirk on his face.

Oh... my... God. It's Ethan. What the hell is he playing at? I guess I told him I would be here but I didn't think he would turn up here. And bumping into us? Wow, that's psychotic. That's Steve-type behaviour, right there.

He doesn't seem bothered that I've spotted him, that I've caught him in the act – instead he looks quite proud of himself. He flashes me a wink before he heads deeper into the dance floor until he's out of sight.

Okay, right, well, obviously I shouldn't mention that I know him to Pat, because it's going to make me seem like a mess.

Yes, Pat, the one with the lady parts permanently inked on his neck. That Pat.

22

Pat sways on his seat. He looks... odd.

As I finish my drink – which was quite strong, to be fair – I wonder how many he's had. Do bar staff drink while they work? I wouldn't have thought so, and he didn't seem drunk when I got here but, oh wow. He's swaying on the spot.

'So you... you're... a wedding?' he mumbles.

'I'm going to a wedding?' I repeat back to him, checking that's what he means.

'You're... wed... mmm...'

Okay, he's really slurring his words now.

'Pat, are you okay?' I ask him.

'I'm...'

Oh boy, his eyes are rolling into the back of his head.

'Pat?' I say, placing a hand lightly on his arm.

I barely touch him but it's enough to make him wobble and after a second or two of swaying he falls off his stool.

I quickly turn to the bar, to catch the attention of another employee.

'Can you help?' I call out.

'Oh, shit, not again,' one of them says, hurrying around to our side of the bar. Another man quickly follows.

'Come on, Pat, let's get you upstairs,' one of them says as they hoist him up.

'He's just had too much to drink, we can take care of him,' the other says.

'Okay, thanks,' I reply. 'I don't know what happened – he was fine, he had one drink, and we were chatting away, and then he just took a turn...'

'Don't worry,' the first man reassures me. 'Happens all the time. Downside to working in a bar.'

I watch as the two of them practically drag Pat away, disappearing into a back room with him.

What the hell just happened? He didn't seem drunk before, I had the same drink as him and I'm fine... Oh my God. He must have taken something – he must be on some kind of drugs. Wow, okay, I know I wanted someone unimpressive to take to the wedding, but turning up with someone who gets himself in this kind of state would not be the vibe. They would just feel sorry for me, or get me in rehab. I want to take (to use their vocabulary) an unsavoury date, sure, but I want to seem like I'm living my best life. Being unapologetically not what they want me to be is how I win, right?

Well, it would be, but I think I'm finally shit out of luck. What are my options? My flight is in less than forty-eight hours, so I could go alone, but not only will that make me look like a loser, I'll be a sitting duck, braving the lot of them alone. I could not go, and stay here, but then I'll be spending my thirtieth birthday all on my own. My mum did invite me over to Connecticut, to celebrate with them, and as lovely as it would be to see her, I don't know, it's expensive, and I just don't quite feel like I fit in there.

Mum has her family, Dad has his family and I just feel sort of... loose.

With nothing else to stick around for, I head for the door. It was a stupid, stupid idea, to think that I could find some random man to take to the wedding with me. I really think something is going on in my brain, some background response to turning thirty, that is making me a little crazy.

'Hey,' Ethan says, popping up from nowhere.

Wow, speaking of crazy...

'Are you spying on me?' I accuse him, cutting to the chase, because he's obviously up to something. 'Stalking me, too?'

'Just a little,' he replies with a smile.

'Okay, Joe from *You*, don't you think that's a bit creepy?' I ask.

'Just a little,' he says again. 'But I'm hoping you'll find it charming.'

He walks with me, as I head for the door.

'You've got ten seconds to charm me,' I tell him.

'Okay, so...' he begins, a quickness to his voice, like he's certain he can give it a go. 'When you told me you had a date earlier, I don't know, there was something in your eyes, or your voice – something that told me you weren't that into it, or you weren't being honest – I don't know. Also – although I've just seen in my emails that it turns out I am sticking around for a few days – I couldn't stand the thought of not seeing you, so, you know me, a voice in my head told me to come here, and I was right to.'

'That was more than ten seconds,' I tell him, keeping my expression blank. 'And I'm not sure if I'm supposed to find this romantic or weird – I suppose you saw my date get carried out almost unconscious?'

I don't know if it's more or less sad at this point to make clear that he wasn't actually a date but I don't suppose it matters all that much either.

'I did,' he says. 'And, honestly, it's super fucking romantic. Okay, so I was watching you, a bit, and maybe that's weird. But if I hadn't been watching then I wouldn't have noticed that dirtbag slipping something in your drink.'

'What?' I blurt.

'That guy put something in your drink,' he tells me. 'I saw him, as he was mixing them. Well, I was like 80 per cent sure. Seventy-five, maybe...'

'Are you serious?' I blurt.

'I know, I shouldn't have turned up, but if there is one thing that pisses me off, it's men who let the side down, who don't treat women with respect,' he tells me. 'So, I admit it, I saw red, and I could have just kicked off, but you might have thought I was doing it out of jealousy, and he could have just covered his tracks, and I could have been wrong, so...'

'So...?'

'So, I switched the drinks,' he tells me, smiling slightly. 'If he hadn't done anything then no big deal, right, but if he had, I would rather he drank it than you.'

Holy shit. So that's what's wrong with him. I don't know what I feel the strongest, upset, terrified, or really fucking angry. I think the last one is winning right now.

'Oh my God, I thought he was just on drugs or something,' I say.

'I guess he was, technically,' Ethan points out.

'Yeah, except there's doing a line of coke, and then there's date-raping yourself,' I point out.

'Well, he really has fucked himself,' Ethan adds. Then his expression quickly gets more serious. 'Look, I can't even imagine how much it must fucking suck, to be in a position where people try to take advantage of you. I've been fighting against guys like that my whole adult life – I can't even imagine having to contend with them. Don't let one arsehole rattle you, he got what he deserved. Let me walk you wherever you're going next.'

I puff air from my cheeks.

'Thanks,' I say simply.

I know, nothing happened, but without people around me, looking out for me, then it could have. Now, more than ever, I appreciate what we're trying to do at work with Redflags, and while I'm not going to use it any more (in the way I've been using it, anyway) I am going to go on and update Pat's entry. He might be the biggest walking red flag I've seen so far.

We head out into the street, the cool air soothing my warm face, taking the edge off the tension headache I've managed to cook up over the last few minutes.

'I just can't believe it,' I say as we stroll up the street. 'I can't believe he – anyone – would do something like that.'

'Did he... did he have an incredibly detailed vagina tattooed on his neck?' Ethan says.

'I think it was technically a vulva,' I joke, feeling a bit better with every step we take away from 24bar.

'What's the difference?' Ethan asks. 'And why would anyone have that there?'

'I mean, if you don't know the difference, the diagram might come in handy,' I joke. 'And your neck is useful, for a quick check in the mirror – if he was smart, he would have had it done backwards.'

'He's fucking backwards,' Ethan adds.

'Yeah, it's always the ones you least expect, eh?' I reply.

Almost everyone has tattoos now, and they're not that deep, they don't tell you anything about the sort of person you're dealing with. But, in hindsight, perhaps each case should be judged individually. The man had the word labia on his neck, for crying out loud.

We stop outside the Corn Exchange. I love the way it looks at night, all lit up. I don't know how to describe it, other than it feels safe here. The city feels so built up these days, with far more packed in than there was when I was younger, and I used to spend my teens aimlessly walking around the shops. Here, outside the Corn Exchange, there's room to think. Wide-open space, bars and restaurants nearby, but not right outside. It's peaceful, but not lonely.

I sit myself down on one of the cold stone steps – even if it's only while I figure out what to do next. Ethan sits down next to me.

'This is one of my favourite spots in the city,' I tell him. 'I love the lights, the cobbles, the stunning architecture. Leeds really is my favourite city. Although I bet everyone says that, about their home town.'

'Nah, I think you might be on to something,' he replies. 'I love London but it's so big, and so expensive. I like that, when I'm here, I can get pretty much anywhere in a few minutes.'

'Imagine having to get the Tube to a Primark,' I reply. 'See that building, over there? That's where Primark is.'

I point along Boar Lane, towards Trinity.

'I can see McDonald's and Burger King from here,' he replies with a laugh.

'Not that you'd get that far, because you have to walk past Five Guys,' I joke.

'True,' he replies. 'What if I wanted a Starbucks?'

'Oh, well, you'd have to trek a little further for that,' I say seriously. 'There's one on the first right, the second right, or left to the train station. You could be outside any of them in under five minutes.'

He laughs.

'See, I like that,' he tells me. 'Everything is just... great. And I'm starting to learn my way around now. I know that my hotel is just behind us, and that the office is just over the bridge from there.'

'Well then, you're practically a Yorkshireman,' I tell him.

I turn to look at him, at his kind eyes, and his soft smile. I love when he is funny and flirtatious but when that side of him goes dormant, and this side of him comes out – I'm in love, so to speak.

'So, you're sticking around a few more days?' I ask, moving the conversation along.

'Yeah, had a meeting with Jennifer today,' he replies.

'Oh, so she wants you now?' I tease.

'She always wanted me,' he says, playfully narrowing his eyes. 'The first version of her really wanted me.'

I sigh heavily.

'Doesn't that feel like a long time ago?' I reply.

'It really does,' he tells me. 'Best Valentine's Day I've ever had though – haven't had a good one since.'

'There has only been once since,' I point out.

'Well, last year I spent the whole day in bed, hot and sweaty, tissues everywhere – I had a terrible cold,' he adds with a laugh. 'What did you do?'

I sigh again.

'I went on a date with Steve,' I tell him.

'Were you two serious?' he asks me.

'No, not at all,' I insist.

If I'm being honest, the only reason I went on a date with Steve last Valentine's Day was because all I could think about was the year before, with Ethan, and how amazing it was, and I was feeling down, and soooo single, and Steve asked – I don't think I'll say that to Ethan though.

'We dated a bit but I only moved in with him recently, when I needed somewhere in a pinch, and he offered. No strings...'

'Let me guess, there were strings?' he replies with a knowing smile.

'Oh, like I'm a puppet, and he's my master,' I confirm. 'But it's not really working out in the way he had hoped. I reckon he's going to kick me out any day, when he realises it isn't going to get me back.'

'Do you really think he would kick you out, just because you won't date him?' he replies.

'Not in so many words,' I tell him. 'But I think he might throw out an ultimatum, to see if that works on me. I'd rather sleep here.'

'That might be a better plan in summer,' Ethan says. 'I can't feel my arse.'

'Yeah, I guess we should move,' I reply – although I really, really don't want to. 'I just cannot face going back to Steve's right now. I'm early, he'll grill me on where I've been, I never know what is the wrong or right thing to say, and I really do not want to talk about tonight. I just want to forget about it.'

'Look, do you want to come back to my hotel with me?' he asks. 'When I say no strings, I really do mean it. It sounds like things are intense, at home, so if you want a night off...'

'I would love that,' I tell him quickly, biting his hand off. 'Thank you.'

We stand up – wow, I really can't feel my arse – and make our way along the cobbles and under the bridge that leads us on to The Calls. And there it is, his hotel, the same hotel he stayed in last time.

'They let you back in then,' I say, referring to what happened the last time we were here together, but without actually mentioning what happened.

'They must have short memories,' he says with a smile. 'No one mentioned it when I booked. But you will be pleased to hear that I not only don't have a ground-floor room this time, but I'm overlooking the river. I haven't spent much time in it, beyond checking in, but it didn't seem like anyone could see in. Weirdly, it felt a bit like being on a cruise.'

I laugh.

'Well, it doesn't get much more private than a cruise ship window, does it?' I reply.

'Actually, I went on a cheap cruise with my mates, and we had digital windows,' he tells me. 'We must have been so low in the ship that we were underwater. So, where a window would usually be, they had this screen with a fake view. Of course, I was sharing a room with my mate Tommo, and you don't get less private than that.'

I laugh.

'Let's just say one night he brought a girl back, and I wanted to jump out of the digital window,' he tells me, widening his eyes for effect. 'I ended up sleeping on a sunlounger, on the deck.'

'I hope you were somewhere warm,' I reply.

He purses his lips and shakes his head.

'Right, here we are,' he says, opening the door for me to step inside.

And suddenly I'm back in time, two years ago, feeling all the same things that I did back then. It's like muscle memory, walking through the door, passing through reception – my body thinks it's going to get a repeat of what happened the last time we were here. Body, you need to calm down!

We step into the lift together. I should change the subject, I know I should, but...

'Do you make a habit of sleeping in places that you shouldn't?' I ask him.

I notice him smiling to himself in the mirrored lift wall.

'Not as often as it would seem,' he replies. 'Although Jennifer's office has to be the weirdest.'

We fall silent for a second again. I open my mouth to speak just as the lift doors ding, so I retreat back into the silence.

We walk along the corridor, finally approaching Ethan's room. He unlocks the door and then steps aside, for me to head in first.

Oh, wow, what a beautiful room. I don't know what this old building used to be but there are exposed wooden beams and pieces of old metal machinery that have been artfully preserved to give the place character. I'm like a moth to a flame when it comes to the windows though. I hurry over, trying not to make eye contact with the super-king bed as I pass it, and look outside. It really does feel like being on a boat – just one that is floating through Leeds city centre. I can see Bridgewater Place in one direction, Brewery Wharf in the other. The water below looks so flat and peaceful, with lights reflecting on it. You can tell it's cold out there just by looking (of course, I already knew that from first-hand – or should that be first-arse – experience), but it's so cosy in here.

Ethan stands next to me, mirroring my position, with his elbows on the windowsill.

'It's even more beautiful now,' he says.

He turns to face me, his chin resting on his hands.

Every instinct I have right now is either telling me to kiss him or to run out of here and never come back.

'What are you thinking?' he asks me.

Should I tell him the truth? No.

'Just about how lovely it is in here,' I reply. 'You?'

'I was thinking about how much I want to kiss you,' he tells me.

'That did pop into my mind,' I admit.

Ethan slowly stands up straight. Then he places his hands on my sides and lifts me up, sitting me down on the windowsill. The glass feels cold on my back so I lean forward towards him, wrapping my legs around his waist, hooking my arms around his neck. Okay, this really is like muscle memory.

He presses his face into my neck but he doesn't kiss it, he just rubs his face up against it for a second, his hands exploring my back – almost like he's giving me a moment to think about it and, yep, thought about it.

'We said we would never do this again,' I remind him – not exactly sounding like I never want to do it again.

'I think it was more that we never *should* do it again,' he clarifies, his voice super soft and silky smooth.

I chew my lip thoughtfully.

I want him. I really want him, but...

'No, you're right,' he tells me – and it's only as he says this that I realise it's the opposite of what I want to hear.

'You love an audience, don't you?' I reply. 'Here, in front of the window...'

'Well, the first time we did it, we were in the bathroom,' he reminds me – as though I could forget. 'No audience in the shower.'

I know I shouldn't, but...

'Maybe we should go into the bathroom then,' I say.

Ethan picks me up gently, only to place me back on the floor. It feels like it takes an hour, to walk from the window to the bathroom, but we get there, he turns the light on and – would you believe it – there's no shower. Just a bath.

'Ah,' I blurt, hoping this isn't a sign from the universe that we need to stop this right now.

'I mean, baths are romantic, right?' he points out. 'Bath? It looks big enough for two...'

'Yeah,' I say, not sounding entirely convinced, but I'm just being silly, right? The universe doesn't give signs.

'I'll run it,' he says. 'You go sit through there.'

Let me tell you now, nothing kills the moment like pausing to run a bath. It's a long pause that we do not need right now, because it's giving me a chance to think things through.

Ethan joins me, sitting next to me on the bed.

'The bath is filling,' he tells me. 'Unless you've changed your mind? Your face looks like it's changed its mind.'

I laugh.

'It's not that I've changed my mind,' I begin. 'It's just that... there's a reason we said we would never do this again, but every time we do, we seem to cause trouble. Last time—'

'Last time we were drunk,' he reminds me.

'I know but, still, think of the chaos we almost caused,' I say. 'I like to have a drink, and a good time, but there's something about you that just makes me absolutely nuts. Like, if you told me to jump off a cliff, and you said it while you didn't have a shirt on, I'd backflip off the thing.'

Ethan laughs.

'It's like you think we're cursed,' he says. 'Like we're doomed to cause a major incident.'

'Can you blame me?' I reply. 'Look what we almost did, in Jennifer's office.'

'That was just a freak accident,' he reassures me.

'It was like a *Final Destination* accident,' I remind him. 'I mean, come on, we caused water damage, then fire damage, then water damage again.'

'Well, that last one was for the fire,' he points out with a cheeky grin.

Honestly, I don't even know that happened. I mean, I do, it was because we were too busy getting busy to realise we had knocked over a bottle of champagne, flooding an electric heater with the contents – which we had on, because it was cold – which started smoking and sizzling and then... it's all a blur, I think Ethan threw water over it, to stop any sort of fire in its tracks, I managed to knock over the framed photo of Jennifer and her family while I was frantically trying to turn the power off, and it was just mess on mess, on chaos, on mess.

'We sorted it out,' he reminds me. 'And no one ever found out.'

'But if they had found out, I would have lost my job,' I say. 'I could have been in even more trouble than that – especially if we had caused more damage. We could have burned the place to the ground.'

'Isn't that everyone's fantasy?' he replies. 'To burn their office down?'

I can't help but laugh because he's got a point.

'We fixed, sure, but the way we fixed – it felt unhinged, what we did. It was psychotic, sociopath shit,' I remind him.

'It was also the coolest thing I've ever done, and the most alive I've ever felt, and just something about doing it together – I don't know – as awful as it was, and as stressed as I was, looking back it only makes it seem hotter. And, hey, we work great together as a team.'

I mean, we did work great together as a team that night. We knew we had made a mess, and that we would be in big trouble if anyone found out, so we set about covering it up. Sure, there was no way to make everything as it was when we found it, so what we needed to do was offer an alternative narrative, a different version of events that could have brought about the same accident. It was the middle of the night and we were still drunk, so I'll never know how we pulled it off, but some careful arranging of a window that was 'left open', and a plant that was knocked over, and a cup of coffee Jennifer clearly never finished (in her favourite 'If I'm too much then go find less' mug) tipped over in just the right (or technically wrong) way and it actually looked like a genuine accident. What's interesting is that Jennifer must have thought it was her fault, because when I came into the office the next day there was no mention of it. She genuinely believed it was a mistake she had made, and so she covered it up for us. It really was the perfect crime and, yes, I do feel like a psycho saying that. It was also the reason we ended up swearing we would never see each other again, if that was the kind of mess we were going to make. We'd already had the incident with the blinds, and the trouble we caused on the night out before that. Thinking about it now just reminds me of how close we came to throwing it all away and for what, a shag? A few shags? A few incredible shags, fair enough, but there's good sex and then there's burning an office block down.

A loud thumping on the door snaps me from my thoughts. I look to Ethan, concerned.

'Stay here,' he tells me.

I don't know what the problem is but I just know it's going to be something – something that we've done, or caused, or happened because of us. Maybe it's the police because they think I drugged Pat. Maybe it's Jennifer, because she's got me bugged, and I just confessed to the crime we made her cover up. Maybe it's Steve with an axe. All I know is that whatever it is, it's bad news, and it's because we're together.

Fuck you, universe.

23

I place my index finger silently over my lips and widen my eyes in Ethan's direction to let him know that I'm being serious. He has to be quiet.

It takes me the best part of a minute to place my key in the lock and turn it ever so softly, making sure that my other keys don't make a tinkling sound, that the lock doesn't make too much noise as it turns, that the door hasn't suddenly developed a new extra-loud creak (or that Steve hasn't fitted it with one of those bells that shops have, so that you know when customers walk in).

I hold up my hand, letting Ethan know to stay put in the door-way, before creeping in to peer around into the living room, to make sure that Steve hasn't sat up waiting for me. It's not like he hasn't done it before.

Without saying a word, I beckon Ethan indoors with my hand. Impressively, he manages to close the door and lock it without much of a sound. Now all that's left to do is make it to my bedroom.

Steve is normally very strict about this being a 'shoes off at the door' home, but do you know what makes him even angrier than that? Me fraternising with boys. The best thing I can do is get the two of us safely to my bedroom, where we can hide out for the rest of the night, and then I'll either sneak Ethan out as soon as it's morning, or I'll keep him here until Steve goes to work. Lucky for me (not that any part of this feels lucky in any way) I'm off work tomorrow, to get the last of my things ready, before flying in the early hours of the next day. This is my last full night of sleep before I catch my flight to Sydney, and this is how I'm spending it. Incredible.

Ethan carries his suitcase so that it doesn't make any noises that might wake up Steve. He's great at sneaking into flats, which makes me wonder if it's a skill he picked up by sneaking out of them.

Inside my room, I close the door carefully behind me and finally exhale.

'So, the walls aren't that thick,' I whisper to him. 'But if we stick to whispering, we should be okay.'

'Great,' he calls back.

I don't turn on the big light – not just because only psychopaths like the big light on, but because it feels more incognito to only turn on the dim light next to my bed.

'Oh,' Ethan blurts – still keeping his voice nice and quiet. 'You only have a single bed.'

'And you don't have any other options,' I tell him.

'I can sleep on the floor, it's all good,' he replies.

I know that's probably the safest thing to do, but I can't be so cruel.

'Don't be daft, it's freezing,' I reply. 'I'm sure we're safe to share a bed. The universe only gets mad if it thinks we're going to have sex.'

Ethan laughs, silently, and rolls his eyes.

'So long as you don't think it will cause a threat to society,' he replies sarcastically.

I take off my things – my clothes and my jewellery, but I decide that my make-up can stay on for tonight – and climb into my sad little single bed. Ethan takes off his shirt, then his trousers, and I'm pretty sure he's only doing it in a normal way, but the thirst trap is real regardless. This is like pay-per-view stuff.

I avert my eyes quickly, although I'm pretty sure he catches me looking because I notice his smile creeping onto his face.

Finally, Ethan gets into bed next to me. At first, he tries to go back to back with me, but he's a muscular bloke, so we struggle to both fit.

'There's only one way you'll fit, you'll have to lie facing me,' I tell him.

'There are definitely other ways we could fit better,' he points out. 'We'd stack on top of each other better than we'd fit side by side.'

I laugh softly.

Ethan does as instructed, spooning up behind me. His body fits with mine perfectly. It feels as though he goes to put an arm around me, almost instinctively, but then he quickly returns it to his side.

For a moment we're just silent. I can feel the heat from his body, his breath on my shoulder, his hips pressed tightly up against my own.

'I can't believe you tricked me into your single bed,' he jokes, lightening the mood.

'I mean, if we're saying things we can't believe – I can't believe you flooded a hotel,' I reply.

'Erm, you mean *we* flooded a hotel,' he corrects me. 'That bath was for the two of us.'

'Okay, but you were the one who left it running,' I point out.

'You were the one distracting me,' he replies. 'It was an honest mistake – I can't believe they kicked us out.'

'They said they were fully booked,' I say, shrugging my shoulders.

'Yeah, well, I would have kicked us out too,' he says, laughing quietly. 'And don't shrug your shoulders because when you do, your bum wiggles – now is not the time to be bumping and grinding on me. Unless you're actually planning on bumping and grinding on me, that is.'

'Sorry,' I say, smiling to myself.

I subtly but intentionally arch my back, pressing myself against him slightly.

'You're doing that on purpose,' he says.

'Doing what?' I reply, making it a bit more obvious this time.

'Hey, you're the one who's too scared to go through with it,' he points out. 'I could do this all night…'

'I know you could,' I reply. 'But having sex with you is like a bin fire.'

'Can I put that on my sex CV, please?' he asks jokily.

'Sorry, I don't mean that as bad as it sounds, it's just that, you know, it's really hot and it's really dirty but it's…'

'A bin?' he replies.

'Yeah, so as much as I want to do this…'

I wiggle back into him with intent, even though I know I shouldn't, and the universe is in there like a shot. My sad little single bed gives way, crashing to the floor with a loud bang. There is no way Steve didn't hear that.

'Shit,' I say under my breath – not that there's much need for that now. 'Can you hide?'

'Where, under the bed?' he jokes as he glances around.

It's too late. The bedroom door flies open.

'Lana, what the hell?' Steve replies.

It's Steve, wearing his green stripy PJs and a face like thunder.

I look to Ethan, just in case he's managed to hide in time, but all he's done is lie face down on the mattress – the mattress that is now on the floor.

'Lana?' he prompts me again.

'Oh my God, I don't know what happened, the bed just broke,' I say with a faux innocence that he's not buying.

'Lana, this is so, so disrespectful,' he replies. 'I generously give you a place to stay and you have sex in my bed? You know the rules about having guests. What's wrong with him?'

Oh, so it's his bed? So he gets to say who can and can't sleep in it? And Ethan is genuinely playing dead right now and, honestly, it's an impressive tactic. Thankfully Steve doesn't recognise him from work.

'He's sleeping. We had nowhere else to go,' I begin, but he's not having it.

'I hear round the back of Wetherspoons is perfect for this sort of thing.'

I know, now isn't the time to make a joke, but do I let a silly thing like that stop me? No. No, I do not.

'Which Wetherspoons?' I ask.

Ethan falters ever so slightly, his chest bouncing as he laughs. Luckily only I notice.

'Lana, you have taken advantage of me for long enough,' Steve barks, not seeing the funny side to this at all. 'I want you out of here. I know you're going to Australia tomorrow so, go, get your trip over with, and then when you come back I want your things gone. And I want him out of here, before I wake up. Clear?'

'Clear,' I repeat back to him.

Steve slams the door behind him, before heading back to bed. Safe in the knowledge that the coast is clear, Ethan rolls onto his back.

'That's—'

'Yeah, yeah, I know what you're going to say,' Ethan interrupts me. 'That's the universe, at it again. You take the floor with the mattress, I'll take the floor without.'

Ethan grabs the extra throw from my bed, leaving me with the duvet.

See what I mean? The two of us create nothing but carnage. This can never happen again.

24

I'm homeless – yay.

Unlucky for me I have no other ex-boyfriends who are willing to put me up in exchange for the faint hope of getting back together, so I'm really up shit creek this time.

I can't afford anywhere, not on my own, because it's not just the bills, it's the huge deposit everyone wants, the references, the good credit score – ironically, I've never had a problem with credit, other than no one wanting to give me any, so that's why my score is so low. The bank of Dad has always been closed for withdrawals, even in emergencies, which only really leaves going to live at Saltburn itself. I could probably live there without anyone noticing, in one of the bedrooms no one goes in, but if Bea didn't take me out with a shotgun then the commute to the office would probably kill me.

My phone vibrates on the bedside table. Of course, I forget that I'm on the floor, so when I reach out to get it I just punch the bottom drawer instead. God, that hurt.

I reach up this time, successfully grabbing it, noticing that it's half ten so Steve must have gone to work. Presumably, he didn't look in here, to see if I – or my gentleman caller – had gone. Ethan is still flat-out asleep on the floor.

'Hello?' I say quietly, answering the call, because it's Faye.

'Hey, so we forgot you weren't in today, and we're dying to know – how did it go last night?' she asks.

'Oh, not good,' I tell her. 'The guy was a total creep.'

'But don't you fly later?' she checks.

'In less than twenty-four hours,' I reply with a heavy sigh.

'What are you going to do? Go alone?' she says.

'Tell her she can't go alone,' I hear Molly's voice in the background.

'One of them must be some good?' Faye continues. 'Who is the best of the bad bunch?'

'I suppose I could ask Joseph if he wanted to come?' I suggest. 'He was only pretending to be a bad boy but, I don't know, I'm sure he could still cause some havoc with me, maybe...'

'Yeah, give him a call,' Faye suggests. 'If he was keen...'

'He was keen on the free holiday,' I reply. 'He wasn't keen on having fun – I'll bet he would behave impeccably the whole time – and I don't think he was keen on me either. I didn't get the impression he was interested in me, just the holiday.'

'See what you can do,' Faye says, her voice turning into more of a whisper. 'Gotta go, bye.'

She hangs up.

Is Joseph really the best I can do? A good boy pretending to be bad? Perhaps I would be better off going alone.

'Good morning,' Ethan says, snapping me from my thoughts.

'Morning,' I reply – well, what's so good about it?

'Reckon your dad has gone?' he replies.

'Yeah, I guess he's gone to work,' I say. 'That gives us a chance to sneak out.'

'So, you're going to Australia?' he says.

'Yeah,' I reply, my tone guarded.

'I heard Steve say so last night,' he reminds me, reading my thoughts.

'Ah,' I say, rolling onto my side to face him. 'Yeah, my sister is getting married there. I actually found out, that night we met. She's tying the knot in Australia – because the moon was fully booked.'

Ethan laughs softly.

'So, who is Joseph?' he asks.

'Huh?' I reply, knowing exactly what he means. Shit, he must have heard me on the phone just now.

'Joseph,' he says again. 'It sounded like you were taking him with you – are you seeing someone?'

The truth sounds horrendous but the idea of Ethan thinking I was going to cheat on someone with him seems far worse.

'Okay, don't judge me,' I begin, taking a deep breath.

'Would I ever?' he replies.

'So, my sister, Seph, is getting married in Sydney – Chester, her fiancé's parents retired there,' I explain. 'But what you need to know, for all of this to make any sense, is that Seph and I had completely different upbringings. My dad's side of the family has money, and when he and my mum split he remarried and had Seph, so she's grown up in that lifestyle, whereas I was raised by my mum, who didn't have much money. That lot are just so, so out of touch with reality – it's embarrassing – but the worst thing of all is that they think that about me, that I'm out of touch with their reality. They think I'm some tacky commoner – the poor relative who they have to include – and seeing as though they're my only family in the UK now, I think they're posho morons who I have to dutifully turn up to events for.'

'Well, that's family, right?' Ethan replies. 'Turning up, doing things, trying to get along.'

'Yeah, and I'm hap... and I'm willing to do it.' I was almost going to say happy to do it, but willing is more accurate. 'Except, they called me over for a pre-wedding lunch, and I thought it was for everyone to talk about wedding stuff, but it turns out it was exclusively some sort of class intervention, just for me, where everyone had a go at me for how I dressed, acted, and to warn me about not bringing a date they wouldn't approve of.'

'So...'

'So, I became obsessed with finding a date to take, who they wouldn't approve of, to say: fuck you,' I reply. 'Obviously, I'm not a monster, I don't want to ruin Seph's wedding, and I do want to be there, but I need to show them that I am me, and I matter, and they have to love me as I am.'

'That sounds like something Jennifer would have on a mouse mat,' Ethan says with a smile, lightening the mood a little.

'The worst thing of all though...'

'It gets worse?' he replies in disbelief.

'Yeah! The worst thing of all is that they've moved their wedding day, last minute because Chester's gran is superstitious or something, and the date they have moved it to is my birthday – my thirtieth birthday, no less – but absolutely no one has mentioned it. I don't know if they don't care, or they've forgotten, but either way I'm fuming.'

'None of that is cool. I'm sorry,' he says sincerely. 'But so much makes sense now – when I saw you with the vagina neck guy, I started to worry about you, like you'd gone off the rails, like you were going to extreme lengths to find a man who gave you as wild a time as I did.'

I smile. He's obviously joking about that last part.

'You say that but, hey, it's almost true,' I point out. 'You fit the bill almost perfectly. You're fun, you're chaotic, I have a good time with you, they would *hate* you...'

'Oh, stop, you're going to give me a big head,' he says with a touch of playful sarcasm.

'Well, they would,' I say with a laugh. 'You're a lot like me, in all the ways they hate.'

'Take me with you then,' he suggests.

'What?' I blurt. 'No, that's okay, you don't need to do that. I've got this one guy, Joseph, who is willing to pretend to be what I need – a free holiday to Sydney will motivate anyone to do anything.'

'I want a free holiday to Sydney,' he says with a shrug. 'Take me. I feel like I'm the man for the job.'

Right, except the problem with Ethan is that while he may be absolutely perfect to cause chaos and piss everyone off, it's that I actually like him, and want him, and when we get together there is too much chaos. Even in separate hotel rooms, I don't know, if we keep our distance we're fine but if we – pardon the pun – rub together, we're like two sticks. Everything goes up in flames.

'No, honestly, I think I'm better with someone things are... easier with,' I continue.

'You think we make a mess when we get together, right?' he says, and I nod. 'So, okay, I get that, we need to stick to being mates. But there's no reason we can't pretend to be together, to go on the free holiday, have a blast. I really, really want to go.'

As fun as it would be to go with him, even if we could pull off keeping things platonic, it's just too much of a risk.

'Don't you have to work?' I reply. 'Are you not doing something for Jennifer?'

'I work remotely,' he tells me. 'I'm free as a bird.'

I think for a second but, no, I need to stop entertaining the idea. Ethan is too much trouble.

'Thanks,' I say, trying to sound like I mean it – I do appreciate the offer, after all. 'But no thanks.'

Ethan scoots across the floor, until he's sitting on the edge of my mattress.

'Have you booked a ticket for this Joseph?' he asks. 'For the flight?'

'Not yet,' I admit. 'It was a while ago when they told me, but Seph and Chester said they had reserved two seats for me, and I would just need to work with the wedding planner, and they would sort the paperwork and put the seats in the right name. So there is a seat reserved next to me, it just needs booking in the right name.'

'Okay, makes sense,' he replies. 'And what about a visa?'

'Hmm?'

'Presumably you have a visa to visit Australia?' he checks.

'Erm, yeah,' I reply. 'The wedding planner basically did all of that.'

'The wedding planner did that for you,' he replies. 'What about your plus-one?'

'Oh, erm, I guess we would sort that when we sorted the ticket?' I say, audibly draining in confidence as my sentence goes on.

'You thought you were going to get a visa for a plus-one today?' he says, raising an eyebrow.

Ah, shit, I think I did. Well, no, it wasn't that I thought I would, I guess it was just that the wedding planner sorted mine, so I didn't really think about it.

'So I can't take Joseph,' I say, stating the facts. 'I can't take anyone.'

'Wrong again,' he says with a cheeky smile. 'There is someone you can take.'

I just stare at him.

'Me,' he says, as though it were obvious. 'You can take me.'

'Why, do you have a secret Australian passport?' I ask sarcastically.

'No, but I have a New Zealand one,' he replies.

Again, I just stare at him.

'That's where my dad is from,' he reminds me. 'So, I have a UK passport and a New Zealand one, and if you're from New Zealand then you don't need a visa before you travel to Australia.'

'Is that true?' I reply. 'Like, is it still true? Could the rules have changed?'

'I spent Christmas there,' he confirms. 'I told you, Australia is my family's supposed midpoint between New Zealand and the UK.'

I laugh. His family sounds almost as interesting as mine.

'So, unless you know Chris Hemsworth's number, it seems like I'm your only hope.'

He grins at me, that cheeky twinkle in his eye that usually precedes him doing something crackers... but it's when he's crackers that he sets my entire body alight (it's just that usually, in my experience with him, the room usually follows suit).

I know him, I like him, I trust him, he's fun to be around, my family will hate him... and, yeah, he's right. He's the only one who can get into Australia, the only real contender.

'Do you have your passport?' I check.

'Yep, I keep it in my case,' he replies, his excited smile slowly powering up.

'And you have your suitcase but it's summer there, right? You'll only have winter things with you.'

'I'll go buy some,' he says, like it's no big deal. 'Someone told me all of the shops are minutes apart, it will take me no time at all.'

'Oh, God, and it's black tuxedos for the wedding,' I add.

'Black tuxedos? In the Aussie summer sun?' he replies in disbelief. 'Does your sis want everyone to die?'

'Probably,' I say. 'So long as they die with a wingtip collar.'

'Right, okay, I'd better get going then, if we're on?'

His question hangs in the air. He sounds like a little boy, asking if he can sleep over at his mate's house.

I guess it's him or it's no one.

'Okay, fine,' I say.

'Yeah?'

'Yeah.'

'Woo, I'm going to Sydney,' he says, punching the air. 'I'll go buy what I need. Lana, you won't regret this. I'm going to be the best worst date you've ever had. I understand the assignment and, truly, I was born to do it.'

Ethan grabs his things and heads for the door, to go and buy his holiday essentials – and a tux, presumably. Oh God, what have I done? But this is what I want, right? I need someone like him on my arm to show them that I'm my own person, they can't tell me what to do, or who to date. Yeah, the more I think about it, the more perfect he seems for the job.

Well, you know what they say: Don't get mad, get Ethan.

25

'Would your son like a bar of chocolate?' a flight attendant asks Ethan.

'He certainly would,' Ethan replies. 'Thank you.'

Ethan takes the bar of chocolate from her and hands it to Jake, who is sitting in the window seat next to me.

'We're sharing, right?' Ethan checks.

'I guess,' Jake says with a sigh as he takes the chocolate.

Ethan doesn't let go of it quite yet though.

'Wait, do your real parents let you have chocolate?' Ethan checks.

'Yeah,' Jake replies – but then his conscience catches up with him. 'Well, my mum doesn't, but my dad does.'

'Which one lives in Australia?' Ethan asks.

'My dad,' Jake replies.

Ethan lets go of the chocolate bar.

'You're a pushover plane dad,' I tell him with a smile.

'Well, we're over international waters,' he reminds me. 'And we're closer to Australia than we are the UK, so I think this falls under his dad's jurisdiction.'

I laugh.

I was grateful, when it came time to board, and the lady at the desk said she would allocate us seats together on the plane. I didn't really think about the fact that we might have a third person with us.

Jake, it turns out, is flying the same route to Sydney as us. He's ten years old and currently splits his time between his divorced parents who live on the opposite side of the world to one another – I suppose that's one way to avoid your ex.

So poor Jake is flying alone – except not all members of the flight crew seem to know that, so most of them keep assuming that Jake is our child, so we've taken on the role of honorary plane parents, and believe me when I say we are not strict.

After sleeping for the first stretch of the flight, it's sort of like our daytime now. The in-flight entertainment system looks decent but it seems like the number-one way they keep you happy and distracted through long-haul flights is by feeding you and feeding you and feeding you – oh, and plying you with drinks, of course.

'We should really make a plan, for how we're going to handle this,' I say to Ethan.

'Isn't the idea of a plan counterproductive to what we're turning up to do?' he points out. 'I thought you wanted to turn up and just kind of piss around.'

'Bad word,' Jake ticks us off.

'Don't swear in front of our plane son,' I playfully remind Ethan.

'Sorry, Jake,' Ethan tells him before leaning in closer to me, lowering his voice to make it more difficult for little ears. 'So, I figured we were just going to turn up and be ourselves. That's usually chaotic enough.'

'That's too chaotic,' I remind him. 'I need a more manageable chaos.'

'Ooh, I'm not sure I can help you there,' he jokes. 'You see, with me, what you get is fires, floods, explosions.'

'Explosions?' Jake repeats a little too loudly.

A woman sitting in the seats over the aisle from Ethan coughs loudly. We glance over at her to see a concerned look on her face. She narrows her eyes at us, trying to work out if we might actually be plotting something. I can't help but notice that she's reading a copy of what looks like it would be a murder mystery (well, you don't have to be a detective to figure out that *The Mysterious Murder of Mr Black* is probably not a romcom) so I'll bet she's the type to fantasise about suddenly becoming a lead character in her own life when she happens upon something story-worthy. I can see her imagination going into overdrive.

'No, no, no, don't say that word on an aeroplane,' I tell him quickly and quietly. 'You'll freak people out. He just means explosions like... fireworks.'

I turn back to Ethan.

'Wow, kids are always listening,' he whispers.

'We just need to talk more... in code,' I suggest.

'Fireworks is code, is it?' Ethan says with a smile. 'Did I give you fireworks?'

Boy, did he!

'You gave me fireworks – it's just that you threw in the bonfire too,' I point out.

'There's no pleasing some women,' he dares to joke.

'I just want to turn up to this wedding, and wear my unsavoury dress, and have my unsavoury date by my side – no offence – and just piss them off by living my best life...'

'Bad word,' Jake chimes in.

'...and just be unapologetically myself,' I continue. 'Living well is the best revenge, right?'

'I thought revenge was a dish best served cold?' Ethan replies.

'Who is getting revenge?' Jake asks.

'No one,' Ethan reassures him. 'We're just doing a bit of role play.'

'What's role play?' Jake asks.

Honestly, how on earth does anyone with children say anything about anything? They're like a smart speaker, always listening – and usually responding with a random reply.

'It's something grown-ups do,' I tell him. 'And it's really boring, so we might just pop to the toilets – but we'll see if we can get you more snacks on the way back. Sound good?'

Jake nods before going back to whatever it is he's watching on his tablet.

'Aww, you're such a great plane mum,' Ethan jokes as he follows me down the aisle. 'But didn't we always say we would never appease them with sweets?'

'Hilarious,' I tell him as we pause in the small space where the toilets are. 'We can probably hover here for a moment, while the loo is occupied, without looking weird.'

'Do you ever think that maybe you worry too much about what people think?' he asks me.

'Do you ever think that you don't?' I reply.

The toilet door opens and a man steps out, pushing between the two of us before heading back to his seat.

'Look, I get it, you want me to turn up, to be myself, to look bad on your arm but you—'

'Oh my God, that woman is coming, the one who thinks we're going to explode the plane,' I tell him in hushed tones. 'Quick!'

I shove Ethan into the toilet before squashing in with him, closing the door behind us.

'What are you doing?' he asks through a laugh.

'If she thinks this one is occupied, she might go to the other one,' I tell him.

'And why don't we want her to see us talking?' he asks, bemused.

'Because she thinks we're up to something,' I reply. 'And here we are, out of the way, talking together, looking all... conspiratorial.'

Ethan gasps theatrically.

'Look, I don't want to risk anything going wrong,' I admit. 'Things around us just seem to go wrong – the last thing I want is for some air marshal to detain us, because he thinks we're up to something.'

'You watch too many movies,' he replies. 'But if it makes you happy, we can wait until the coast is clear.'

'What were you going to say before?' I ask.

'Hmm?' he replies.

'You were talking about what you were going to do, on the trip, and then you said but...'

I shift on the spot, trying to get more comfortable. It's such a tiny toilet with barely enough standing room for one person. Our bodies are pressed close together, our faces just inches apart.

My heart is beating like mad and as I breathe in the air feels much heavier than usual. We just need to focus on the task at hand – that way I can get my mind out of the gutter, and we can de-escalate this situation. We both just need to calm down.

'Oh, I was just going to say, you might not want floods or fires, but what about explosions and fireworks?'

He flashes me a cheeky smile and, oh God, why did he have to say that? We're supposed to be calming down, not whipping each other up.

Ethan wraps an arm around my body and places his other hand on my face. I gaze into his eyes as he strokes my cheek lightly – my face cheek, that is... wait... scratch that, his other hand has settled on my bum.

I swallow hard. Obviously I want him, how could I not? But things always seem to get so messy, if we so much as think about getting it on. It's like we're jinxed or cursed or something. That's silly, right? There's no such thing. It's just the two of us, alone, in a room. If we were to just kiss, just this once, just to see...

Ethan reads my mind. He leans in, his lips parting ever so slightly, and my common sense vanishes. All I can think about is kissing him but, come on, what's the worst that could happen? It's not like we're going to make the plane fall out of the sky, is it?

I take a deep breath before mirroring his body language, leaning in, and I swear the anticipation alone sends a shock wave through my body.

Of course, right on cue, a loud banging on the toilet door interrupts us before we can actually kiss.

'Come on now, that's enough,' a woman's voice calls out. 'Come on, get out, both of you.'

'Shit,' I say quietly.

Ethan purses his lips, like he's trying to hide his amusement from me.

'What do we do?' I ask him.

She bangs on the door again.

'Come on, come out,' she demands.

We do as we're told, opening the door and stepping out one after the other, like a couple of naughty schoolkids.

'So sorry, I was just feeling so sick, so my partner brought me to the toilets,' I tell the furious-looking flight attendant.

'Do you think I was born yesterday?' she asks, looking down her nose at us.

'Honestly,' I insist.

'Even if I were to believe you – even if I didn't see couples like you trying to get away with... this all the time – it was your poor son who gave you away,' she replies.

'What?' Ethan says.

'I asked your son where you were, and he said that you had both gone to the toilets to do role play,' she tells him. 'Your poor son...'

'Oh, no, he got the wrong end of the stick there,' Ethan tells her. 'You know what kids are like.'

'I do,' she replies. 'Their brains are like sponges – you need to be more responsible. Do I need to sit the two of you apart?'

We shake our heads.

'Then go back to your seats, please, and don't do this again,' she tells us.

Ethan and I skulk back towards our seats.

'Well, that went well,' he says with a laugh, now that it's just the two of us again.

'What that did was remind me why we need to keep things platonic,' I tell him.

'What?' he says with a laugh. 'Come on...'

'No, I'm serious,' I tell him firmly. 'You plus me equals disaster. I can't have a disaster while we're here, okay? We really do need to just stick to being friends.'

'Okay, well, if that's what you want,' Ethan says.

'It is,' I reply.

I sit back down next to Jake.

'Kid, you really shouldn't just repeat everything you hear,' I tell him, semi-amused. I'm sure it will seem funnier when the embarrassment wears off.

'Okay,' he tells me. 'Did you bring me more snacks?'

'I'll get you something,' Ethan tells him. 'I'm starving too.'

I slump down in my seat a little. I'm not crazy, am I? The two of us almost just kissed and, right on cue, disaster struck. Imagine if we had started kissing, if we'd started tearing off each other's clothes – ugh, imagine that! – she could have caught us in the act and then what?

I know that I'm doing the right thing, keeping things friendly, I'm just really not sure how easy it's going to be – for both of us. It definitely felt harder a moment ago...

26

There is something so magical about getting on a plane in the middle of winter and getting off again in the height of summer. Of course, it feels like the months have passed by in real time because the flight felt like it was never going to end.

Oh my days, it is boiling here. I think the screen in the airport said it was 26°C, which, yeah, I've felt that in the UK, but I think the fact that I've been living in winter (for what feels like a year) and then the plane being so cold – I was not ready for this at all.

It's intense, but it's lovely. I feel like the sun is seeping into my skin, warming my bones, thawing me out. I guess the downside is that, when I do fly back home, it's going to be a more unpleasant shock to the system, going from summer to winter again.

As a big fan of a small city, I feel almost intimidated by the size of Sydney. I think when it comes to places you've only ever seen in the movies or in photos, it really builds them up, they feel almost fictitious. Seeing them in person, it's uncanny.

I have to admit, I'm almost relieved to see the urban landscape shifting into something more coastal. This is what I need, for my shitty mental health, I need to see the sea.

'I'm just going to come out with it,' I begin, because if I don't say it now, it will only be on my mind. 'Is the spider thing true or is that just in the movies?'

The taxi driver stifles a laugh.

'What do you mean?' Ethan asks, laughing too.

'Pop culture has taught me that Australia has lots of big, scary, dangerous spiders,' I reply. 'And I'm scared of daddy-long-legs, so...'

'Well, yeah, there are spiders here, and some of them are bigger than back home, and some of them are dangerous, but it's not going to be a part of your day,' he says. 'You've definitely seen too many movies.'

'So, when you lived here, you never had any memorable interactions with spiders?' I check.

I notice Ethan's jaw tighten in a way his smile can't mask.

'Only once,' he replies. 'I can tell you about it?'

'I would rather you didn't,' I quickly insist.

'Everybody has one story to tell about a spider,' the taxi driver chimes in. 'If this fella has had his, I'd stick by him.'

'I will absolutely do that, thank you,' I reply.

'Right, well, this is where you're going,' the taxi driver eventually says. 'Have a great time here in Australia – and watch out for those spiders.'

It is exclusively all I am doing right now.

Ethan drags both of our cases behind him, up to the door of the building. I don't see any signs or anything but I gave the taxi driver the address that Seph gave me. You would think there would be something to give away that this was the right spot.

Seph's high-pitched squeal somehow manages to echo, despite us being in a wide-open space. Perhaps it's just my ears that are ringing, or alarm bells going off in my head.

'Lana banana,' she calls out. 'You came! I was almost worried you wouldn't.'

I exchange glances with Ethan. Already I feel like he knows what I'm up against.

'And who is this big, strapping fellow?' she asks, turning to Ethan, playfully batting him in the chest.

'Seph, this is Ethan. Ethan, this is my sister, Seph,' I say, making the introductions.

'Seph is an interesting name,' Ethan replies. 'Beautiful, but I haven't heard it before.'

'It's short for Persephone,' she tells him.

'I always say Persephone is short because she's got tiny legs,' Chester adds. 'Chester Brimble-Plaskitt. Good to meet you, pal.'

Chester gives Ethan one of those almost aggressive, manly handshakes – the kind that makes everyone's knuckles turn white.

'Ethan Paul James,' Ethan replies, clearly throwing in his middle name to make the whole thing sound longer.

'You've got three forenames,' Chester points out, amused.

'Paul is my middle name, James is my surname,' Ethan tells him.

'Extraordinary,' Chester replies. 'I like it – EPJ, that's what we'll call you.'

'You could just call him Ethan,' I suggest.

'Lana banana, come here,' Chester says, ignoring me, pulling me in for a hug. Again though, even his hugs are aggressive, like we're two big blokes on a rugby pitch.

Apparently Lana banana is something Seph used to call me, when we were kids, but my only memories of it are her calling me it as an adult and me hating it.

'Lana,' Dad says, joining us on the path. Bea isn't far behind him.

'Oh, Lana, you came,' she says – and she sounds surprised too.

Seriously, did they all think I would bail? I'm glad I didn't now, so I didn't give them the satisfaction.

'Yep, hello, I'm here, and this is Ethan,' I say. 'Ethan, this is my dad, Walter, and my stepmum, Bea.'

'Stepmum, deary me,' Bea says as she greets Ethan with a peck on the cheek. 'Always keeping me at arm's length.'

Wow, okay. Best I just ignore that.

'Hello,' Dad says, shaking Ethan's hand – and it's another grippy one. 'Glad you could both make it.'

When I was younger I always used to think that a stiff upper lip was a literal thing – because my dad has always spoken a little bit like his lips are frozen in place.

'Don't be silly, carrying those, there is staff for that,' Bea tells Ethan as she slaps his hand.

'Oh, okay,' I say. 'I was worried this wasn't the hotel, when I didn't see any signs.'

'This isn't a hotel,' Chester says with a laugh. 'This is my rentals' place.'

I know he means parents but Ethan looks puzzled.

'This is your parents' house?' I reply.

'Yeah, we're having the wedding here,' he replies. I notice him beckon a woman and a man from the porch, indicating for them to take our cases. 'And we're all staying here.'

'Oh, I thought we'd be in a hotel,' I can't help but say – because I did think that.

'Lana, don't be rude,' Bea tells me off. 'The whole family is staying here.'

Still biting my tongue.

'Mum and Dad are getting ready for this evening – actually, we should too, Seph,' Chester says.

'So, Mum and Dad – *my* mum and dad – will show you to your room,' Seph adds. 'Catch you later.'

I can't help but notice that she said room – as in one room. I mean, why would they give us two rooms, they thought I was bringing a date.

'Is it possible for us to have separate rooms?' I ask. 'We're, erm... we're old-fashioned.'

'Oh, Lana, don't be ludicrous,' Bea replies. 'And don't make fun of us. It's quite all right for you to share a room, isn't it, Walter?'

Dad pulls a face.

'Quite all right,' he replies.

'My love, go prepare for the evening, I will show Lana and Ethan to their room,' Bea tells him, patting him gently on the cheek. 'You two, do follow me.'

'You asked for this,' I whisper to Ethan.

'So did you,' he replies with a cheeky smile.

This house is huge. It's dark grey, with columns that give it a real sense of grandeur, and super modern so there are huge glass windows with balconies on almost all of them. We must be near the ocean because I can hear it roaring, so I'm guessing we are really close to the beach right now – if not on it.

'Wow, this is some house,' Ethan says as we step into the hallway with Bea.

'It's not a house, it's an estate,' she corrects him.

The hallway has brilliant white walls and shiny black marble floor tiles. The décor is clean but opulent, mixing minimalism with what I can only describe as big chunks of gold and silver. I'm talking cabinets, sculptures, frames – the place literally looks like it's made of money.

'This is the ground floor,' Bea explains. 'The living space is downstairs, on the lower ground floor – which is how you access the gardens, pool and the private beach. This floor has bedrooms, as does upstairs, which is where the two of you are.'

God, I can't believe we're going to have to share a bedroom. I know what you're thinking, we've literally slept together, but that's the problem. We're comfortable together – give us a bed and a closed door and we might slip into old habits (I don't even think we'd need the bed to be tempted, or the door for that matter, but you take my point).

'You're late, so I'll show you straight to your room,' Bea insists.

'We're late?' I reply. 'The plane was the plane – we couldn't have got here any faster.'

She selectively ignores this as she leads us up the stairs and along the hallway, finally stopping outside the door.

'This is your room,' she says. 'You will find your en suite inside, just around the corner. I'll leave you both to settle in but, Ethan, I'm looking forward to getting to know you much better.'

Bea says this almost suspiciously. Okay, fair enough, this situation isn't what it seems, but she should respect me enough that if I turn up with a man and say he's my boyfriend then that's that, right? There's nothing to be suspicious of.

Ethan and I head into our room, closing the door behind us.

'Holy fuck,' he blurts. 'Look at this.'

Ethan charges past the big-screen TV, the super-king bed, and the welcome basket full of food – no, scratch that, he grabs a packet of biscuits as he rushes past it – and heads straight for our balcony.

I drop my handbag, hurrying after him.

'Okay, wow,' I say – my words seemingly made of nothing but breath. 'This is unreal.'

Chester's mum and dad's house sits elevated, above the beach, and it looks out over nothing but sand, sea and sunshine. If you look a little further down the beach you can see people walking, playing sports, sunbathing, surfers in the water, boats. We're in paradise.

'Oh, I am so ready for a holiday,' Ethan says, wrapping an arm around me.

'I'm so ready for a nap,' I tell him. 'Flying really takes it out of you.'

'It's a long flight,' he replies, following me back indoors.

I sit on the edge of the bed before dramatically flopping down onto my back. Ethan does the same next to me.

'So, we're sharing a bed, huh?' he says.

'Let's try not to break this one,' I reply.

Right on cue, I realise Bea is back in the room.

'In bed already?' she says. 'I forgot to say before, you need to dress for dinner, right now, as we're headed out soon.'

Oh, but all I want to do is sleep.

'We're going out for dinner?' I reply.

'Yes, and do dress in your best,' she adds. 'The boat has a very strict dress code.'

And with that she's gone.

'Boat?' Ethan says.

'A fancy boat,' I reply. 'I am dreading it.'

'Really? Because I can't wait,' he replies.

Ha. All he needs is time and he'll soon change his tune. But for now, I guess we need to get ready.

27

'Dinner on a boat,' Ethan says, clapping his hands together.

'Didn't you say you'd been on a cruise?' I check.

'Yeah, a cheap one with a fake window,' he reminds me. 'For a cheap-o holiday. This is a boat just for dinner – dinner on a boat.'

Okay, he's adorable when he's excited in a dorky way.

'If you want to fit in, pretend there isn't even a boat there,' I tell him as the taxi pulls into wherever it is you board a boat to dinner in these parts.

'Well, I don't want to fit in, do I?' he reminds me.

'An excellent point,' I reply as we get out of the car. 'So, it's just like we talked about, okay?'

'Got it,' he says. 'Just be the worst version of my best self.'

'Are you two the late ones?' a man in a white shirt (who looks like he works here) calls out.

How are we late? We came here exactly when they told us to, in the car they booked for us.

'I guess?' Ethan calls back.

I hook my arm with his as we approach.

'Ethan, no matter what I say, do your worst,' I tell him. 'Even if it seems like I'm chickening out – because I always soften, and then they always do something that makes me wish I hadn't.'

'It would be my pleasure,' he replies.

It turns out that the place you board a boat to dinner is like a snap from a Sydney postcard. At first it's a slow reveal – blink and you'll miss it – and then it's there, all at once, Sydney Opera House, and the Sydney Harbour Bridge, and they're somehow bigger than I imagined them, although that's probably because I've only ever seen them in photos or videos.

'Dinner on a boat,' he whispers to me, nudging me with his elbow.

Boat feels like a very small word for a very big yacht. God, it does look inviting though. The buzz of activity, the pretty lights, the unreal backdrop. The only thing that could ruin it really is the people – and you know they're going to give it their best.

'Do you know all of these people?' Ethan asks as we walk along the gangway to board the yacht.

'I know as many people as you do,' I tell him. 'Actually, no, that's not true. There's the chief bridesmaid, Eleanor, and cousin Tiggy should be here somewhere.'

'Do we like either of them?' he checks.

'Eleanor, no, she's a supervillain,' I tell him, in no way exaggerating. 'Tiggy, we love. Don't get me wrong, she's as bourgeoisie as the rest of them. She's a boarding-school brat, she's never worked a day in her life, and she's probably had to leave a holiday for this holiday. But she's actually nice. She loves a drink and a dance and a roll around with a "working man" – so watch your back. It is, of course, fine for Tiggy to be a party girl because she's on a champagne budget.'

'You've got to love that double standard,' he says.

Now that we're on board – the two late ones – the gangway comes away from the yacht. There's no turning back now, we're trapped. I supposed there's always jumping overboard but hopefully it won't come to that.

'Welcome drinks,' a server says, presenting us with a silver platter loaded with various cocktails. He's wearing a black tuxedo which I think is funny, because if this were the wedding then he would look like a guest. Not on a boat though, on a boat it's (very) smart casual.

I'm wearing a navy strapless midi dress with silver accessories – yes, silver, not white gold or platinum, which to this lot is as bad as turning up in clown make-up. Ethan, accidentally, is almost perfectly coordinated with me. He's wearing a navy suit with a crisp white shirt unbuttoned at the collar. He looks seriously fit in a suit, like he should be in an advert for aftershave – a suit which he assures me he already had in his suitcase, just in case, but I'm not sure I believe him.

I take a drink from the tray. Ethan takes two.

The server doesn't bat an eyelid – he's either not being paid enough to care, or being paid more than enough to let everyone do whatever they want.

'You made it then,' Bea says as she greets us. She's wearing a cream twinset – very Queen Camilla chic – while Dad wears a dark green suit.

'Ethan,' Dad greets him. 'How about you and I take a stroll, have a chat?'

Tell me my dad isn't dad-ing right now!

'Yeah, okay, cool,' Ethan says.

He polishes off one drink, so that he only has one to carry.

'I like to get blotto at these things too,' Dad tells him as they walk off.

Unbelievable. So, apparently it's fine for men to drink too much.

'Best behaviour tonight, Lana,' Bea warns me. 'Remember what we talked about.'

Ha. I remember. It's the main thing that's motivating me right now.

Finally alone, I knock back my drink.

Normally I'd worry about a boy talking to my dad – or more specifically my dad talking to a boy – but with Ethan I have nothing to lose. Not just because we're not a real couple but because, well, the worse the conversation goes, the better it is for what I'm going for.

I walk across the deck, running a hand along the gleaming silver railings. It isn't the only thing that's glittering – everyone here is dolled up to the eyes, in their diamonds and expensive watches. Everyone is catching the light.

Most people I don't know, some look vaguely familiar, but generally it's the same bunch of people who rarely give me the time of day – although at Dad's sixtieth birthday one of his friends did tell me to top up his glass before asking if I offered extras (which simultaneously boosted and destroyed my self-esteem).

Oh, but he's new though. I haven't seen him before. A man in his late thirties maybe. He's tall and slender, with hair to his jawline that he wears tucked behind his ears. I can tell that he's one of this lot from his posture and – and this is going to sound stupid – the angle of his chin. He's good-looking, and I don't usually find anyone who associates with this lot good-looking, so he really is something special. He's eating a canapé, treating it almost as though he were kissing it, sucking the leftovers from his thumb when he's finished.

'Drooling over the earl, you horny bitch,' a familiar voice whispers into my ear.

I'd know that foul mouth anywhere.

'Tiggy,' I say, turning around to give her a squeeze. 'Oh my God, it's been forever.'

'Totes,' she replies, giving me a big sloppy kiss on the cheek. 'I've been – oh, you know, I don't know. Who cares? We're here now.'

Tiggy looks amazing, as always. She's leggy and slim, and she often mentions how much she spends on hair extensions but you would never know. She used to (I assume) joke that it was cocaine that kept her svelte, although her cheeks have sucked in, in that way you typically see if there has been… pharmaceutical intervention, shall we say. Who cares though? She looks fantastic. She's unbelievably forty next year – but no one is allowed to talk about that. Here's me, whining that my milestone birthday is going by unacknowledged, and there she is, threatening to stab anyone who mentions hers.

'How have you been?' I ask.

'Fucking amazing, as per, but don't change the subject,' she says, playfully slapping my arm. 'Are you perving over the earl?'

'Is he actually an earl?' I ask curiously.

'The Earl of Fuck Me He's Hot,' she jokes. 'Yes, that's Lord Beaumont Cunningham, the Earl of Wrancaster.'

'He is a hot earl,' I admit.

'Is it the good looks or the title that is doing it for you?' she grills me.

'It was the looks at first but, now you've said the title, it's kind of sexy – who knew titles were sexy?'

'Me,' she sings, raising her hand. 'Do you want introducing to him?'

'Oh, no,' I say quickly. 'No, no, no.'

'Let me introduce you and you won't be saying no, no, no. You'll be saying yes, yes, yes.'

Tiggy takes me by the hand, dragging me to the deck below.

'I know, I'm just awful,' she says, not sounding all that cut up about it. 'But trust me.'

I trust Tiggy in many ways – like with secrets, for example – but when it comes to her actions I would say I actively fear her. I like a drink and a good time but I don't have the spectacular confidence (or the even more spectacular bank balance) to be dangerous with it. She does.

'Beau, you miserable ass, how is it you haven't tracked me down to say hi yet?' she practically shrieks at him.

'Tig, come here,' he commands.

Oh my God, the way he greets her, the way he places his hand on her lower back as he kisses her on the cheek – it makes me want to bite my lip.

'You've met cousin Lana, right?' she asks him, knowing full well he hasn't.

'Oh, another Pemberton girl?' he replies, smiling at me.

I just smile back. Why am I not saying anything?

'Guilty,' Tiggy says on my behalf. 'The only single Pemberton girl left, if you're still looking to take a wife – add another surname to the collection.'

'Hilarious, Tigs,' he says in a voice that makes Hugh Grant sound kind of like an extra in *EastEnders*. 'Well, Lana, we haven't met, but we're family.'

As he says this he leans in to give me a couple of these charismatic kisses. He holds the small of my back with his hand as he pulls me close.

'*Like* family,' Tiggy corrects him. 'No blood relation – not that that bothers our lot, hey?'

I appreciate her pointing that out quickly, lest I realise I was accidentally lusting over a cousin.

'And no, Tigs, no wife as of yet,' he tells her.

'The burden of being an earl,' she replies. 'Having to find the perfect good girl and... oh, excuse me, I've just spotted a fitty I need to go and sink these dagger nails into, before someone else does. Catch you both later.'

Oh, shit, she's leaving me alone with him. She's leaving me alone with the bloody earl.

'Your cousin is fun,' he says with a Prince Charming smile – I'm surprised his teeth don't sparkle and make a little ding noise as he does it.

'She's great,' I reply, finding myself changing my accent, stripping out the Yorkshire charm that I have (unlike the rest of my family), instead going for some kind of newsreader-style RP that makes me sound closer to my family than I actually am.

'Do I detect a slight hint of an accent?' he asks curiously. 'Have you worked abroad? Canada, perhaps? I'm picking up on something.'

A thinly veiled cover-up of Headingley's finest.

'Oh, I've been all over,' I reply. 'You know how it is.'

'I do indeed,' he says. 'Tiggy and I are the same age – not that any of us are allowed to disclose such a classified number – and suddenly everyone is always telling me it's about time I settled down.'

'Oh, me too,' I reply. 'Especially with Seph tying the knot.'

'That just means you'll have your pick of the bachelors,' he points out.

'Well, there is that,' I say with a smile.

God, he's beautiful. Ethan is broad, muscular and rugged, but the things that make Beau attractive are completely different qualities. He's more subtle, more refined, with more beautiful features. I suppose it just depends what you're into. I always thought I was more into the Ethan type but, I don't know, now that I'm here, chatting to an actual earl – maybe a Beau is for me. Plus, as much as I want Ethan – or think I do anyway – that just can't happen. I need to get that out of my head and crushing on someone new could be the cure I need. Actually, that's a great idea, because if I throw all my energy into crushing on someone else – someone I could actually date without causing a forest fire or a landslide – then it will keep things between me and Ethan strictly business and I won't go slipping into old habits...

'We shall have to look out for one another at this wedding – single solidarity,' he tells me.

'I'd like that,' I reply with a smile.

He's almost too beautiful to look at, I have to avert my eyes, but it's as I glance sideways that I notice who Tiggy is talking to, the fitty she – what was it? – wanted to get her dagger nails into. Shit, it's Ethan. Oh, God, he's just her type too.

'I, ahem, I need to step away, and assist Tiggy with something, briefly,' I say, almost every word sounding like not quite the right one.

'Of course, go ahead,' he says. 'I'll see you later, I'm sure.'

'Absolutely,' I tell him.

I walk off slowly, as sexily as I can, until I'm out of his line of sight and then I do the most unladylike run back over to where Tiggy and Ethan are chatting.

'Hey,' I say, rocking up to them, trying to play it cool, although I can't quite hide how out of breath I am.

'Lana, Lana, Lana,' Tiggy says, waggling her index finger at me. 'You kept lovely Ethan here a secret, didn't you?'

'I, er...'

'You know Lana,' Ethan tells her. 'She doesn't like to make a big deal out of things.'

'No, I know,' Tiggy replies seriously. 'Nor do I.'

She gives me a look – one that says she's dying to know more.

'Well, I need to go and get a top-up, but I look forward to hearing more about the two of you later.'

'Of course,' Ethan tells her. 'See you later.'

Okay, so I know that once we have a private moment together I can tell Tiggy that Ethan isn't *with me* with me (although the thought of the two of them getting it on really does make me want to jump overboard), and I think she already knows I have a bit of a crush on Beau, so she probably already knows that things aren't as they seem.

Wow, I really am not usually one to go for the kind of guys I meet at these family events but I could make an exception for an earl, right? However, as we all know, I am not the kind of girl that an earl would go for. Maybe I should be? I mean, come on, I've got the family name. How hard can it be?

'Ethan, listen, while it's just us, I need to tell you something,' I say in hushed tones.

'What's that?' he replies.

'We need to abort the mission,' I tell him.

He just laughs.

'I'm serious,' I reply. 'There's been a change of plan. I don't want to cause any trouble, at all, I want to be good – for my sister.'

The second part is a line but the first part is absolutely what I need to do, if I want to woo an earl.

'This is a test, isn't it?' he says with a knowing grin.

'No, it's really not,' I insist.

'Yeah, okay, sure,' he replies. 'Like I'm falling for that one. Don't worry, you're going to get what you sort-of paid for – what your family paid for, I guess.'

Okay, so now isn't the time or the place, but I can explain it to him, that the plan really has changed.

I came here thinking I was going to make a mess. Now, I guess I need to clean up my act.

28

'So... our first night sharing a bed together,' Ethan points out.

'Except it isn't,' I remind him.

'It's the first time we've done so in the normal way,' he replies.

'Because this is *so* normal,' I add.

If we were actually in bed together *like that* then the scene would be perfect. I'm wearing one of my more attractive sleeping-vest-and-shorts combos – one of the ones that I don't somehow lose a boob from while I'm sleeping – and Ethan is wearing a tight-fitting pair of boxers, not that I've noticed (of course I've noticed). It's warm but it isn't too warm. There's a breeze drifting in through the open door that leads out onto our balcony. It's so relaxing, watching the sheer curtain blowing gently. The room smells like an expensive diffuser with a name like 'ocean bliss' and the only thing I can hear is the roar of the ocean (and maybe my heart thumping in my chest a little stronger than it usually does).

The scene is set for romance. Proper Mills & Boon-type shit. If I weren't thinking straight I could just pull back the covers, climb on top of him, and forget about everything else. I am, however, thinking straight and I know that if we did it would probably result in us – I don't know – dislodging a block that sends the entire house crashing into the sea, just bringing it all down like the end of a game of Jenga.

'So, how was your day, honey?' he asks me.

I laugh.

'Don't do that,' I tell him.

'What?' he replies, chuckling innocently.

'Turn us into some old sitcom, where we're both lying here, side by side – essentially like we're in twin beds – wittily debriefing our day. I'm half expecting to hear a laugh track.'

'I'm just asking,' he insists. 'But I'll drop the honey. I'm taking my role as your fake boyfriend very seriously.'

'Right, but I meant what I said, I don't want to do that any more,' I tell him.

'I thought that was a test,' he replies.

'No, I really don't,' I insist. 'Like, stay, enjoy the holiday, have a lovely normal time – but I am officially abandoning the plan.'

He laughs to himself, ever so quietly.

I roll onto my side, to face him.

'What?' I ask, getting the feeling he's keeping something from me.

'Well, if it's not a test, and you really do want to call it off, then I can only assume it's because of that lanky lord I saw you drooling over.'

'He's an earl,' I point out.

'Oooh,' he teases. 'Someone sounds exactly like the rest of their family.'

I know he's joking but that prods at a soft spot.

'And I notice you're not denying that you were drooling over him,' he adds.

'Well, we're just friends, so I'm free to drool as I please,' I remind him.

'You are, that's true,' he tells me. 'But I was brought here to be your boyfriend, and everyone thinks I am your boyfriend, so I can't let you make me look bad, can I?'

I laugh.

'You can say and do what you want,' I tell him. 'I'll just make out like you're like Steve – a desperate ex, deluded in thinking we're still together.'

'But you brought me here,' he reminds me.

The tone between us is wildly flirtatious, given the conversation we're having.

'Yeah, but it's like, when you know the dog needs putting down, and you love it so you give it an absolute dream few days, to say goodbye. I'll just tell everyone I'm doing that.'

'You'll tell everyone you love me?' he replies, selecting the part of the sentence he knows will bug me. 'Interesting.'

'Ethan, the plan has changed, and you're right, I fancy the earl, so I'm going to see what happens there,' I tell him firmly.

Telling him this can only help, right? Because if he thinks I'm completely uninterested in him, and that I'm all in on someone else, then he won't do anything that tempts me back over to the dark side... right?

Ethan rolls onto his side, so that he's facing me – sort of like that thing they make boxers do before a fight where it looks like they're going to kiss.

'In that case I am going to "toff block" you at every opportunity I can,' he replies with a smile. 'I'm doing the job I came here to do.'

I should have known, really, that if you shop for crazy, you buy crazy. Ethan is here and he's doing exactly what the plan was, in a way that is better than I could have imagined... but the plan has changed so, if Ethan wants to play dirty, that's what we'll do. And we'll all ignore just how oddly hot this all is.

29

They say breakfast is the most important meal of the day. In this house, it's a little too important.

'You're saying I can have anything?' Ethan checks with the member of the housekeeping staff who is taking our breakfast orders.

We're all sitting around the dining table – all of the key players in the wedding – and first things first, breakfast is being ordered.

'Yes,' the young woman replies.

'So, if I said I wanted lobster bisque...'

'Then I would get it for you,' she confirms – of course, you can see in her eyes that she thinks he's an arsehole.

'Holy shit, that's wild,' he replies. 'I'll just have a bagel, with scrambled eggs, but wow.'

You can see a small puff of relief come out as the young woman exhales.

See, if the plan were still the plan, then Ethan really would be doing an incredible job. He's being kind of uncouth, and ridiculous, but he still knows who the enemy is.

'Lobster bisque for breakfast – a man after my own heart,'

Chester tells him. 'Beau, do you remember that morning, while we were still celebrating Maximus's stag, and we dared you to drink French onion soup from Digby's brogue?'

'As I recall it, it wasn't French onion soup, it was, ahem, vomit,' Beau replies. 'And in the end, I think it was Maximus who enjoyed a sort of *shoey* for breakfast that day.'

'Disgusting,' Seph says with a roll of her eyes. 'Boys are disgusting.'

'I'm not surprised he and Briony got divorced,' Tiggy adds as she sips her second espresso. 'Given what they both enjoyed for breakfast the day before their big day.'

'Why, what did Briony have?' Chester asks.

'Fellatio, I believe,' she says, incredibly casually. 'With the gentleman whose villa we had commandeered for the weekend.'

'Right, Antigone, we get the picture,' Bea tells her firmly – you know you're in trouble when you get your full first name thrown at you. That's a verbal warning. A written warning is, to have a guess stupid enough to be true, wills being changed.

I glance at Ethan, who is so very clearly having the time of his life. He's gripped, like he's watched an upper-class version of *Hollyoaks*. They could actually put lobster bisque down in front of him, and I don't think it would steal his attention.

'Not in front of the rentals, Tig,' Chester says with what I think is technically a chortle.

Chester's rentals – aka his mum and dad – seem nice enough, but almost everyone at this table is cut from the same cloth. Joan and Richard are old money, stiff – clearly not fans of Tiggy saying 'fellatio' at their breakfast table.

Tiggy is... I don't know how to describe it. I swear, I make dirty jokes, I like to have a drink and a laugh. The thing is though, when I do it, it's common and unacceptable. When Tiggy does it, it's okay, that's just Tiggy being outrageous. There are so many double standards, in that same way, where it's classy if you're wealthy, but in incredibly poor taste if you're a lowly commoner. Drinking too much, talking about sex, stories from wild nights out – badges of honour for this lot. But you can guarantee if I decided to tell the story of when Ethan and I were getting it on and the blinds opened, it would get a reception that would fit seamlessly into *Pretty Woman*. Not that I want to tell them, I want to seem like a whole new me, the kind of me who fits in.

'I want to know more about our new friend,' Chester says, looking across the table to Ethan. 'What's your story?'

'Oh, I'm not sure I have a story,' Ethan replies.

'Everyone has a story,' Chester replies. 'A list of conquests, achievements and such.'

'No one wants to hear about my body count or my criminal record over breakfast,' Ethan replies.

'I certainly do,' Tiggy says before flagging down a member of staff for another coffee.

Oh, fuck, he's being perfect – for the *old* plan. But I don't want that now.

'I am committed to your daughter, sister, cousin, basic stranger,' Ethan tells everyone, glancing at them one at a time, working his way from my dad to Seph to Tiggy to Beau.

I can feel the uncomfortable look creeping across my face.

'Ha ha, yes, of course you are,' I say. 'Daddy, Ethan and I work together.'

Daddy! I just said Daddy! Seph – of course – still uses Mummy and Daddy to refer to her parents and it always makes me cringe. Well, look at me now, trying to use the word 'Daddy'.

'I know we do,' Ethan replies – then he stops in his tracks. 'Sorry, she calls me Daddy too, I thought she was talking to me.'

My actual daddy doesn't look impressed, although I think (and this is a relief) he thinks this is Ethan saying he's like the dad I never had, rather than it being a sex thing.

'Ethan, I like you,' Chester tells him, laughing wildly.

'Me too,' Tiggy adds. 'We need more fun people in this family.'

'I don't know, you can never have too many sensible heads in the room,' Beau adds. 'What do you think, Lana?'

Oh my God, he's talking to me.

'Are you with me and Seph or Chet and Tigs on this one?' he asks.

Speak!

'Er, yes, sensible all the way,' I reply.

'So, you're an office worker too?' Bea enquires – very much with a tone.

'Well, I don't work in the office,' Ethan replies. 'But I do make apps for a living.'

'Is that a real job?' Seph enquires. 'I know Lana is a secretary, or similar, but they have those everywhere. But the app-making side – is that a job?'

'Where do you think they come from?' Ethan asks her with a smile.

'I don't know,' she replies. 'I thought they just sort of... appeared on the phone,' she says.

'Ignore her, EPJ, she thinks money grows on trees,' Chester says.

Oh, so the nickname is happening then. I don't know if that's a good or bad sign but Chester only gives nicknames to those who he deems worthy of his time.

'It's made of paper, you idiot, of course it grows on trees,' Seph tells him smugly.

'It actually isn't,' Ethan corrects her. 'It's made of polymer now.'

'Ha!' Chester says loudly, pointing in his future wife's face smugly. 'You're so out of touch, you don't even know what money is made of.'

'So, it's plastic?' Seph asks. 'Because I do a lot of philanthropy, and they say plastic is bad.'

'I think polymer is polymer,' Beau chimes in. 'And that plastic is a polymer, but not all polymers are plastic. What kind of second-rate boarding school did you attend?'

He's joking – imagine being able to joke about who went to the best exclusive, expensive school.

'So, really, money is terrible for the environment,' Seph says. 'I am a better person than all of you, for not handling it.'

'Money is bad for the environment, but not in the way you think it is,' I reply.

'All right, Lana, can we save your "eat the rich" mentality until after breakfast please?' Bea insists.

'Yeah, Lana, it's a bit of a buzzkill,' Chester adds. 'I'll bet you were on the side of the orcas, when they went on their yacht-sinking spree.'

I mean, I had more in common with them.

'Lana has a point,' Beau says, jumping to my defence. 'Emissions data says—'

'Lana, why do you always have to do this?' Seph asks angrily. 'We're just trying to enjoy breakfast.'

Neither the first, second nor third things that pop into my head to reply are very demure so I just hold my tongue.

But, as I look around the table, and notice Beau looking my way, I see him subtly raise his coffee cup to me, as if to say cheers.

I notice Ethan noticing too.

Okay, well, maybe the earl doesn't think I'm a total loser. I can work with that.

30

I think, if this were any other wedding, then an all-expenses trip to a beautiful country would be a dream come true. But this isn't any other wedding, it's Seph's wedding, and so all of the forced fun beforehand feels like it will be anything but fun.

Today we're going for a walk in the Blue Mountains National Park.

Here's another example of how the rich and the not rich differ – to me, walking is first and foremost free transport. To them, this is exclusively a social activity. There's a big difference between strolling around the most beautiful places in the world while on holiday and hurrying down Briggate on a Saturday morning – stepping over takeaway litter and dodging puke from the night before – because you're running late.

Still, I'm focusing on the bright side. It's somewhere I've never been, that I would love to visit. And the great news is that because we're all travelling there together on the same luxury coach, and because Chester and Beau are sitting with their new bestie – EPJ – that means I get to sit with Tiggy, away from everyone else, to talk etiquette.

'You want what?' she blurts. 'You want me to teach you how to shag an earl?'

'No,' I say quickly, laughing. 'I could take it from there – what I want is for you to teach me how to woo one.'

'Why would you want some aged, overpriced filet mignon when you have the world's best burger?' she asks.

I really can't tell if that's complimentary or offensive or both.

'Ethan is not what you think, okay, we're not together,' I tell her.

'Oh, right, so he's free for the taking?' she replies.

I hesitate for a second.

'He's my ex, sort of, and I told him he could come for a free holiday – that's it. And, well, that he could pretend to be my plus-one. But that's really it.'

'You're not over him then,' she points out.

'What? No, I absolutely am,' I insist. 'What the two of us had was just a weird sex thing, but it was too much. We just cause trouble, whenever we get together, so we agreed to just be friends.'

'Cuz, all I'm hearing is that you brought your ex – who sounds frankly like the shag of a lifetime – to a family wedding. You are not over him. But, sure, I'll help you shag the earl. What are cousins for? And I suppose they say the best way to get over someone is to get under someone else – and there aren't that many titles above earl.'

She might not think I'm over him but there's nothing to get over. We were never anything but sex.

'Tell me what an earl's girl is like,' I say, moving the conversation along.

'Not you, I'm afraid to say, lovely,' she says frankly. 'Nor I, so you're in good company.'

'Ah,' I reply.

'The interesting thing is that while our lot just have money because we do, being an earl is a whole thing,' she explains. 'Beau is – I forget – the right honourable sixteenth... or maybe seventeenth... earl of Wrancaster. Beau to his friends, Lord Cunningham to everyone else.'

'So, you call him Lord Cunningham, not Earl Cunningham?' I check.

'Darling, I've never called him anything other than Beau or other unrelated four-letter words,' she jokes. 'But yes, he's a lord. He owns an estate – and the most beautiful twenty-bedroom manor house. It makes Uncle Walt's place look like a shack. He runs the estate which, really, is a real job. He owns thousands and thousands of acres, with residential properties and farms paying him rent, so he makes plenty of money; however, he isn't fulfilling his obligations, as an earl, and that's a no-no.'

'How do you mean?' I ask.

'Well, these sorts of titles are hereditary, so the title and the estate go to the eldest male heir. Beau has no children, no partner, no prospects,' she continues.

It's a crying shame when you can be an actual earl, the owner of a huge estate that makes lots of money, and still be considered someone with 'no prospects'.

'He has no brothers, no uncles,' she continues. 'You're supposed to have an heir and a spare, so the pressure on him to get married is humongous.'

'But he must be inundated with offers?' I reply.

'Well, yes, but honestly, the pressure to choose the right kind of girl – he needs a lady, but someone he can live with, someone he can start a family with, who isn't a gold digger. And of course, image is important. He has this PR person trying to make him relevant, but Beau says he would sooner remove the sword from the wall of the drawing room and impale himself before he'll dance on TikTok.'

I laugh – a man after my own heart.

'If he likes you, he likes you,' Tiggy says sincerely. 'You'll soon be able to tell. But I'd curtsy, just in case.'

'Oi, Lana.' I hear Ethan's voice from the back of the bus.

I turn to face him as he throws me something and my reflexes kick in just in time to catch it. It's a pack of Tim Tam biscuits.

'Aw, he brought snacks for the bus,' Tiggy teases. 'Adorable. What's he going to do when you ride off into the sunset with Beau?'

'He reckons he's going to try and stop me,' I say with a smile.

'I think you want him to stop you,' she tells me. 'I think this is all to make him jealous.'

'Tiggy, Beau is a handsome earl – a regular Prince Charming,' I remind her. 'Ethan is a Buttons kind of guy. Have you never read a fairy tale?'

'Have you never seen *Shrek*?' she claps back.

'We're here,' Bea sings. 'Time to disembark.'

'Incidentally, I am familiar with *Cinderella*, and your ugly step-mother is very much as expected,' Tiggy whispers.

'I think it's the sisters who are ugly,' I tell her. 'I think the step-mother is just wicked.'

'Well, you got both rolled into one,' she replies. 'Ugly on the inside and definitely wicked. I miss Aunt Liz.'

'I'll give her your love, the next time we speak,' I reply.

It must be at least ten years since Mum last saw Tiggy but they always got on really well.

'I can't believe this lot have talked me into a walk,' Tiggy says with a sigh. 'I've had to borrow flat shoes from whatever Chester's mum's name is. My feet are like a Barbie's, they don't know what to do.'

'I don't love walking either,' I tell her. 'We'll stick together.'

'We will – after you chat with Beau, of course,' she replies, egging me on. 'Don't worry, I'll take care of Ethan, and I know just to look, not to touch.'

We all filter off the bus, grabbing the fancy matching water flasks Seph gave us all for the trip, and stand in the car park awaiting further instructions.

Car park is a grand name for it, I suppose, because really it's just a sandy patch off the road from the town, where vehicles pull in to drop off walkers.

'Darling, you know your dad isn't getting any younger,' Bea tells Seph, although I suspect from the tone of her voice she is equally if not more worried about herself.

'Mummy, you have nothing to worry about,' Seph assures her. 'I chose the easiest walk – no dangerous cliff-edge walking or difficult hills – simply a stroll through the forest where we can take lots of lovely photos and go at a relaxed pace until we reach the waterfall.'

Easy, not dangerous, stroll, lovely, relaxed – words that are all music to my ears, and going to see a waterfall sounds great. I just need to make the most of it.

'Okay, everyone, let's get into pairs, so we each have a walking companion to look out for us,' Seph suggests. 'Chester and I will stick together, of course. Mummy and Daddy. Mummy and Daddy-in-law to be.'

Eleanor hasn't come with us (no, I'm not disappointed) because she's allergic to some kind of tree sap? Apparently she hasn't interacted with a tree since the nineties and, because this is her, I kind of believe her. I also think it's plausible that she didn't fancy a hike.

'Oh, may I walk with Ethan?' Tiggy pleads. 'I'd love to get to know him better – and Beau less.'

'Hilarious, Tigs,' Beau replies. 'But I am happy to accompany Lana.'

'Yeah, er, yes,' I say, correcting myself. 'Yes.'

I need to try not to sound so keen but I am, and I'm grateful to Tiggy for giving me the opportunity.

'Yeah, that's fine by me,' Ethan adds with a smile, although I suspect he knows what is going on.

'Right then, shall we?' Bea suggests.

We all set off along the sandy path that leads into the forest, two at a time. It's a gloriously hot and sunny day – and I think I saw on Instagram that there is snow back at home, so I feel incredibly smug to be here. I'm in Australia, with an actual earl, walking through the mountains in the sunshine, when really I should be back in snowy Leeds, in the office, running around after Jennifer and doing my best to avoid Steve.

Ah, Steve. I've just reminded myself that I am homeless, which is just stunning. I wonder, even if it's just a one-off birthday gift, if Dad might give me some money to get a place of my own. Not to buy one, obviously. Just to help me out with a deposit and maybe my first month of rent. Honestly, just when I feel like I'm getting back on my feet, and like I might have the money to get a place of my own, something comes up – like an expensive wedding gift and to buy a very specific dress to attend said wedding.

I don't know – we'll see. I'll have to work up the courage to even ask but who knows? Maybe if he sees me on my best behaviour (even if it is only to impress Beau) he might be more likely to say yes.

Beau and I are the last ones to join the line but I'm happy to walk at the back because not only does it mean that I can keep an eye on Ethan, it also means he can't keep an eye on me.

'Lana,' Beau says with a welcoming smile.

Everything Tiggy told me surges to the front of my brain at once.

'Lord Cunningham,' I say, curtsying slightly. Whenever I see people doing it on TV, curtsies and bows always seem – small? Not much of a movement, just a subtle acknowledgement. God, I hope all of that was right.

Beau laughs.

'Hilarious,' he says. 'You're very funny, Lana. I love the sarcastic little curtsy – did Tig put you up to that?'

To the curtsy? She did. Oh my God, I feel like she set me up with that one.

'Surely we know each other well enough to drop the lord,' he adds with a smile. 'Don't make fun of me, I know I'm awfully old-fashioned and stuffy.'

Okay, he thinks I'm being cute. He thinks I'm teasing him for being an earl and he seems into it. Amazingly my faux pas has worked in my favour.

'Sorry, m'lord,' I say, actually teasing him now that I know he enjoys it. 'I don't think you're stuffy at all, it's a cool job.'

He smiles.

'Most people don't think it's a job,' he says. 'They think I'm some sort of playboy when, really, they don't stop to consider that I live alone in an enormous house, that has tens of thousands of visitors a year – generously, a third of it is still private, but the rest of it is usually teeming with tourists.'

'That must be so strange,' I reply. 'Opening your house to strangers.'

'Thankfully you don't get many hooligans driving out to visit stately homes,' he replies. 'I don't really notice – sometimes I'll look out of the window and see people and for a moment it's like I can't remember why they're there.'

I laugh.

'It must be strange, living in such a big house, all on your own,' I say – and, yes, I am still doing my best to talk without a hint of an accent.

'It's strange,' he replies. 'I've always lived there, so it's just home, but I would be lying if I said it never felt a little spooky. The long, dark corridors can feel especially terrifying of an eve. Of course, it's never truly lonely there. With various staff, cleaners and the nightwatchman about the place seven days a week.'

'I thought Daddy's house was big,' I reply – internally cringing at my use of Daddy, again. 'But you must need a map to get around.'

'I found a new room – a few years back, but even so, it was very bizarre,' he replies. 'It's a strange place to live alone but I know that I have to do my turn, looking after the manor. It's not real hardship, it's a beautiful place... I just need someone to share it with me.'

I honestly cannot tell if everything he just said sounds amazing or awful. He makes it seem like a mixture of both, which probably makes me like him a little bit more.

'It is of course the best place to host parties – I'm very popular in the summer,' he says with a smile. 'I hire a chef, a DJ – and I have enough bedrooms for everyone to stay over. I believe I was second choice for Chet and Seph's wedding.'

'I mean, Chester's parents' house is very lovely,' I reply. 'You don't see many stately homes on the beach.'

'Anything old enough would have most likely washed away by now,' he says. 'A word of advice – though I'm sure you know. Don't mention global warming to that lot – flat-earthers, the bunch of them. If their holidays get a little warmer and the ski slopes a little cooler then they welcome it.'

'An earl with a conscience,' I say, impressed.

'Needless to say, I'm very good about turning lights off when I leave a room at home.'

I laugh.

He's a funny earl too. It's hard to believe he's single, so I suspect it's by choice but, I don't know, I do get kind of a lonely vibe from him.

As we walk and talk, hanging back a few paces from the others, it's just nice. The conversation is easy, about everything and nothing, although I would be lying if I said I wasn't keeping an occasional eye on Ethan and Tiggy.

'Here we are,' Seph – who is leading the crowd – announces.

Oh, wow, we've finally reached the waterfall and it's beautiful. The kind of crystal-clear, sparkling water that looks so inviting – the intrusive thoughts are telling me I would feel so nice and cool if I were to jump straight in.

'A truly wonderful place for a picnic, darling,' Bea says, patting her on the head. 'An excellent find.'

'Thank you,' Seph says, super pleased with herself.

'Well, all this walking has made me positively famished,' Chester says. 'Let's get the grub out.'

Everyone exchanges glances, all eyes darting around to see who has the food.

'Wait, who brought the lunch?' Seph asks.

'What do you mean?' Dad replies.

'Daddy, the lunch we packed for everyone – it was on the bus,' she replies. 'Where is it?'

'Who was supposed to bring it?' Ethan asks.

'What do you mean?' Seph replies, cocking her head.

'Whose job was it, to carry the lunch?' I add. 'How was it supposed to get here?'

Seph just stares at me.

Oh my God. Seriously, do this lot even know how to function without someone wiping their arse for them?

'Who did you ask to carry it, darling?' Bea checks.

'No one, Mummy,' she admits. 'I... I just assumed...'

'No food?' Chester's dad says. 'Because my blood sugar...'

'I'm sorry,' Seph says, emotion building in her voice.

'It's okay, darling, it's just that everyone is so terribly hungry, from the walk,' Bea tells her. 'It was a lovely thought, and we can eat it when we get back to the bus.'

'We have been walking for over an hour,' Dad says, in hushed tones, of course we can all hear it.

'It's okay, I think I have a solution,' Ethan says with a smile as he plonks his backpack down on the floor.

He unzips it and opens it widely to reveal that it is absolutely stuffed full of Tim Tam biscuits.

'Why do you have a bag full of biscuits?' Seph asks him, her face scrunched up in confusion and – I think – mild disgust.

'I lived here, when I was a kid, and I was obsessed with these,' Ethan says, ignoring her tone. 'I haven't had one in years so, when we stopped at that shop on the way, I bought pretty much every pack they had.'

'That's so silly,' Bea points out, siding with her daughter.

'Maybe it is,' he says. A smile slowly creeps across his lips. 'But no one else has any food so it doesn't seem so silly now, does it?'

'Tim Tams for everyone,' Chester declares. 'Nice work, EPJ, you've saved the day.'

'None for me,' Seph says, holding up her hands. 'I won't fit into my dress, if I start eating biscuits.'

'Biscuits will only make mine look better,' I tell Ethan as I take a pack. 'Thank you.'

'Anytime,' he tells me with a smile.

Everyone takes a pack – I even notice Seph nibbling one of Chester's biscuits when she thinks no one is looking – and takes a moment to rest before the walk back.

'I just knew, when I bought them, that I wouldn't regret it,' Ethan says, now that it's just the two of us.

'Yeah, I mean, if I had seen you buying so many I definitely would have asked you what you were doing,' I reply.

'It was the food on the boat,' he says. 'Everything was so tiny. I ate all the things I liked, the bits I didn't like, and I was still hungry so I didn't think it would hurt to keep a pile of biscuits in the room – I'm going to have to replenish the reserves now.'

I laugh.

'I'll buy you more biscuits, I feel like I owe you,' I say. 'You've saved the day.'

'It's just biscuits,' he replies. 'But, yeah, I'm definitely a hero.'

I playfully shove him away, only for him to grab me and pull me close to a squeeze. I can't help but burst into laughter.

'Oh, aren't they adorable,' Tiggy calls out. 'Couple of the year.'

Chester clears his throat.

'After the two of you, obviously,' Tiggy tells him.

I look over at Beau – I can't help myself – to see if he looks bothered. He's smiling, like everyone else, but then I see it. That flicker of tension in his jaw, the brief narrowing of his eyes. Is he jealous or am I deluded?

It's probably the second one but, come on, a girl can dream.

31

Dinner – tonight of all nights – was a very welcome sight.

After a hike powered exclusively by biscuits, and a packed lunch that had to be thrown in the bin after being left to sweat on the hot bus for a few hours, everyone arrived home absolutely starving.

It's funny, because I suggested we stop somewhere to eat on the way home, but it was pretty much universally agreed that everyone was too inappropriately dressed and needed to shower and get changed. So Bea called ahead and arranged for dinner to be prepared slightly earlier than usual... however, she did still factor in enough time for everyone to wash and change. When I suggested we didn't need to 'dress' for dinner tonight she laughed – I honestly think she believes I was cracking a funny joke.

So we're here, we're in our dining attire, and the food is out. It's funny because now that the food is out all formalities have gone out of the window. People are helping themselves from dishes placed in the centre of the table, piling their plates high – Chester was so hungry he used the 'wrong' fork, apparently. As far as this lot are concerned they're eating like savages right now. Ethan and I, on the other hand, feel a lot more relaxed. I can tell from his body language that this is more his style.

I'm sitting between Ethan and Beau – and then there is Tiggy, to Ethan's right, which makes me think she may have had something to do with the seating arrangements this evening. I like to think that she has done this so that I can sit with Beau but, I don't know, she's all over Ethan like a rash. Part of me wonders whether Beau is my distraction so that she can get to know Ethan better.

'...there's one particular painting, in the private side of the house, called *Waiting by the Sea* by Antonelli – and it is indeed an original Antonelli...'

I'm trying to focus on what Beau is telling me – he's been talking about the various artworks in his house for about ten minutes now – but it's hard not to be distracted by Tiggy laughing wildly at every word that Ethan says. I keep trying to listen in, to work out what he is saying that is sooo funny, but with all of the chatter at the table it's impossible to focus on just one voice.

I don't know if it's because he essentially saved the day with biscuits or what, but Ethan isn't going down the way I thought he would. Honestly, I thought this lot would hate him. He's a cheeky boy-next-door, he swears, he drinks, he doesn't care about any of the silly formalities everyone else at the table lives and dies by. So why does everyone seem so accepting of him? And, well, I don't know... of me and him. I don't think I've ever introduced a boy to them (good or bad) that they haven't instantly disapproved of. It's strange.

I notice Bea staring at me as she swirls her wine around in her glass – almost menacingly.

'Lana, Ethan, I for one am dying to know something,' she says, capturing everyone's attention. 'How did the two of you meet?'

My heart drops so low I think I might technically be sitting on it right now. I quickly look to Ethan but he isn't gripped with panic like I am, instead he's got a devilish smile on his lips and a mischievous look in his eyes. Oh, God, what is he going to say? Whatever it is, I can't give him the chance to say it, I need to tell the story first – of course, I have to make up a story first, because telling them the actual way we met isn't a good idea, is it?

'It's actually a really funny story,' Ethan begins.

I open my mouth to speak but nothing comes out, and Ethan is off on one now.

'We met at work,' he tells them.

Shiiiit. Is he actually telling them the truth? Oh, please tell me he isn't.

'The first thing I saw was her bum,' he continues with a cheeky laugh. 'I wasn't looking or anything, she had it stuck up in the air – it turns out she was bent over, in front of the vending machine. It's only as I got closer that I realised she had her arm trapped in it.'

I think this is what you would call a stunned silence – and from me too. Did he really just say that?

'In a vending machine?' Seph checks, as though she might have misheard him – although for what, I have no idea.

'Yep,' Ethan says with a chuckle. 'She had her arm wedged right up in there. She got it stuck trying to retrieve a Twix she thought the machine had screwed her out of.'

And now everyone is staring at me, judging me, clearly questioning what the hell is wrong with me.

'Oh, Lana, really?' Tiggy says with a laugh. 'Why didn't you just buy another one, to dislodge the one that was stuck?'

'Yeah, why didn't I do that?' I reply – mostly for Ethan's benefit. 'That would have made much more sense.'

'Lana hates injustice,' Ethan says. 'And, honestly, she looked so cute, stuck there, all helpless, clutching at her Twix like it was the last piece of food on earth. I knew I needed to help her.'

Oh, can you think of a more sorry sight than me with my arm trapped in a vending machine, just for a Twix? I'm not saying I don't have form for it, but it didn't happen, and it is not making me look good right now.

'So, while she was stuck there, I told her I would help her get free, and I would buy her another Twix, but only if she agreed to go for a drink with me later that night – and the rest is history,' Ethan concludes. 'She said yes.'

Bea is sitting with her hand over her mouth. 'Lana, are you so hard up that you're trying to steal chocolate from vending machines?' she asks.

'No, I get it, we've all been in a situation like that,' Beau says, gallantly coming to my defence – have we? 'I almost fell in a river once, trying to catch a bottle of wine that was rolling down a hill. I completely understand.'

'Really?' I reply, laughing with a girly little squeak.

'That's hardly the same thing,' Seph says.

'I'm with Seph, sorry, Lana,' Tiggy adds. 'There's a big difference between trying to stop a 2009 Château Margaux from rolling into the Seine and getting trapped in a machine with a bar of chocolate.'

'Tiggy, come on, that's not fair. You're so wrong,' Ethan tells her firmly. 'A Twix isn't a chocolate bar, it's a biscuit.'

His face contorts into that grin that makes me want to punch him and kiss him at the same time – the dick.

I can't help but roll my eyes as Ethan laughs at his own little joke.

Still, I suppose I dodged a bullet there. Ethan obviously told that story to make me look silly and – ha! – it didn't work, if anything it seemed to endear me to Beau, and did you see how he came to my defence? He put himself out there for me, he didn't make fun of me – he was on my side when he didn't need to be.

That's something, right?

32

'Well, today was interesting,' Ethan says as we lie in bed together.

A laugh track plays out of nowhere.

I push myself up on my elbows, looking around the room suspiciously, before my eyes settle on Ethan and the cheeky look he has on his face.

'Did you...'

He holds up his phone, showing me the laugh track video he just played from YouTube.

'Hilarious,' I say, lying back down.

'What? You said we were like an old sitcom,' he replies. 'I'm just making it feel more authentic.'

I try to make myself more comfortable. It's a little warmer tonight, the kind of warm where a good night's sleep feels just out of your reach.

'I see you and the earl are getting along,' he says.

'I see you and Tiggy are getting on,' I reply.

'I'm getting on with everyone,' he replies. 'Your family are great.'

'You say that, but just remember what motivated me to invite you along on this trip in the first place,' I remind him.

'Has anyone mentioned your birthday?' he asks, his tone especially gentle, like he already knows the answer.

I shake my head.

'If you could spend it anywhere, where would it be?' he asks curiously.

'If the answer doesn't have to be logistically or financially realistic, then Paris,' I reply. 'I've always wanted to go. If I was an old-money snob, that's where I'd throw my party.'

Ethan laughs.

'Remind yourself that you can go to Paris whenever you want,' he says. 'And don't let this wedding ruin your birthday – you will celebrate it, even if it's late.'

'It's not that I think my birthday is more important than Seph's wedding – even though it's obvious she thinks her wedding is more important than my birthday – it's just the fact that it's a milestone birthday, and milestones are supposed to show how far you've come, and what do I have to show for my thirty years?'

'We could all say that,' he insists. 'Think about it – when we sit with the others, no one from our generation is married. Tiggy, Eleanor – even your lord.'

'Earl,' I correct him. 'But it's not just that, it's everything – maybe it's anything. I don't have anything.'

'And I'm guessing marrying an earl is your best shot at ticking some boxes in life?' he says, with a hint of a tone, but one I can't quite decipher.

'I've got as much of a chance as anyone,' I point out firmly.

Ethan doesn't say a word, he just plays the laugh track again.

Dick.

33

Everything about this wedding is so very clearly eye-wateringly expensive – except the entertainment, because that's seemingly free.

It's unofficial entertainment, of course, but it's entertaining nonetheless.

My family – with the exception of me, of course – is one of those families that takes sports and board games far too seriously. Everyone is so competitive to the point where it isn't actually fun to play with them. In fact, the last time I spent Christmas with them, I went to bed during a late-night game of Monopoly and woke up the next morning to find some of them were still playing!

So, today's unofficial entertainment is... fencing, because of course it is.

'Get him, Chester,' Seph calls out.

'He's no match for Beau,' Tiggy tells her.

They've got quite the little crowd around them, in the back garden, and they fight it out. In any other scenario it would be surprising to find out people just had fencing gear to hand but, no, not with this lot. They could have been playing polo on horseback and I wouldn't have been all that shocked.

Beau lunges as Chester parries – it's funny, they almost look like they're dancing. It's surprisingly elegant, considering they're trying to stab one another.

Their blades clink a little longer before Beau lands the hit that ends the match.

Chester pulls off his mask before playfully staggering around, holding his stomach, as though he's been fatally wounded. Seph runs to his side and kisses him on the cheek.

'You're still my hero,' she tells him.

Cringe.

'And I'm still unbeaten,' Beau announces as he takes his mask off. 'There is no man on this entire island who can beat me.'

'Oh, please,' Tiggy says with a roll of her eyes. 'I could beat you – if I had a baseball bat.'

'Touché,' Beau replies.

'I'll give it a go,' Ethan announces.

I whip my head around to look at him so quickly it almost gives me whiplash. Did he really just say that?

'Have you ever fenced before?' Beau asks him, his eyebrow raised curiously.

'No, but how hard can it be?' Ethan replies as he picks up Chester's sword.

A wave of laughter passes through the group.

'You really don't have to play,' I tell him.

I don't know if he's doing this because he sees Beau as some kind of rival or if he just thinks it looks fun but, either way, Beau is clearly very good, and Ethan has never tried it before. It's a disaster waiting to happen.

'It's cool,' Ethan reassures me. 'I'd love to have a stab.'

'Hilarious, EPJ,' Chester tells him as he hands him his mask. 'Solid joke.'

Beau twirls his sword in Ethan's direction with a menacing flare.

'All right, Ethan,' Beau says. 'Let's see what you're made of.'

I don't know whether I can't look or I can't look away. It's a confusing mixture of both. The only thing more surprising than the fact this is happening is that Ethan actually seems to be quite good at it.

'EPJ, if you've never fenced before, how are you so good?' Chester calls out.

'It's not too different to a lightsaber,' Ethan calls back as he puts Beau through his paces.

'Lightsaber?' Chester replies. 'Like *Star Wars*?'

'Yeah, I'm a huge fan,' Ethan tells him.

'A sword is nothing like a lightsaber,' Beau replies, clearly annoyed. 'It's real, for one.'

'Well, they are real,' Ethan replies. 'At least, the ones at the conventions are. We dress up, re-enact the battles – people take it really seriously.'

'There is nothing serious about what you just said,' Seph tells him with a snort.

Ethan remains unbothered though and, I'm no expert, but it does sort of seem like he has the upper hand right now.

'*Star Wars*,' Beau says with a scoff. 'You sound like a bit of a loser, friend.'

'If that's true, friend, then why does it feel like I'm winning?' Ethan claps back.

I notice Beau's body language change all at once. For a moment it's almost like he loses focus, but then his back straightens, his shoulders stiffen, and he charges at Ethan. He almost seems to force him in a particular direction, forcing Ethan to fall backwards into a garden table. It crumples under his weight, breaking his fall but, you know, breaking itself too.

'Ethan,' I blurt, running over to help him.

He rolls onto his side, keeping one of his elbows elevated as he cradles it with his other hand. As soon as he's sitting upright he pulls off his mask and you can see the pain on his face.

'That was a bit of a dirty play, old boy,' Chester teases Beau.

Beau removes his mask. His expression is blank as he looks over at Ethan.

'Ethan, are you okay?' I ask as I crouch down next to him.

'Yeah, I'm okay,' he reassures me. 'I smacked my elbow on something. It smarts, but I can move it.'

'We should put some ice on it,' I insist. 'Come on.'

I offer Ethan my arm so that he can pull himself up. He keeps hold of it as we head towards the house.

There is an ice dispenser in the bar in the dining room so I place a bunch inside a napkin and twist it shut.

'Sit there,' I tell Ethan.

He does as he's told, taking a seat on a dining chair, while I kneel down in front of him, holding out the ice for him to gently rest his elbow on it.

'I'm okay, really,' he tells him. 'I think it's just bruised.'

'Well, a bit of ice won't hurt either way, will it?' I say with a smile.

He winces as I place the ice on his elbow, but then his face dissolves into a soft smile to let me know he's pretending. I kind of love it when he messes with me.

'As impressive as you were – and we'll get into the fact that you're a *Star Wars* nerd later – you know that you don't have to prove yourself to that lot, right?' I say as I look up at him.

Ethan shrugs.

'I could say the same to you,' he replies.

'Erm, I'm not trying to prove anything other than a point,' I remind him.

I notice Ethan's usual playfulness and cheeky smile fade away, sort of like when the sun goes behind a big cloud and everything does dark.

'Lana, why are you so determined to show everyone what a terrible person you are when, really, you're anything but?' he asks seriously.

I pause for a moment, chewing my lip as I think carefully about his question.

'Because if people think you're something, and they spend years telling you that you're something, eventually you just get to a point where you want to prove them right,' I say with a sigh.

'Hmm,' he says, his smile slowly creeping back. 'Well, a wise woman once told me that living well was the best revenge.'

I can't help but laugh.

'She sounds like a dummy,' I tell him.

I rest my chin on Ethan's lap for a moment, as I look up at him. He reaches forward and tucks a piece of hair behind my ear as he looks back. It's like there's a magnet in his shorts, pulling my face closer and closer – wait, no, I don't mean that as dodgily as it sounds. Just... I don't know. Sometimes it feels like I'm quite literally stuck to him, like I don't want to let him go.

He parts his lips slowly and I don't know if it's because he's going to say something or because he's going to lean forward and kiss me so I panic and quickly pull away from him.

'So, I think we can safely say that my fencing career is over before it's even really got started,' he jokes.

'Well, it would be annoying if you were good at everything, wouldn't it?' I reply. 'Sometimes it's better to just let things go.'

'Sometimes, yeah,' he replies. 'You're soaking my shorts, by the way.'

'What?' I reply.

He nods towards the ice that is rapidly melting through the napkin.

'Shit, sorry,' I tell him, springing to my feet.

'That's okay,' he replies with a laugh. 'At least it's not a flood.'

That's true – but I bet it would have been, if I'd given in to my instincts and kissed him.

34

'You're going to have to explain it to me again,' Ethan says. 'I don't think I'm getting it.'

We're currently standing in the back garden – the beautifully sculpted, pristine gardens that lead down to the beach. We're next to the pool, watching the scene outside the pool house. Dad, Chester's dad, Chester and Beau are currently un-packaging something.

'It's a bench,' I tell him again. 'We have a family tradition that the eldest child gets married on this bench, like it's the thing the happy couple sit on during the seated parts of the ceremony, and then they have custody of it until their eldest gets married. My grandad's grandad – maybe even a step more than that – hand-made it, right down to the intricate little carvings in the wood.'

'But... aren't you the eldest child?' he checks.

'I am indeed,' I say with a sigh. 'Apparently we're changing the rule, to the child who gets married first.'

'That's rough,' he says.

'Oh, no, honestly, I really don't care about a bench,' I assure him. 'Much less getting married on one.'

'I can't believe you've had this shipped over from England,' Chester's dad says. 'It must have cost a fortune.'

'It did,' Dad confirms. 'We had to pay extra, for special care, because it's so fragile.'

I know how it feels.

'It means the world to Seph,' Chester tells Dad, slapping him on the back.

'Anything for my little princess,' Dad says with pride.

Beau looks over at us, giving us a wave.

'Why don't I like that guy?' Ethan says.

'Jealousy?' I suggest.

'I'm about as jealous of him as you are of Seph getting that bench,' he tells me.

'Will it be safe in here?' Dad checks.

'Completely,' Chester's dad replies. 'Not only do we have multiple locks on all of the doors, but see that?' He points above the door. 'CCTV. Anyone who goes through that door is going to get picked up.'

'Good, good,' Dad replies. 'It means such a lot to us.'

I don't know what it is but I just can't stand to watch any more.

'I need to pop in, Seph is showing the girls her wedding dress, and that includes me,' I tell Ethan, not sounding at all enthusiastic.

'Have fun,' he replies. 'I'm just going to watch from a distance here, then join in when they start drinking.'

'It's for the best,' I joke. 'The two of us standing this close to anything to do with the wedding feels like an accident waiting to happen.'

I'm joking, kind of, but it's true. As platonic friends, the fireworks that come from the two of us just aren't going off. Together we generate too much heat but if we keep things cool then it's all good.

We just need to make sure we keep it that way.

35

Here comes the bride...

Well, here apparently comes the bride. I've been sitting here waiting, on the bedroom floor, for so long now that my arse is completely asleep.

I lean back, resting my weight on my hands, as I try to wiggle the feeling back.

Bea and Joan are sitting on the bed, chatting between themselves, with not a whole lot to say to little old me. Not that I mind, of course, because with Bea I generally find that the less I speak to her the better.

The heat of the day is letting up a little now, and the gentle breeze is making the curtains dance in the wind, which is like some kind of mindfulness app, ASMR shit that makes me feel calmer than I usually would in this situation.

'Are you looking forward to seeing the dress, Lana?' Bea asks, dragging me into the conversation.

I mean, I'm about as interested as you would expect. I'm not one of those girls who loves wedding dresses – I couldn't see myself tying the knot in a white dress, if I'm being honest, although if you asked anyone in my family they would say there was probably a very good, very obvious reason for that.

I am, however, a polite human, so I'm happy to play along.

'Absolutely,' I reply. 'Can't wait.'

'There's no need to be sarcastic,' she ticks me off.

Tiggy has somehow managed to get out of being here, despite being female (the only requirement for being here, it seems) by saying she was meeting a friend this evening. Of course, Tiggy being Tiggy, I'm sure she does have a friend in every country so she probably wasn't just making an excuse (although I'm sure she will deem it a happy coincidence).

'Did you manage to find yourself an appropriate dress?' she asks me.

I smile as I think about the fuck you/fuck me dress in my case.

'Yes,' I say confidently.

'Describe it,' she says, narrowing her eyes.

'You'll just have to wait and see,' I tell her. 'Find out the fun way.'

'We're ready,' Seph sings from behind the curtain. 'Three... two... one.'

The bathroom door swings open and out step Seph and Eleanor in their dresses, holding hands, and I gasp involuntarily.

The thing is that while there is absolutely nothing shocking about Seph's floor-length white wedding dress (she actually looks really nice), the thing that has taken my breath away is the fact that Eleanor's bridesmaid dress is also white.

'Oh, you both look simply divine,' Bea says.

'Beautiful, really beautiful,' Joan says, dabbing her eyes with a tissue.

'You look... like you're marrying each other,' I can't help but blurt.

'Lana!' Bea says, horrified. 'Take your mind out from the gutter, for once in your life.'

'Lana, you silly goose, everyone is wearing black or white to match the wedding aesthetic,' Seph explains. 'Everyone is wearing black, except members of the bridal party, who are wearing white.'

'But there are only two of you,' I point out – because I honestly feel like they haven't thought of this. 'So it looks like the two of you are the happy couple.'

'Don't be so childish, Lana,' Bea warns me. 'Everyone at the wedding will of course be there by invitation only. Everyone knows all too well who is marrying whom.'

'Right,' I reply. 'But, I'm just thinking, if Chester is wearing a black tux like all the other blokes, and the women are all wearing black dresses, then it's just Bea and Eleanor wearing white, and even if people don't assume they're a couple, it's still going to look like there are two brides in the wedding photo, no? Even if you know, at a glance, it won't be obvious which one is the bride.'

I say all of this from a good place but I can tell by the looks on everyone's faces that it isn't quite going down that way.

I notice Eleanor's teeth clench, her chin moving slowly from side to side – I'm obviously getting on her nerves, although that's nothing new.

'Very well,' Eleanor says. 'I wouldn't want to be accused of stealing the attention from Bea on her special day – *I* would never do that – so I shall have to find another dress.'

I think the insinuation there is that I would try to steal the attention from her.

Seph turns to face Eleanor, placing her hands on her arms, looking into her eyes – see, they look even more like they are getting married to each other now.

'El, please don't listen to her,' Seph insists. 'I want you to wear white too. It's only silly Lana banana who can't tell the difference between white and pearl white – everyone else will see that we are very clearly wearing different colours. It would mean the world to me, you're my best friend – you're like a sister to me.'

Eleanor smiles – I want to say smugly.

'Oh, of course, I would never let you down, Sephy,' Eleanor replies.

I purse my lips lightly, a physical reminder to myself not to say a word.

I do wonder if Seph knows she's been hurtful, when she tells Eleanor she is like a sister to her, when I am quite literally a sister to her, and she clearly doesn't even really want me here.

It's not that I want to wear a white dress – really, I don't – it's just that Seph doesn't want me to. And I'm not taking the piss, by pointing out that in the photos it's going to be a sea of people wearing black and then two women wearing white – even if one is wearing white and the other is wearing pearl white, because I really can't tell the bloody difference.

She would probably rather I wore a white dress than the one I've packed, that's for sure, because... shit! My black fuck you/fuck me dress was all well and good when the plan was to turn up to this wedding unapologetically myself. Now, however, that I'm trying to pass myself off as a respectable, earl-friendly lady, there's no way I can wear it.

Great, so now I need to buy *another* dress. I'm never going to get on the property ladder, am I?

36

Dinner this evening was roast chicken and vegetables – which means that, thankfully, Ethan is well fed enough not to wake me up by crunching biscuits at 3 a.m. In fact, it was only as he served up his third portion of broccoli that I begged for mercy, reminding him that I'm the one who has to share a bed with him.

We've just finished our dessert – fresh fruit and more cheeses than I can name – and our coffees, and now it's time to retire to our rooms.

I always find myself getting a little anxious, as the sun goes down, and bedtime draws closer and closer. It still feels so peculiar, to be in a bed with Ethan. That's the only word I can think to describe it because it's not that it's awful, or all that awkward, it's just that it feels... incorrect. It's almost as though my body isn't working with the same information as my brain, so while I know that Ethan is absolutely a no-go, and that really I should be focusing on getting to know Beau better, my body hasn't got the memo. I know, this is going to sound crazy, but it's like they're working separately. I'll find one of my limbs edging toward him, my hand creeping toward his as he lies next to me, my legs slinking across the bed like snakes, trying to intertwine with his. It's like they're possessed, and I have to really mind-over-matter them back over to my side of the bed.

Speaking of Beau, it's only tonight, when I'm seeing him sitting next to Eleanor, that I am noticing just how much she flirts with him.

'Everyone knows it's the best man and the principal bridesmaid who ride off into the sunset, at the end of the day,' she tells him flirtatiously. She's talking quietly, just to him, and while everyone else is distracted talking amongst themselves, my ears are fully tuned into their channel.

'Is that so?' he replies.

He sounds like he's smiling but I'm scared to even look. I'm enjoying getting to know Beau, and there's something about him that I really like. Everyone else here (apart from Ethan, of course) seems so two-dimensional, like there is nothing to them but money and image, but Beau seems like he has something going on behind his eyes.

'Oh my goodness, stop the press, someone call *Tatler*, because I think we might have a hot new couple on the horizon,' Seph sings, turning everyone's attention toward Eleanor and Beau.

'Sephy, you are awful, stop,' Eleanor says, batting her hand, clearly not wanting her to stop at all.

Beau looks a little embarrassed maybe, although he doesn't seem like the kind of guy who likes to have eyes on him in this way. I feel like he's a very private person but, then again, I know how many people visit his house each year.

'I would just D-I-E if my best chum and Chester's best chum got together,' Seph says.

'You could do a lot worse than an earl,' Chester tells Eleanor. Then he turns to Beau. 'And we all know you need a wife ASAP.'

Oh, I don't like this. I don't like this at all. I can feel my shoulders rising, my head tipping forward as I grip my bottom lip between my teeth just a little too hard.

'I can't wait to marry you,' Ethan tells me.

I almost get whiplash, turning to face him. What is he talking about? And the way he said it, sort of quietly, but definitely loud enough for everyone to hear.

'Oh, sorry, I didn't realise you were all listening,' Ethan says, feigning mild embarrassment. 'It's just all this talk of weddings... it really, really makes me and Lana want to finally make this official.'

'Are you two engaged?' Dad asks, raising an eyebrow.

'No,' I say quickly.

'No, not yet,' Ethan replies, taking my hand in his. 'But watch this space.'

'Well, it's about time,' Chester says. 'Lana is like Beau, growing dusty on the shelf – of course, Lana has EPJ blowing her cobwebs off.'

Oh, my dad doesn't like that.

I look over at Beau. He's staring at us, glancing back and forth between my eyes and Ethan's hand on top of mine.

'We are very much looking forward to tomorrow, Ethan,' Bea says.

'What's tomorrow?' I turn to him to ask.

'A surprise,' he tells me, his eyes twinkling as they widen for effect. 'I've planned something for us all to do.'

'Seph had arranged an activity for us all, but the place has closed for work on the electrics, so Ethan stepped up, he says he's got something good for us,' Chester tells me.

'Like what?' I ask Ethan.

'It's a surprise for you too,' he replies.

'Right, well, time to retire,' Bea says – I think she hates it when she feels like Ethan and I are becoming main characters.

We all exchange polite goodnights before heading to our

rooms. The second I close the door behind me and Ethan, I whip around to confront him.

'What the hell was that?' I ask him.

'What?' he replies.

'You, telling people we're getting married,' I reply, my voice squeaking with disbelief.

'Oh, that,' he replies. 'You're welcome.'

'I'm... what? Why am I welcome?'

'You want Beau, right?' he asks – of course, I don't answer. 'And Eleanor was flirting with him, and everyone was talking about them getting together, so I said that to make him jealous, and it worked – didn't you see the look on his face? So, yeah, you're welcome.'

For a moment I don't know what to say. Wow, that's really... nice of him? What even is that? He's helping me to bag Beau now?

'And the thing tomorrow...?' I say.

'Oh, it's nothing, Seph had booked some group thing – it sounded shit anyway – so when she was upset that it had been cancelled, I said I'd sort something, it's no big deal,' he replies.

Again, I'm speechless for a few seconds.

'It is a big deal,' I tell him. 'Look, this family don't think much of me. They think more of that stupid bench, that they've got locked away, protected by cameras, like it's in some kind of vault.'

He laughs.

'Really, it's nothing,' he insists. 'Now, come on, wifey, bedtime.'

He strips down to his boxers, completely comfortable in my presence, before heading to the bathroom to get ready for bed.

For a moment I just sit there, on the edge of the bed, trying to make sense of everything in my brain.

Is Ethan working with me or against me now? I really can't figure it out.

37

It occurred to me, when I woke up early this morning, that opinion of me is already quite low, so I could probably get away with a lie-in – even if it was just this once.

Ethan was starving so he went to join everyone for breakfast, which meant that I could spread out in bed, going full starfish, taking up every corner of the bed, and it was glorious. It was almost a shame that I had to get up at all. I know, I know, I'm in a beautiful country and I should be exploring, but you know that feeling where your batteries desperately feel like they need charging? I felt like that, totally flat, and with no remote control to steal the batteries from then a bit of extra sleep seemed like the best thing for it.

I'm up now though and it's strange. I feel like Kevin, in *Home Alone*, because the house is completely empty.

'Hello?' I call out as I explore the rooms downstairs.

There's no sign of anyone – well, I can hear the staff working in the kitchen, so I can rule out a zombie apocalypse. Actually, no, I can't, because I'll bet Chester's parents would make the staff keep working, apocalypse or not.

There's no one on the patio, no one around the pool – oh, I can hear voices though, coming from the beach, so I make my way down the garden and onto the sand.

And here they all are – playing cricket. Oh yay, another sport!

Chester is the centre of everything, as usual, standing in the middle of the 'pitch' waiting to bowl.

'Lana, there you are,' he calls out.

'We thought you might sleep all day,' Bea adds.

'It's a shock to the system, adjusting to the time difference,' I point out.

'We all did it,' Bea points out.

'Join us,' Dad insists, keen to move the game along.

'Yes, you're missing all the fun,' Chester adds.

Funny, because it looks like all I'm missing is playing cricket with my family – aka the opposite of fun.

'I don't even know how to play,' I reply.

'It's easy,' Ethan tells me with a smile. 'I'll help you. You pretty much just hit the ball and run.'

'There's more to it than that,' Beau replies. I don't think he likes it, when Ethan makes his hobbies seem like silly little games that anyone can play.

'Honestly, you all keep doing what you're doing,' I insist.

'She's always been a bore,' Seph says. 'If she doesn't want to join in, let her watch us all having fun.'

'Actually, while we don't have anything planned, I thought I might go for a walk,' I reply. 'I've never been here before – I'd love to see more of the sights.'

I notice Ethan open his mouth, as though he's going to say something, but Beau gets in there first.

'I'll come with you,' Beau says. 'I fancy a stroll – and I make an excellent tour guide.'

'Oh, okay, thank you,' I reply politely. 'Sounds great.'

'Don't worry, Lana, we'll look after Ethan for you,' Tiggy calls out. She's currently standing with the bat in her hand, wiggling her bum as she waits for Chester to bowl.

Tiggy looking after Ethan is absolutely something to worry about.

'So, what are you in the mood for?' Beau asks as we stroll.

'I would love to visit Bondi Beach,' I tell him.

'Bondi it is,' he replies. 'Let's go.'

I glance back at Ethan, who gives me a small wave – but then the ball flies in his direction so he turns his attention back to the game.

I'm sure he'll be fine and, to be honest, some time apart might do us good. Even if it just means nothing bad can happen…

38

Bondi Beach is really something else.

I've seen plenty of photos of it, and scenes in TV shows and movies, but being here is just so surreal.

I feel like I'm on a film set, oddly, like my entire day is a page ripped from a movie script. I mean, come on, I'm strolling along Bondi Beach with a fucking earl.

I'm carrying my shoes in my hand, so that I can feel the warm sand beneath my feet. It sounds silly but the sand here is perfect – like, if you could buy bags of beach sand, this is exactly how it would look and feel.

It's like its own little area of perfection. It's touristy, sure, but not in the same way that, like, Blackpool beach is – as though the two places are at all comparable.

Beau took me into what is essentially an Aussie chippy. It had a vibe of a UK chippy, with its wall-mounted menu and stainless-steel surfaces, but the food is a lot different.

I have fish and chips – although the fish is in breadcrumbs, not batter – and Beau is tucking into calamari and chips. We're eating them out of cardboard containers, using wooden forks, as we stroll – not very earl-y at all. I'm probably the most relaxed I've felt – apart from when I'm with Ethan, obviously.

He's currently telling me more about the manor house he owns and I'm not sure if I'm jealous or it sounds like a nightmare. I'm guessing the reality is somewhere between the two.

'So, theoretically, there are twenty-one bedrooms,' he says. 'Not that I've ever actually counted them. I have my own bedroom, of course, and I've turned one of the libraries into a private living room. It's a big old thing – about 15 metres long – but it's full of books and I've got a television in there. That's probably where I spend most of my time, when I'm home.'

'Wow, it's like you live in a hotel,' I reply.

'Quite,' he replies. 'Especially in the seasons when the house is open to the public. The place is either crawling with people or it's just me and the staff – I would go mad, if I didn't have my dogs. Of course, with the staff, it never quite feels like company, though they are friendly enough.'

'No, I totally get that,' I reply.

'That feeling, of coming home to an empty house, it's something I've never quite got used to – since Father died,' he continues. 'It's the reason why I know I need to settle down – aside from the silly pressure to procreate, to produce an heir – just to have someone to come home to, to have someone to live life with. What's the use in having twenty-one bedrooms and no one in them?'

'It's a tale as old as time, needing to find someone to knock up, so you have a boy to inherit your title,' I joke, instantly regretting my choice of words and my tone. I can't help but find all the old-fashioned nonsense kind of daft.

He laughs – possibly just politely.

'There should be an app for that, really,' I joke. 'A dating app that is exclusively for finding partners befitting the upper class.

People could put things on their profile like "lady material" and "marchioness in training".'

'Such an app does indeed exist,' he points out – and he isn't joking. 'I had a quick look once, egged on by my friends, and it really was quite intense. You had to meet certain criteria – to show wealth, as though that is a measure of anything. There are some incredibly rich people from working-class backgrounds, and I know plenty of noblemen who can barely afford to get by – there's a reason we open our big houses to the public – so it really is a rather pointless measure of a person. Money should never come into it, when it comes to finding true love.' He laughs at himself. 'I don't know if that makes me sound terribly old-fashioned or just frightfully corny, but that's the way I've always looked at it. I want someone who loves me in spite of the title, the house and the expectations – not because of them.'

I smile back at him. Is it possible that Beau could be a rare creature in a world full of beasts? The rest of them all feel the same: preoccupied with class, money and status – and they're all interlinked. Beau seems to look at the world in a different way. He knows he's rich and privileged but he doesn't seem to think it matters. I mean, really, it's all just down to luck, isn't it? He was lucky enough to be born to an earl who passed the title (and the big house) on. My fortune played out differently, and I had a normal upbringing with my mum, and it may seem like I missed out but I wouldn't change a thing. I know, it's easy to say when you're on the outside looking in, but the idea that I could have been as out of touch and (let's not beat about the bush) snooty as Seph makes me feel kind of sick.

'Ah, now, speaking of apps – did I hear someone saying you and Ethan build them for a living?' he asks.

I mean, I'm a part of the machine, sure, but I don't build apps any more than the people who clean the building or do the accounts do.

'Yes,' I say – because that sounds much better.

'Any I might have used?' he asks.

Oh, I seriously doubt that.

'Potentially,' I reply, trying to think of a way to move the conversation along. 'I'm actually working on something of my own. It's only at the planning stage right now but I think it's something really special – a must-have app for women. It might be something I work on separately from my day job though.'

Because the idiots at work don't take my ideas seriously.

'You know, I have multiple revenue streams – one of which comes from investing in small businesses and entrepreneurs. I would love to know more about your app – later, when we're not supposed to be relaxing, of course – and, well, if it sounds good it could be just the venture for me. I want to get into tech.'

'Wow, really?' I reply, trying not to sound too keen. Isn't it silly how we've been conditioned over the years to downplay our emotions, especially to men? 'Yeah, ahem, yes. Yes, I would love to talk more about it later.'

As we approach a bin, Beau takes my rubbish from me and places it inside.

'Now then, any requests, or would you like me to make some suggestions, for what we do next?' he asks. 'I know some women favour scenery over shopping, playing games over peace and quiet – I'm sure we could still participate in the cricket, if we head back now.'

He laughs, letting me know that he's joking about that last part, and I laugh too until I realise something. Shit. I do actually need to go shopping, and the reason for that is because the only thing I brought with me was the fuck you/fuck me black dress, and Beau may be more down to earth than the rest, but that dress

is not befitting someone who you might find on the arm of an earl.
No way. It is not a dress for royalty, it's a dress for royally pissing
people off. So I need to buy a bloody dress.

Let's think, let's think... how do I spin this?

'Well, I'm not usually one for shopping while I'm on holiday,' I
tell him, which is only true in that I can rarely afford to go on holiday, and when I can – as a direct consequence – I can't afford to
shop. 'However, I do need to buy a dress for the wedding.'

I notice Beau's eyebrows rise as he wonders why I don't have
one so late in the day.

'The airline lost one of my bags,' I lie. 'And of course it was the
one with my wedding attire within it.'

Yes, I'm still trying to keep my accent as neutral as possible
and, yes, whenever I try to fancy up my sentences they only seem
to make less sense. I swear, everyone else throws unnecessary
words into their sentences, and it just makes them sound sophisticated. When I do, it sounds like I'm drunkenly slurring my words.

'Oh, nightmare,' Beau replies.

'So I am going to need to go shopping, in fact,' I say – ugh,
even that sounded ridiculous. 'But thank you for a lovely walk.'

'I'll come with you,' Beau insists.

'Oh, no, don't feel like you have to trek to the city with me,' I
reply.

'Bondi Junction isn't far,' he replies. 'As I recall, they have a
Chanel, Dior – plenty of lovely little designer boutiques. You'll be
sure to find something.'

The only thing I'm going to find in a Chanel or a Dior is that I
cannot afford anything.

'Okay,' I say, my voice shooting up in pitch, so high it's like
even my own mouth is surprised to be agreeing to it.

'Marvellous,' he replies. 'Come, this way.'

Oh, God, what am I getting myself into now?

Beau wasn't exaggerating when he said that Bondi Junction was close by – we're there before I know it, before I've had a chance to think of what the hell I'm going to do.

Well, when he walked past Zara without even acknowledging that it was a shop that sold clothes, I realised I was in big trouble.

'Oh, this one,' I say, clocking a boutique that says it sells vintage items. Obviously there is the kind of vintage where it's worth a fortune but sometimes vintage just means old and used. If I'm smart, perhaps I can find a bargain. It's not going to be easy, finding something that is cheap, meets the dress code, and looks and feels good on me, but I'll give it my all.

I try to look like I'm casually browsing when what I'm actually doing is skimming the rails for the cheapest black dresses I can find. I'll try a bunch on and then I guess I'll take the cheapest one that fits – and then I'll go into overtime, faking it, making out like I love it.

'Okay, I'm going to try these on,' I tell him, holding up the four cheapest dresses I could find, smiling to try to make it seem like I'm excited about them.

'Right, well, I'll wait here,' Beau says as he lingers outside the fitting room. 'In case you want a second opinion.'

I step behind the curtain – the only thing separating me from Beau as I get changed – and I do my best to keep steady on my feet, because it would be so like me to fall over, into the curtain, and rip it from its hooks as I tumble out of the small fitting room and onto the shop floor, in my underwear, before – I don't know – knocking over a decorative nuclear warhead that just so happened to be nearby. Well, that's what would happen if Ethan was with me, and we dared to flirt.

Meh, one of the dresses is okay, I guess. I like that it doesn't cost a fortune more than I actually like it but it's demure and it covers all the bits that need covering, so this might be as good as it's going to get.

'I think I've found the one,' I announce, not sounding at all like I mean it. I need to up the enthusiasm. 'It's great! Would you like to see?'

'It would be an honour,' Beau replies.

I step out in the long, plain black dress. It has a very high neckline that doesn't quite play well with my 'tacky' cup size but, hey, it covers them.

'Well, you do look beautiful,' Beau tells me. 'But something tells me that's not the dress for you.'

'No?' I reply.

That's funny, because my bank balance tells me it is, and if I tried to buy anything more expensive, my bank wouldn't think twice about telling the cashier that it wasn't the dress for me – because my card would be declined.

'That's not the reaction to a dress you love,' he tells me. 'If I may...'

Beau reveals a dress that he has been hiding behind his back. He holds it up in front of him and, I swear, my breath catches in my throat.

'That's the reaction to a dress you love,' he points out with a grin. 'I asked the lady who works here if she had anything special. She tells me it's vintage Chanel, from the nineties. She tells me it's from Coco Chanel's neutral palette collection, that she believed black was empowering and that this dress represents freedom and independence.'

It also probably represents a month's wages for me.

'Oh, it's very nice but I have this one, and I really do think it's the one for me,' I tell him – sounding even less convincing now.

'Indulge me,' he insists, handing it over. 'The lady who recommended it said it looked like it would be your size, so it should fit.'

The next thing I was going to say was that it might not be my size.

'Okay, yeah, I'll give it a go,' I say – well, what else can I say? I'll just humour him, I'll try it on, and then I'll tell him I like the cheap one so much more, and I really will say it in a convincing way this time.

It's a black midi dress with layers of material. It has a mesh overlay, which makes it look like my trashy dress's classy sister. One strap is thicker than the other, giving it a stylish asymmetric neckline that flatters my chest the second I get it on and, wow, okay this dress is... wow. The back is a mesh panel – hilariously, if I were to wear my dress backwards, it would give a similar effect. It's just... wow, it's perfect. I can't stop looking at it, twirling around on the spot, looking myself up and down, twirling again.

'What do you think?' Beau calls out.

'Erm, not for me,' I reply.

Beau laughs.

'Can I come in?' he asks.

In? Into the fitting room?

'In here?' I check.

'Yes,' he says simply.

'Erm, okay,' I reply.

'Oh my goodness,' he blurts as he claps eyes on me. He closes the curtain behind him. 'Lana, you look phenomenal.'

'Do you think so?' I ask in a breathy voice, like I can't quite believe he's paying little old me such a compliment.

'I think you do in fact love this one,' he tells me.

'What makes you so sure?' I ask, trying to play it cool.

'Lana, I saw your feet, under the curtain, and I could just tell,' he points out. 'I know why you're hesitant.'

Does he?

'You're worried about upstaging the bride,' he continues.

Ah, he doesn't.

'I just think the other is more... wedding-appropriate,' I say simply.

'And I just think that you love this one,' he tells me. 'So I'm buying you it – consider it a gift.'

'Oh, no, you don't have to do that,' I insist.

'It was paid for before you tried it on,' he says with a smile. 'I had a feeling.'

Before I can even really think about what I'm doing, I throw myself into Beau's arms and squeeze him tightly.

'See, you do really truly love it,' he points out.

I really truly would never afford it and now, thanks to Beau, I'm actually going to feel like I fit in.

I release him and step back.

'I'd better take this off, before I destroy it by squeezing you too tightly,' I joke. 'But thank you so much.'

'It's truly nothing,' he says. 'I'll give you some privacy.'

Right, I need to get this dress off, ASAP, because there is a strong chance that I could destroy it – this is me. I let it carefully fall to my feet just as Beau steps back inside.

'Oh, goodness, I'm so sorry,' he says as he averts his gaze. 'I didn't think you would take it off quite so quickly.'

I don't know who is more embarrassed, me or him, but I'm sure that me pretending that I'm not bothered will go a long way to smoothing out the awkwardness.

'Oh, that's okay,' I reassure him. 'No apologies needed – my bikini covers less.'

I say this like I'm joking but that might actually be true.

'I just popped back to see if you needed shoes,' he says, trying to keep his eyes level with mine.

'Ah, right, no, my shoes were in my bag that made it, so we're all good,' I tell him.

'Good,' he says. 'That's good. Very good. Yes.'

He's babbling. Is he just uncomfortable or... is he into me? If he was just a regular bloke and he bought me a vintage Chanel dress then I would think he was madly in love with me but he isn't, he's a loaded earl, so maybe this is truly nothing to him. Maybe, when he said that, he meant it quite literally.

I need to test the waters, to see if I'm imagining things, just – you know – to know.

'I really can't thank you enough,' I say as I hug him again.

As Beau wraps his arms around me he holds me close, pressing my body against his own, his hands daring to explore my back as they move down ever so slowly.

'Did she need shoes?' the shop assistant calls out.

Beau clears his throat as he releases me, stepping back, clearly flustered.

'No, thank you,' he calls back. Then he turns his attention back to me. 'I'll give you some privacy – I promise not to barge in again.'

He says this with a bit of a laugh to make me feel at ease.

'Don't worry about it,' I reply with a smile.

Alone again, I look at myself in the mirror, looking myself in the eye – almost like I'm conferring with my reflection. Was something happening then? Was something about to happen?

I know, it sounds crazy but... I think the earl might actually like me!

39

'Ethan, you're a true hero, aren't you?' Tiggy says flirtatiously as we step off the minibus.

I glance at him and smile. I think he's a hero too. Well, when Seph's planned activity – a group dance class – was cancelled due to the venue needing to close, Seph got herself in a bit of a flap about having nothing for us all to do together. Ethan stepped up and said that he would find something else for everyone to do, that he had something in mind, and that he would make it happen. As far as I'm concerned, he's a hero because he's sorting us something to do other than a dance class. I cannot think of anything more cringe than taking a group dance class with my family.

'Well, what are we doing instead?' Bea asks as we all gather next to the bus.

'We're walking across Sydney Harbour Bridge,' Ethan replies.

'We're just walking across the bridge?' Dad replies, unimpressed.

He really is a man of few words, and the words he does say are always to the point.

'Yes,' Ethan says with a grin that gives me a nervous feeling in the pit of my stomach.

'That's not really an activity, is it, Ethan,' Bea points out.

'That's so dull,' Seph practically sulks. 'I wanted to get people dancing, get their hearts pumping...'

'Oh, this will get everyone's heart pumping, don't worry,' Ethan reassures her. 'When I said we're walking across the bridge, I should have been more clear. We're not walking on the path. We're climbing it and we're walking across the metalwork. Up there.'

He points up at the bridge which, truly, has never seemed higher. Is he serious right now? He's Ethan. Of course he is.

'Wow, really?' Chester replies. 'Is that... safe?'

'Yeah, they harness you up, it's perfectly safe,' he replies. 'And it's just... a really high walk – kids can do it. It promises the best views in Sydney.'

'It sounds more like it promises the best way to die in Sydney,' I can't resist replying.

'Ah, come on, it will be fun,' Ethan insists. 'I'm doing it. You'll come with me, won't you, Lana?'

I have to admit, it does seem kind of cool – just terrifying. It's like that thing they used to say at school though: if Ethan jumped off a cliff, would I do it too?

'Well, I'm going to have to politely decline,' Beau chimes in. 'I couldn't do it even if I wanted to. My insurance doesn't cover me for these sorts of risks, not without an heir.'

'That's the weirdest thing I've ever heard,' Ethan replies. 'Anyone else?'

'If I'm being completely honest, I did get rather tipsy at lunch,' Tiggy replies. 'I'm talking to two of you right now so perhaps it's not the best idea for me. I'll keep Beau company, make sure no harm comes to him.'

He's statistically more likely to come to harm with a tipsy Tiggy looking after him but the risk is still probably less than, you know, walking across the top of Sydney Harbour Bridge!

'I can't believe what a bunch of chickens you all are,' Ethan says, and that really is all it takes to convince Chester.

'I'm no coward,' Chester tells him. 'And I'm not marrying a coward. Count me and Seph in.'

'I'm intrigued,' Dad adds. 'I'm in too.'

'Yes, well, so long as it is safe,' Bea adds. 'I never would have thought of this but... yes, intrigued is the word.'

Wow, I think they actually really want to do it.

'Come on, Lana,' Ethan prompts me. 'I might have a surprise up there waiting for you...'

'Okay, fine, I'll do it,' I give in.

'Awesome,' Ethan says. 'Let's do it.'

It all happens so fast – we're strapped into our harnesses and sent on our way.

The word climb threw me, because I was imagining actually climbing, but really it's just walking up a bunch of small steps, until we're at the top.

The view reveals itself, getting more and more spectacular the higher you go, and by the time we're finally at the top my fear has evaporated. Everyone seems so relaxed and happy, all taking in the truly unique perspective together.

'Okay, you were right, this is a lovely surprise,' I tell Ethan. 'I feel on top of the world.'

'You haven't had your surprise yet,' he replies. 'And I feel on top of the world too – not just up here, but down there too, and it's you, Lana. You make me feel like I'm on top of the world every day. You make me a better man and I like to think I make you a better woman – who knew that was possible? I've always thought you were perfect.'

Ethan slowly gets down on one knee and my heart stops. I hold my breath. I feel like I'm going to drop into the water below. What on earth is he doing? What's he playing at?

'Lana, will you marry me?' he asks.

I can't reply – of course I can't, because I have no idea what he's doing. We didn't talk about this, this wasn't part of the plan.

'Oh, nice play, chap,' Chester calls out. 'Ask her while she's stranded up here, so she can't say no.'

I assume he's joking.

'Something like that,' Ethan says with a grin. 'So, Lana, what do you say?'

'How about I give you a reply when we're back on the ground,' I suggest. 'That way you'll know I mean what I say.'

'Fair enough,' Ethan replies. 'But don't keep me waiting.'

'No, don't keep him waiting,' Bea replies. 'Eligible suitors aren't common.'

Does she mean generally or for me?

'You didn't ask my permission,' Dad reminds him, totally straight-faced. But his stern look dissolves into a rare smile. 'But you have it.'

Oh my God, they are – bizarrely – all on board with this. Even Seph is smiling.

As we continue our walk, Ethan keeps giving me these little glances. His eyes are somehow saying everything and nothing. Honestly – what is he playing at? Obviously he isn't serious, he isn't actually asking me to marry him, and this wasn't part of the plan, so what's the play? Is he working for me or against me? With Ethan, from one minute to the next, I feel like I can never quite tell.

40

As we walk into the dining room, to have another family dinner, Beau catches my arm, gently pulling me to one side.

'Lana, are you and Ethan getting married?' he asks. His expression is serious, his eyes full of concern. There might even be a little hint of jealousy in there – or maybe I'm reaching.

His question catches me off guard. I don't know what to say. Actually, yes, I do.

'No, no,' I insist with a bat of my hand. 'Ethan is just... he's trying really hard, to get back together, but we're long over. He's just having a difficult time accepting it.'

All I really need to do is think about Steve and then swap out his name for Ethan's.

'Is that so?' Beau replies.

'Absolutely,' I tell him. 'We've had this trip planned for some time so I thought it might be nice to bring him along, give him one last good holiday, something nice to remember me by, before we're over for good. He knows this.'

'Well, that is incredibly kind of you,' he tells me. 'Listen, we'd better catch the others up, but I was wondering if you might like to come to my room tonight, to spend a little more time together, just the two of us?'

Another question to catch me off guard.

'Oh, yeah – yes, okay, sure,' I reply, my accent a bit like a boomerang, going in a different direction, then coming right back.

He nods towards the dining room, as if to tell me to hurry, before the others notice we've hung back.

Okay, I'm not misreading this one, am I? Is this actually something? Does he really want me?

It's all I can think about, as I take my seat at the table, and as the conversation flows I find my mind wandering off, going to Beau's room, thinking about what I might find there.

'So, is this a celebration?' Tiggy asks. 'Are you two really getting hitched?'

'I told him I would think about it,' I reply.

Beau makes eyes at me. He gives me a knowing smirk, now that he thinks he's in on our little secret.

'Never keep a man waiting too long,' Bea says. 'You're not getting any younger – the offer won't be on the table forever.'

'It will,' Ethan says with a smile. 'I'll wait for her to see that we're meant to be – as long as it takes.'

'That's rather sweet,' Tiggy says. 'If you're into that sort of thing. I would be looking for a parachute, if someone said that to me – I don't know why I'm in a jet in this scenario.'

I do. Because she's Tiggy.

'Well, Lana has a great idea for an app for that,' Ethan tells her.

'Ah, yes, I've heard about this app,' Beau chimes in.

'Oh, go on?' Tiggy says. 'I love an app.'

'Basically, if you're in a situation you need to get out of, you can get a fake call or a fake text, with a fake emergency, saying you need to leave ASAP,' Ethan tells her.

'Er, what?' Seph says.

'That's hilarious,' Chester adds. 'Surely no serious human would need that.'

I can see from most of the expressions on the table that they think my idea is completely dumb.

'It's supposed to be for safety,' I say, defending it. 'If you're on a date and you're worried, or you just want to leave and you don't think the guy will take it well.'

'Well, if you will only date psychopaths,' Bea adds.

'None taken,' Ethan jokes.

Bea just ignores him.

'Is this the business we talked about me potentially investing in?' Beau can't help but ask.

'Run a mile, chap,' Chester warns him. 'She's going to bleed you dry with that one.'

'Yes,' I reply, ignoring Chester. 'It's a safety thing.'

'That does sound a little silly,' Beau says as tactfully as he can. 'I can't imagine much of a market for it.'

'It's not silly, it's all part of something bigger, to keep women safe,' I insist. 'That's not the whole idea – there would be a button that will message your friend, giving them your real-time location, in case something happens, and a panic button in case something really bad happens. Maybe even something that links to a rape alarm, in your bag, so that if you're in trouble you can just hit something on your phone – it's not always easy to rummage around in your bag. The phone – or even a smartwatch – is more subtle.'

'Where on earth do you spend your time, Lana?' Bea asks me, genuinely horrified. 'Because it sounds like you're trying to make a safe way to fraternise with murderers and sex offenders.'

'The world is full of murderers and sex offenders,' I remind her. 'And they don't always look like they belong on *Crimewatch*, most of the time they look like you and me. I almost had my drink spiked recently and, honestly, I still think about it, even though I got off lightly...'

'Can we not talk about sex offenders over dinner,' Dad insists.

Yes, because that's the takeaway from that sentence.

'Sorry,' I say flatly.

'Well, I think it's a great idea,' Ethan says firmly.

'To be fair, EPJ, you want to marry her, so you would,' Chester teases him.

The dinner conversation moves on from sex offenders, unsurprisingly, but all I can think about is the reaction from everyone. What planet do they live on, where they think that women don't need to keep themselves safe? And Beau especially – I'm surprised at him. One minute he's all about helping me follow my dreams but then he's telling me my dreams are silly?

When dinner is over, I can't wait to leave the table.

'Lana, I was thinking, we could watch a movie,' Ethan suggests. 'Go to the kitchen, grab us some snacks, and I'll go upstairs and get something ready.'

He's too excited to wait for a response. He dashes off upstairs, just as Beau walks off in the other direction.

For a second, I wonder which one to follow. I've been trying to get Beau to like me and he seems like he might, so you would think I would want to go to his room, but then I think about how dismissive he was of my app, and how small he made me feel. Ethan, on the other hand, is like my cheerleader, and we might even be together now, if we weren't such a car crash when we were together.

I take a deep breath as I make my decision – the only real choice – and head up to the room that I'm sharing with Ethan. He gets me, and he thinks I'm great as I am, and that's the kind of person I should be spending time with.

Yes, Beau is an earl but, really, I'm not sure what else he has to offer apart from empty charm.

Ethan is the one for me. Tonight, I mean. Although, now that I think about it, he really does seem perfect for me. Apart from the car crash thing, of course. It's a shame that might always get in our way.

41

Ethan seems different tonight.

He was his usual self at dinner, and then when we came up to our room and put the movie on, but around two-thirds of the way through *Step Brothers* his laughter seemed to die down, and now that it's finishing he seems positively frozen in time.

'So, are we going to talk about you proposing?' I ask with a laugh, now that the movie is over.

He flashes me a little smile.

'Tell me that wouldn't have been romantic, if it were real,' he replies.

'Oh, no, super romantic,' I agree. 'Plus you have the tactical advantage of threatening to undo a girl's safety harness if she says no.'

He laughs at my joke but then it's like someone hits the mute button again.

'So, did you do that to help or hurt?' I ask curiously. 'Although I guess your help does always seem to hurt.'

I give him a playful nudge with my elbow, to let him know that I'm kidding.

'I don't know,' he replies.

'Like, I didn't know if you were doing it to make Beau jealous, or to keep him away from me,' I say, making my point even clearer.

'Yeah, I don't know,' he replies. 'I was trying to be trouble, as ordered, but...'

'Don't worry about it,' I tell him. 'It was funny. Exactly what I ordered.'

Ethan dangles off the bed, the muscles in his back rippling as he reaches for his backpack. He grabs a packet of Tim Tams, takes one out, and then takes a huge bite – there is more in his mouth than there is left in his hand.

'Something weird is happening,' he says with his mouthful. He pauses to swallow. 'You know me. I love the chaos, I love the games... it's just I keep getting this feeling, like I don't want to mess around any more.'

What is he trying to say? Does he want to leave?

'Okay...' I say, hoping he'll say more.

'I know, I know, we said we would keep away from each other,' he continues. 'But it was never really about the holiday, I just wanted to spend time with you. And I know, you think we're a bin fire – I'll shut up.'

'Hey, I don't think that we're a bin fire,' I insist. 'Just that we cause them.'

He laughs.

'Maybe you don't get the heat without the fire,' he says simply. 'Maybe sometimes it's worth risking getting hurt. Anyway, I need to brush my teeth again.'

He hops to his feet and heads for the bathroom.

When Ethan and I first got together it was a sex thing... except it wasn't just that, was it? I liked him. I really liked him. It was just too much, too powerful, too chaotic, too scary. Too much like something real. Too much like something I would be terrified to lose.

He went home and I didn't hear from him, but I did tell him not to contact me again. I know I think that we're getting clear signs from the universe, that we shouldn't be together, but what if him turning up right when I need him is the sign?

Did Tiggy have it right, when she said I was only going after Beau because I wanted to get over Ethan, or because I wanted to make Ethan jealous? Well, yeah, but it was more than that, right? Beau's good-looking, he's a fucking earl, for fuck's sake.

He's no Ethan though, is he?

Shit.

42

The house seems so quiet as I walk down the stairs. I suppose it is still early – Ethan is still fast asleep.

I, however, could not sleep last night. Ethan's words were going round and round in my head as I tried to figure out exactly what he meant. Does he want something to happen between us? Something real, that is. That was all I wanted, before... everything! But has too much time passed by? If it's a choice between wildfire and a well-maintained log burner in a stately home, I would be crazy to choose the former, right? Right?

The main problem with me and Ethan is that we're too similar. We don't balance each other out, we razz each other up. There's no voice of reason, no caution – no adult in the room when we're together. But the way I feel about him is like nothing I've ever felt before. I just don't know what that feeling is.

It's never a bad idea to caffeinate yourself – especially when you haven't slept – so I head for the room where breakfast is served, to see if anyone is knocking around.

I'm not expecting to find my dad sitting at the table, the sun shining in on him as he drinks a coffee and reads the newspaper.

Then again, one of the things I remember about him was that he seemed like he was always up late and early. I've inherited that from him, I think, but only when it comes to staying out late and then getting up for work the next day.

'Good morning,' I say brightly.

'Morning,' he replies.

Dad calls out for a member of staff and asks them to bring me a coffee with milk.

'Did you sleep well?' he asks me, his eyes back on his paper already.

'Yes, thanks,' I lie.

As he folds up his paper and places it to one side, I wonder if he has some kind of fatherly instinct that can detect that I'm really going through it right now.

'How are you doing?' he asks me, looking into my eyes.

'Fine,' I lie again.

His brow furrows.

'Have you responded to Ethan's proposal yet?' he asks.

'Not yet,' I say with a laugh.

'For what it's worth, I approve of him,' Dad says – and I wasn't expecting that.

'Really?' I practically squeak in disbelief.

'Yes, you seem to have met your match,' he replies.

Do keep in mind that I only brought Ethan here specifically because I thought my family would loathe him.

'Although I have noticed you and Beaumont spending a lot of time together,' he adds.

Beaumont. Imagine screaming that name in bed. Beau, sure, but Beaumont. Oh, Beaumont, harder, Beaumont, harder. It's giving me the ick just thinking about it. I can see why he goes by Beau.

'Now, he is a fine suitor,' Dad says.

Speaking of the ick – he makes it sound like I'm his prize bitch that he's looking for a mate for. Hmm, maybe that's exactly what it is. Absolutely hilarious.

'I'm glad you're here, alone, I was hoping to talk to you,' I say, moving the conversation on from my love life because: ew.

'What's wrong?' he asks.

'I was hoping to ask a favour,' I begin, because now might be my only shot to ask him when it's just us.

'What favour?' he replies, his eyes narrowing slightly.

'I need somewhere to live,' I explain, keeping it as easy-breezy as I can, but I suppose I did just tell him I was basically homeless.

'What's wrong with where you've been living?' he asks.

'My flatmate needed the room back,' I say simply, and we'll leave that at that, I think. I can't imagine the truth being more sympathetic.

'What have you done now?' he asks, that knowing tone in his voice. Oh, it pisses me off, that his instinct is to think the worst of me.

Okay, yes, in theory I have pushed Steve into kicking me out, but I was only there in the first place because he wanted to be together – would my dad rather I prostituted myself for a room? Ha, probably, he probably thinks it's a more useful profession than a secretary.

'Nothing,' I insist. 'He just needed the room back. It's about time I got my own place though, so, I was just thinking if you could help me with the deposit? I can pay you back, when I can...'

'Lana, you know the rules,' he says firmly. 'We said we would never help you kids out with handouts, that you needed to make your own way in the world.'

Jesus wept, Beau's dad gave him a title and an estate – my dad won't even give me a few hundred quid for a deposit.

'I know, but—'

'Is she asking for money?' Bea says as she joins us.

Great, my wicked stepmother is here. This is going to go in my favour, I'm sure.

'You needn't waste your breath, Lana, we have nothing to spare at the moment,' she says firmly. 'This wedding is costing us a fortune.'

So Seph gets her entire lavish wedding paid for, but I can't even get help with my rent.

'Forget I asked,' I say, pushing my chair back out, and leaving the room before either of them can say anything – not that either of them seems to try.

Well, that didn't solve that problem. What next? I suppose I should go see Beau, to apologise for standing him up last night, and to explain why.

The end room on the ground floor, right? The more money people have, the earlier they seem to like to rise. I wouldn't be surprised if he was up already.

His door is open, great, because that means I can get this over with. I'm not exactly sure what I'm going to say, I'm hoping the words will just come out exactly as I need them to. That said, that strategy didn't work with my dad.

'...and what are you doing with Lana anyway?' I hear Eleanor's voice coming from his room as I approach it.

I keep hidden, behind the wall, standing just close enough to listen in without getting caught.

'Lana is fun,' Beau tells her with a bemused laugh.

I shouldn't be listening in, should I? This is a private conversation. A private conversation about me though, so...

'Fun?' Eleanor replies in disbelief. 'Roller coasters are fun.'

She says that like a Martian – definitely like someone who has never been on one in her life.

'Lana is a car crash,' she continues. 'A nightmare. A tornado. A total mess. She is a lot of things, but what she isn't is the kind of girl that a man of your standing settles down with. She's no lady. I don't care what your PR team says about you seeing a "normal" girl, to seem more "cool" and "accessible" – it's madness.'

I feel my eyebrows shoot up.

'Lana is anything but normal,' Beau says in my defence. I smile to myself. Fuck you, Eleanor, thinking you can put him off me – he's not listening. Ha. 'She may seem normal, but she's a Pemberton girl. She has that girl-next-door appeal, but she's from good stock.'

Good stock? Ew, ew, ew. What is wrong with these people? He's talking about me like I'm cattle. Really good cattle, I guess, but cattle nonetheless. Do all of the men in this world think women are just complicated animals or something? It's really starting to seem that way. I hate it. I really, really hate it.

'I'm just saying, you can do better,' Eleanor insists. 'What sort of heir will you get, from a girl like that, if she will even give you one at all. Girls like Lana are just selfish party girls, who are only out for themselves. It will be your money she wants, not you – you know that, right?'

'Eleanor, will you stop getting your knickers in a twist,' Beau tells her through a laugh. 'Do you really begrudge me having a little fun at a wedding? You know that's my favourite sort of fun. What are you, jealous, hey?'

His tone is something different, something I haven't heard from him yet. I hate it. Wow, he really is just like the rest of them. I can't believe that I thought he might be different.

I don't need to hear anything else so I slink off back to my room.

Genuinely, I would rather be 'normal' than be anything like any of this lot. And I would rather be with someone 'normal' too.

43

The party that we're having is absolutely not the party Seph planned – and, would you believe it, it was good old Ethan who saved the day.

Seph wanted us all to get together, to have a party on the beach, and although she arranged food and entertainment, the whole thing just fell flat.

For starters – well, there were no starters, no food at all, because the caterers didn't show up. The entertainers – an acoustic band – did show up, but their singer had lost her voice, so she wasn't there.

Seph was trying to keep calm but you could see it all going on behind her eyes. She looked like she might be about to burst when Ethan swept in, telling her he had thrown plenty of last-minute parties, and that he was sure he could make the best of it.

He was right. He went to a local Mexican restaurant and not only got them to agree to cater, but to bring it to the beach too. And as for the singer-less band, well, the spin he put on that was: live karaoke. Ethan was, of course, the first person to take the mic, performing an acoustic cover of 'Toxic' by Britney Spears that was as impressive as it was hilarious. Astoundingly, it was my dad – yes, my dad – who took to the makeshift stage next. I never thought I would see the day I would see him standing there, a mic in one hand, a taco in the other, while he covered an Elvis song. Honestly, I've never seen Dad like this – I've never seen any of this lot having fun like this. It's like Ethan brings out the best in them and, now, it's hard to believe I ever thought there was a chance they might not like him. They love him. And as strange as it sounds, I feel like they like me more for being with him.

The party has a more chilled-out vibe now. I'm sitting on the sand, drinking margaritas with Ethan, Chester and Seph. I've never really hung out with them – not in a chilled-out way – so this all feels so surreal.

I am, of course, avoiding Beau like the plague, now that I know how he really feels. He tried to talk to me earlier and I was cold with him so now he's giving me a wide berth. I don't know if he knows why, or if he's guessed, or what, but he's taking the hint. I'm avoiding Eleanor too, not for any new or specific reason, just because I really, really don't like her.

'So, what did you do for your stag do?' Ethan asks Chester, genuinely curious.

'Oh, I didn't have one,' Chester replies with a shrug.

'What?' Ethan replies. 'Are you serious? What about you, Seph, did you not have a hen party?'

'No,' she says, sounding almost self-conscious now. 'That's not really our sort of thing.'

'It's any sort of thing you want it to be,' Ethan tells them. 'It's just a party – one last party, to send you off into married life.'

'It does sound quite fun, when you put it like that,' Seph says, as though she'd never really thought about it like that.

Ethan looks at me and smiles. Oh, I can read him like a book. I give him a nod.

'How about we throw you stag and hen parties?' Ethan asks them. 'I'll take care of the boys, Lana can sort something for the girls – right, Lana?'

'I never say no to a night out,' I reply.

Seph lights up at the idea – yes, the same Seph who has always kept me at arm's length. She looks at me with a smile, like she might actually want to spend time with me.

'That does sound fun,' she says.

'Yes, I'm on board, EPJ,' Chester adds.

'Then let's do it,' I say.

Ethan looks at me and smiles. I love that he's doing this for them, like he doesn't want them to miss out on something.

Of course, this does mean that I have to now organise something for the girls, for tonight, but even I'm looking forward to it now.

The only downside is that, well, as silly as it sounds, I'm actually disappointed that I'm not going to get to spend the evening with Ethan. Oh, boy, I really am disappointed, I wish we were all going out together. Then again, me and Ethan on a night out, that's a recipe for disaster.

I suppose it's not only my family who are loving having Ethan around, I am too.

Of all the ways I expected this week to turn out, today really has been the most surprising one yet.

44

_____

Thankfully, between me and Tiggy, we managed to find an upmarket nightclub with a free booth for Seph's impromptu hen party – or 'bridal shower' as she is calling it.

Thankfully Seph approves – well, with crushed-velvet seats and a rope separating us from everyone else here, I'm sure she feels right at home.

Seph lounges back in her seat next to me, eventually resting her head on my shoulder. She's clutching a piña colada like it's the last liquid on earth – her, I don't know, sixth, I think.

'I can't believe you've dragged me to a club on the night before my wedding,' she says. 'This is so, so not me any more.'

'Are you not having a good time?' Tiggy asks her as she sips her champagne – it takes a lot more than six drinks to get Tiggy off balance.

'I am... loving it,' Seph says, building suspense into her sentence. 'Aren't you, Eleanor?'

'Of course,' Eleanor replies, although I suspect she's annoyed because Seph and I are getting along.

'I used to be fun,' Seph says, slurring her words. 'In fact, do you want to see my party trick?'

'Always,' Tiggy replies.

I don't know who is the most stunned as Seph climbs up onto the round table in front of us and starts dancing.

'See, I've got moves,' she calls back.

'You really do,' I reply, stunned. 'But we don't want you hurting yourself before your wedding, so maybe come back down, yeah?'

'I thought you were the fun sister,' she teases as she joins us.

'Right, come the fuck on, Lana, what's the deal with you and Ethan?' Tiggy asks. 'We're all dying to know.'

'There's no deal,' I insist.

'You two clearly really like each other,' Seph points out.

'Even if you're trying to pretend you don't, for some silly reason,' Eleanor adds. You can tell she wants to get involved but that she also doesn't want to give me the satisfaction, so her words come out through gritted teeth.

'I do like him, of course I do,' I reply. 'It's just... it's a strange feeling. I don't really understand it.'

'What do you mean?' Tiggy asks.

'Well, sometimes I like him, sometimes I want to kill him,' I begin. 'Sometimes it feels good, sometimes scary, sometimes I feel physically sick, like something is wrong with me. I get this heavy feeling in my stomach.'

'Not lower?' Tiggy jokes.

'Ah, I know that that is,' Seph says seriously. 'I've had that before – I have it now, actually, I don't think there's a cure.'

Oh, God, don't tell me it's some hereditary family illness that I've been cursed with.

'Is it hard to breathe properly sometimes too?' she checks.

'Shit...' I say softly. 'Yes.'

'Don't look so worried,' she says with a laugh. 'You're not ill, you're in love.'

'Oh,' I say simply. 'No. No, no, no. It's not that.'

'I think it might be, cuz,' Tiggy says, wincing.

'They are all of the classic signs,' Seph says. 'Have you never been in love before?'

'No,' I say. 'Is that... Is that really...? Oh, God. What do I do?'

'You have to go and tell him, you silly goose,' Seph says. 'Go, now, get it over with today, don't do it at my wedding.'

No, we mustn't forget the most important thing.

'Go,' Tiggy tells me. 'You have your diagnosis; your prescription says that you need to tell him. I'll take care of these two. Go, figure it out, but just be bloody happy.'

I smile at her.

'Okay, sure, I'll go figure it out,' I reply.

I will go, back to the house, but... am I really going to tell Ethan I love him? Do I love him? I like him, a lot, but none of this changes the fact that we are incompatible, does it?

I'm going to head back to the house, mostly because I feel too flat out to party now. This should feel like a good thing, surely? If so, then why does it feel so bad? I am definitely not ready to tell Ethan I love him, if I even do, but I do need to say something to him, because it feels like limbo right now.

I guess I'll just have to hope the words come to me when I need them. And that they don't trigger a nuclear war.

45

The house still looks alive, as the taxi drops me outside. It's late – the early a.m. – and the night before the wedding, so I'm surprised to see that all of the lights are still on.

The gravel path crunches beneath my feet, as I head for the front door, but I can see Bea on her phone in the hallway, so I decide to slink around the back instead, and head in through the back door.

Of course, once I'm around there, I realise that the large sliding doors are wide open, and the grown-ups are hanging out in there, drinking and chatting. Now there's a group of people I don't want to hang around with right now.

I suppose a bit of air might do me good. I could walk through the garden, down to the beach, maybe dip my feet in the sea and try to wash away my stress.

As I walk through the multilevel, perfectly manicured garden, something catches my eye by the pool – or rather, someone catches my eye. It's Ethan.

'Hello, you,' I say cheerily as I approach him.

He's lying on a sunlounger – not that there's any sun – with his hands behind his head.

'What are you doing here?' I ask.

'Just vibing,' he says with a smile.

He looks and sounds about as drunk as I am – enough to feel it, but still sober enough to feel everything else.

'Are the others still out partying?' I ask.

'No, they've both gone to bed,' he tells me. 'Posh boys can't handle their drink.'

I laugh as I linger next to him.

'Thanks for taking them out,' I tell him. 'And for encouraging me to take Seph out. I can confirm: posh girls can handle their drink.'

'I know – I've seen you drink,' he says with a smile.

'Oi, I'm not a posh girl,' I insist.

He looks me up and down and smiles.

'No, you're nothing like your family,' he says. 'And I mean that in the best possible way of course.'

'Don't worry, it's music to my ears,' I reply.

'Although an earl does seem like the kind of bloke you should end up with,' he adds, revealing what's really on his mind.

'Is that really what you want for me?' I ask.

'I just want you to be happy,' he replies.

I chew my lip for a second or two.

'What if I could be happy with you?' I say. 'What about that?'

He smiles ever so subtly as he stands up, walking over to me.

'I thought you said we were cursed,' he reminds me.

I don't say a word. I just beckon him closer with my finger – alcohol is great for stuff like this.

He stops in front of me, his lips just inches from mine, so close I can almost remember what they feel like.

'I don't care about curses tonight,' I tell him, my voice breathy and hopefully inviting.

A cough drags us out of our moment. It sounds like it came from one of the balconies, maybe.

'Quick, let's go in here,' Ethan suggests, opening the door to the pool house.

He takes me by the hand and pulls me inside with him, closing the door behind us.

Finally safe inside, hearing nothing but the sound of my heart beating in my ears, I look around.

The room is all decked out for the wedding ceremony tomorrow. Ceremony here, and then the reception in a marquee in the garden. Rich people, I swear, they have the money to get anywhere and then do it at home – although I guess they do have very nice homes.

Rows of chairs are lined up neatly, ready for the ceremony. Everything is covered with ribbons (black or white, of course) – I've just realised we're technically walking down the aisle.

'I thought this place was locked,' I say.

'It was,' he replies. 'I got the key, to get a cushion out of the storeroom, for one of the sunloungers. I was thinking I might sleep outside tonight.'

'Don't you want to sleep with me?' I ask him.

For a second or two nothing happens and then, all at once, it's like the starter pistol has been fired. Our bodies snap together. We kiss for a few seconds before I leap into his arms, wrapping my legs around his waist. Ethan drops to the floor – in what I think was supposed to be a controlled way – but we knock over a bunch of chairs in the process.

'I'll stand those back up, I swear,' he mumbles, his words almost inaudible as I pepper his lips with kisses.

Now that we've started, it's impossible to stop. It's for the best though, that we're reuniting out here.

Down in the garden, in the dark pool house, with the ocean roaring nearby, it's sort of like a horror movie: no one can hear you scream.

46

'I don't ever want to move again,' I say with a sigh.

'And you wouldn't have to except – a few small things – one being that we don't live in Australia, and we have to go home, the other being that there's going to be a wedding ceremony here in a few hours, and the two of us lying naked on the floor might kill the mood,' Ethan replies.

'Perhaps,' I say. 'I suppose we could take this party inside.'

'Okay but I hate to break it to you, we do need to move all the chairs back into place first,' he says.

'I guess I can handle that,' I say with a smile.

It's dark but I don't have to search for long to locate my bra. I quickly put it on, throwing my dress over the top, and I've located one of my shoes when I realise Ethan isn't moving.

'Shit,' he says softly.

'What?' I reply.

Oh, God, don't tell me he's regretting it already. I thought we'd turned a corner, that this was going to be the start of something.

'The bench,' he says. 'Your family bench... we've broken it.'

Shiiiit. Suddenly I wish it really was just Ethan having cold feet, that I could deal with.

'What? How?' I ask.

'I don't know if we landed on it, or we knocked it with a chair but... look,' he says.

Sure enough, the bench is in three pieces.

'Can you fix it?' I ask him, panic consuming me.

Ethan gets down on his knees and tries to click the bench back together. I grab my phone from my bag and shine my torch on it. Oh, thank God, I think he's done it.

Ethan turns around and cautiously tries to put his weight on the bench, but the second he gets near it, it falls apart again.

'Shit,' I blurt.

'Look, it's okay, we—'

'It's not okay though, is it?' I snap back. 'I knew this would happen, I knew we should stay away from each other, that we shouldn't do this, that—'

'Do not say we're cursed, or that it's the universe, or whatever,' he tells me. 'It's not that.'

'What's the alternative?' I reply. 'That we're both fuck-ups? That we're both losers, with no direction in life, nothing to show for our time on earth, just making a mess everywhere we go? Because, newsflash, that's what we are. I should never have brought you here, look what we've done. I think you need to go, you need to leave, before we fuck anything else up.'

'Lana—'

'Ethan, I'm serious, we're nothing but trouble,' I tell him.

'Okay, fine, I'll go,' he replies. 'But, just so you know, every-thing you just said about me, it's not true.'

'You think you're better than me?' I reply.

'No, I don't,' he says seriously. 'And I would never say anything like that about you, but perhaps if you did care a little more about your job you would know that I don't work there. Redflags is my app, your company built it. They work for me. I've just put in an offer on a new flat – I don't feel like I'm doing all that bad in life. I'm sad to hear you don't feel the same.'

I know that I should apologise for what I just said but I'm not wrong about one thing: we are trouble together.

'I'm going to bed,' I tell him. 'Just... balance that thing together, lock the door and put the key back where you found it.'

'We won't get away with that, will we?' he says.

'No,' I reply. 'They'll realise it's broken, and maybe I'll come clean, or maybe I'll be too scared and they'll end up checking the CCTV, and they'll see that it was us and... and I'll deal with it alone.'

'Lana—'

'Just... leave it,' I tell him. 'We were never supposed to do this.'

I grab my bag and hurry out of the pool house, slinking back around the house to go in through the front door now that Bea isn't lingering there any more. It seems like most people have gone to bed now, but this is definitely the best way to get in, without bumping into anyone.

Oh, I have really fucked up this time.

47

Have you ever woken up from a bad dream and felt that relief when you realised that it was actually just a dream, and everything is fine? Yeah, well, I just did that in reverse. One minute I was in bed with Ethan, cuddled up close, our hands on each other's bodies, one thing leading to another, and then I woke up to realise that it was just a good dream, and the real nightmare is what I've woken up to.

I feel the other side of the bed, just to check, but I can already tell that he's not next to me before I even open my eyes.

Eventually I do give in, to face the day, and slowly open my eyes so that they can adjust to the light. Nope, he isn't here, and it doesn't look like he's been here either.

Well, I guess he listened to what I said, he went away and stayed away... of course, now that he's done it, I'm really not sure it's what I actually wanted at all.

I know, I should feel relieved, because the two of us really are nothing but trouble when we're together, and today is an important day, it needs to go well. This is what I wanted, and what I told him to do – I have no right to feel regret. Not when the only thing I should be feeling is guilt about the bench.

I sit up in bed and rub my tired eyes before climbing out and stretching. How is it always the nights when you feel like you've had the least sleep that you have the most vivid dreams? That doesn't seem fair. Nothing seems fair, but I need to pull myself together, put my big-girl dress on, and get on with things.

I glance at the dress Beau bought me. It really is beautiful. I wonder, if things hadn't gone so chaotically last night, if I would be looking forward to wearing it. Right now I don't feel like I deserve it. Everything feels like a mess and every instinct I have is telling me to make a run for it, but I know that I can't. That would only make things worse – which is why I'm surprised that Ethan did as I asked, and bailed on me, but like I said, he did as I asked. What more did I want?

If there is one thing I don't have time for right now it's dwelling, obsessing, and overthinking, so I need to snap out of it and crack on. I'm supposed to be joining the girls, so we can all get ready in one room which, again, sounds like it would have been really nice if everything hadn't gone to shit last night.

So I grab my things and I take them to Seph's room. It's her who greets me, when I arrive. She places a glass of champagne in my hand and a kiss on my cheek.

'Oh, Lana, I had such a fabulous time last night, thank you,' she tells me.

'Ah, it was nothing,' I say with a smile. 'You deserved it.'

'Did everything go okay, with you and Ethan?' she asks me. 'Did you tell him?'

'I decided to wait,' I lie. 'Until after the big day. This day should be all about you.'

'Okay, but you know that I don't mind sharing elements of it with you, if it means you'll be happy,' she replies. 'We are sisters, after all. It's been so lovely, spending time with you this week. I don't know why we don't do things like this together more often – a belated New Year's resolution, perhaps?'

'That sounds good to me,' I say with a smile.

'I just love, love, love your dress,' she replies. 'I know Mummy was being silly, with all the things she said, but she will agree that you look divine.'

'Thanks,' I say simply. I don't quite feel myself now that I'm here wearing it but, hey, it really is a beautiful dress.

'Well, come in, everyone is getting glammed up – don't worry, we have protective gowns, to cover our dresses,' she explains.

I step into the bedroom and the first thing I see is Tiggy and Eleanor standing on either side of Bea, fussing over her freshly styled hair. Bea is sitting between them, with a face like thunder. She's clearly not happy with her hair but of course she isn't, it's Bea. It looks fine – in fact, it looks like it always looks, but she's the sort of person who will worry about things not being perfect. On a big day like today, I suspect she will worry about things not being perfect until the day is actually over. Only then will she stop fretting.

The room does feel thick with her nerves – and not just from me. Even though she hasn't said a word, you can tell that Seph is clearly anxious. Excited, but definitely nervous with it.

'Oh, and by the way, happy birthday!' Seph says.

Shit. As stupid as it sounds, I had completely forgotten that it was my birthday. So this is thirty, eh? What a mess.

'Oh, thank you,' I reply.

'I know today is my wedding day, and that we've kind of hijacked your birthday, but it's an honour to share this special day with you,' she says, warm and genuine, and it truly takes me aback. 'Don't worry, okay, because we do have plans for your birthday tomorrow, we *will* celebrate it, but it's a surprise, so don't let on that I said anything.'

I grab her and give her a big hug.

'I won't say a word,' I reply. 'Thanks.'

'Well, if you do say anything to anyone, make it a thank you to Ethan, because it was him who reminded us that it was your thirtieth birthday, and insisted that we do something special for you. I hadn't realised it was an important one – you don't look or act your age at all.'

Ignoring what is possibly a compliment, maybe an insult – the thing that hurts me is the mention of Ethan's name. I can't believe he's stepped in and got them all to do something to acknowledge my birthday. Actually, I can, because he's amazing, and he really cares about everyone, and I am the horrible cow who sent him away.

'You've got yourself a good one, with Ethan,' she tells me. 'I hope you do say yes to him, and I hope you never let him go. Now, come on, let's get this party started. Tiggy has had almost a whole bottle – of course, being Tiggy, it has had almost no effect on her whatsoever.'

Wow, I didn't let him go, I sent him away. And I really, really regret it.

Actually, scratch that, I haven't let go of him at all. He's all I can think about. That and what happens when Seph and Chester sit on that bloody bench.

I don't know what I'm going to do.

48

I fidget in my seat, trying to calm my nerves. I'm not the one getting married, but I'm probably the most terrified person in the room.

There is an empty seat next to me that was supposed to be for Ethan. The gap, despite being just one space, seems huge. It just goes to show what a difference one person can make because his absence is really apparent – and it's not just the physical space that stands out, I feel like he's going to be really missed, not just by me but by everyone.

'If you would all like to stand,' the wedding official says. 'The bride has arrived.'

I should hope so – she only came from upstairs.

I glance down the aisle where Chester is shifting his weight between his feet. He looks nervous – I don't think I've ever seen him look nervous before. Beau gives him a sort of pat/rub on the back, to steady him.

And there it is, the bench, still exactly as we balanced it last night, so I'm guessing no one has noticed yet. I don't know if that's good or bad. God, Chester would be even more nervous, if he knew about that, and how it's not going to take one person's weight, never mind two.

Perhaps I'm worrying over nothing – perhaps they won't even sit on it. Wedding ceremonies aren't as long as they used to be, right? It isn't a religious ceremony, and they don't seem like the type to have singing and stuff. Perhaps it's just a symbolic, ornamental bench. God, I hope so.

As the music starts, I feel someone's arm brush next to mine.

'Ethan,' I blurt in a whisper, my heart skipping a beat or two.

'We're a team,' he replies. 'If you go down, I'm going down with you. Happy birthday, by the way.'

I can't help but smile. He could have run for his life but he hasn't, he's here – and he's here for me.

The violinist picks up the pace as Seph and Dad begin their journey down the aisle.

Seph looks so beautiful, and Dad looks so proud, and I feel... good? Wow, it really does feel like things are good. But then my eyes dart back to the stupid bench and I know that if they sit on it, everything (metaphorically and literally) is going to come crashing down. I wonder if they'll think I've done it on purpose, as an act of sabotage, because I'm jealous, or because it should have been mine, or because Dad wouldn't lend me money – they could pin it on anything, not that it matters. Even as an accident, it feels unforgivable.

'Please take your seats,' the wedding official says.

It feels like my heart and my stomach swap places.

'And the bride and groom, take your seats too,' the official says, once Dad has handed Seph over to Chester.

Oh, God, I can't watch. No, God, please, do not sit on that bench. I feel sick as they lower their bodies, their bums heading for the seat in what feels like super-slow motion, and while I'm sure I would probably make things worse by calling out and telling them not to sit down, I don't think there's time to warn them anyway.

I wince as they make contact but... nothing happens. The bench holds their weight. They're sitting on it, exactly as they should be, and nothing bad is happening.

I quickly whip my head around, to look at Ethan. He just smiles at me, winks, then gestures for me to turn my attention to the ceremony.

I don't know how he's done it, but he's fucking done it. He's fixed it. I could kiss him.

And to think, I brought Ethan here thinking he could ruin the wedding. It turns out that bringing him here has saved it.

49

It's been non-stop since Seph and Chester said, 'I do.' If weddings are this exhausting for the guests, I can't even imagine how knackering they must be for the happy couple.

The ceremony went well – and without a hitch – which was a huge relief. I know that Ethan must have done something to fix the bench but I was on the edge of my seat, willing them to stand up and not sit back down again. It was all good though, nothing bad happened, but I'm still waiting to hear how he pulled it off.

After the ceremony the bride and groom went off for their photo shoot while the rest of us were ushered into the marquee to start eating and drinking – I don't think we've stopped doing that since.

It's fortunate that the garden is so big here because, I swear, there must be at least one hundred guests – and if there aren't, it certainly feels like there are.

Ethan and I are very much main characters at the wedding – much to Bea's annoyance. She and Dad approached me earlier, said that they had been talking and that, if I needed somewhere to live, that I could move back in with them. They were keen to insist that this would only be temporary, while I got set up somewhere new.

No – obviously. I didn't say that though, because I felt Ethan's reassuring hand on the small of my back, so I just thanked them for the offer. They did wish me happy birthday, as an afterthought, so at least there's that.

The two of us have been mingling with guests all day. It's like people are drawn to us – although they're probably drawn to Ethan specifically, because everyone seems to love him. Well, what's not to love? It's nice though. I've never felt so welcome and accepted with this crowd – almost like we're more palatable as a team, like I'm no longer the odd one out. There's two of us now.

It's been good though – the food was great, all four courses of it, and Ethan liked it too so he didn't need to sneak Tim Tams (although I wouldn't be surprised if he had some in his pocket).

The speeches were... interesting. Well, Beau's especially. He talked about waiting for the right person, about how settling down didn't actually involve settling – it sounded way more sophisticated when he said it, but you take my point. He's not wrong.

He tried to talk to me earlier – to both of us – but it was only polite small talk. I think he's taken the hint, that I'm not interested, after I gave him the cold shoulder yesterday.

I'm not – definitely – and I know that for sure now. I was initially attracted to him, obviously, and it would have been kind of cool to date an earl, but he was only ever a distraction from what I really wanted, that I thought I couldn't have – Ethan.

We're sitting at a large round table – and it is undoubtedly the singles table – not that we care. It's kind of nice, sitting over here, looking at my family all together on the top table. It feels sort of like watching an old TV show, where you feel like you know the characters. They're all in their own little bubble, and I know I'm not really a part of it, but I suddenly don't mind being on the outside looking in. I think sometimes too much emphasis is put on the family you're born into. I think accepting that we might not have much in common, or get on, or be all that close, is okay. Trying to get people's approval – or kicking up a fuss in the opposite direction – isn't the way to go. It's all about being happy with yourself, and not giving a damn what anyone else thinks. Sure, it's nice to have had better interactions with them, but I'm happy with the way things are. I couldn't imagine doing this full-time, that's for sure.

'Would you care to dance, m'lady?' Ethan asks in a silly posh voice, offering me his hand.

'I would love to, m'lord,' I reply.

It's getting dark outside the marquee now. Honestly, the day has passed by so quickly – again, it must go even quicker, if it's your own special day.

The music is soft and romantic – and the lighting above the dance floor is made to complement the music – so we slow dance. I think this might be the first minute we've had alone together all day.

'I figured this might get us some privacy,' he says with a smile.

'It's a good idea,' I reply. 'Unless someone wants to cut in.'

'I'll just say no,' he says, laughing it off. 'You look incredible, by the way. That's a beautiful dress – different from the one you've had hanging in our room all week though. I really liked that one too.'

I can tell by his tone that he liked my original dress more, but he's being very polite in saying he likes both.

'Yeah, well, I thought this one might be more appropriate,' I reply, like it's not a big deal.

'The Lana I met didn't care what anyone thought,' he reminds me.

'The Ethan I met pretended he didn't have a job,' I reply.

'That's not true,' he says with a grin. 'You never asked.'

'So, Redflags is your app?' I confirm.

'Yeah,' he replies.

'You know, I used it to try and find a bad date for the wedding,' I tell him. His eyebrows shoot up. 'It's very good at identifying the freaks.'

'That's not its intended use,' he reminds me with a smile. 'But I'm glad that it works. And I'm definitely going to try to integrate your ideas – your extra safety measures. I think they would be a really good addition.'

'Oh, God, you don't have to do that,' I reply. 'I know they're dumb.'

'They're not dumb ideas at all,' he insists. 'People don't appreciate how hard it is to keep safe. I want to do my bit to help.'

'You're a regular hero, aren't you?' I say with a smile. 'Which brings me on to my next question. The bench. How did you fix it?'

'Well, I wish I could say that I did it with brawn and manliness,' he begins. 'But I didn't. I went around all the local bars until I found a carpenter, with a romantic streak, who wasn't too drunk. That said, he definitely did it for money, not love. There's some sort of old-fashioned technique, of putting them together – he tried to explain but I was just trying to get him in and out as quickly as possible.'

'So, we just need to hope no one has any reason to check the CCTV outside,' I say with a grin.

I feel like we might have actually got away with this one.

'They have no reason to check it,' he says. 'It will probably get overwritten, eventually, but if not, well, I'm sure we'll come up with something between us.'

I can't help myself any longer. I lean in to kiss him, to seal the deal, but he subtly pulls away from me.

'I think it's probably safest we don't do that here,' he tells me with a smile. 'You never know with us – there's still time to ruin the wedding.'

'Oh, okay,' I say, trying to hide how devastated I am. Have I completely misread this?

'Instead, how about you go upstairs, you change into the dress you want to wear, and then you meet me down on the beach,' he suggests.

A smile spreads across my face.

'Okay, sure,' I say, trying to hide how giddy I am, but probably doing a terrible job.

I duck out, as instructed, heading up to our room where I step out of my sophisticated dress and into my trashy one – I mean, I think both are lovely, but you take my point. I check my make-up is perfect (or close, after a warm day), spritz myself with perfume, and then make my way back outside.

I pass the marquee, heading down the garden, and out on to the sand. I've no sooner taken my shoes off, to feel the sand between my toes, when I spot him.

The beach is quiet, between the buzz of the party and the roar of the sea. There's just Ethan, standing there, next to a pop-up table for two. It's covered with candles and there's a white box in the centre.

'What's all this?' I ask him.

He starts singing 'Happy Birthday' to me, as he lifts up the white box to reveal the most delicious-looking chocolate cake.

'Happy birthday,' he says. 'Happy *thirtieth* birthday. I got you a cake.'

I place a hand over my mouth.

'Did you think I was going to let it go by unacknowledged?' he says.

'Everyone else was,' I reply. 'Thank you so, so much. This is so sweet. I don't think I could have asked for anything more perfect.'

I launch into his arms, giving him a big, grateful squeeze.

'Thank you for this, for earlier, for coming – for everything,' I babble at him.

'Have you not realised by now that I would probably do anything for you?' he says, pulling back just enough to look at me. I'm not letting him go though. 'Look, I know you think we're cursed, or that the universe is conspiring against us, but that's just not true,' he tells me. 'And if you really believe it, well, I'm going to have to prove you wrong.'

I would love him to do that, but...

'But we live in different cities,' I remind him. 'It won't be easy.'

'Unless the reason I was back in Leeds was because I was buying an apartment,' he tells me. 'Because I'm moving there, because I want to work more closely on the app, and turn it into something much bigger.'

My heart slams against my chest as I just stare at him. Is he really, really saying what I think he's saying?

'Of course, I'll probably need a local tour guide,' he adds, his tone playful. 'Maybe a lodger, to begin with. Do you know anyone who might want to rent a room from me? No strings attached, of course. Just the usual ones, when someone rents a room – no deposit needed though.'

'I just... are you...?'

'I'm saying there's a single bed with your name on it,' he says with a laugh. 'I know you're in a tough spot, let me help you. Move out when you're back on your feet, or don't, but I want us to be together.'

'We don't have a good track record, when it comes to single beds,' I point out, grinning from ear to ear.

'That's true,' he replies. 'Then I guess I'll have to let you in my bed, occasionally, for safety – if you're good.'

I'm practically laughing now, I'm smiling so widely. I just can't believe it.

'Is this my birthday present?' I ask.

'Yes,' he replies. 'Oh, actually, I have another. I almost forgot. We're stopping off somewhere on the way home.'

'Where?' I ask.

'Paris,' he replies simply. 'It's all booked.'

Oh my God, he's amazing.

'Do you think it's safe for me to kiss you now?' I ask him. 'No tidal waves, wildfires, shark attacks, or fireworks of any description?'

'I'll risk it if you will,' he tells me, moving his face closer to mine.

Screw it.

Our lips meet and it's like everything clicks into place, like a wave is washing over me but it's warmth and relief and genuine, comfortable happiness. And – wait – can I actually hear fireworks? Am I imagining this because the moment is so perfect? No, okay, there are actual fireworks going off, probably from the wedding, but still, the moment really is perfect.

We kiss a little longer before pausing to watch the rest of the fireworks, Ethan's arms still wrapped around me. The big colourful lights pop and crackle in the sky, reflecting so beautifully on the water below.

And... nothing bad happens, not yet at least. Perhaps our luck really is about to change but, if not, I know that with Ethan by my side we can figure anything out.

ACKNOWLEDGEMENTS

Thanks so much to my lovely editor, Megan, to Nia and to everyone else at Boldwood HQ.

Huge thanks to everyone who takes the time to read and review my books – I can't thank you enough for all your lovely messages, it really makes my day.

Thanks to my family for their love and support – to the wonderful Kim and Pino, to the amazing Aud, to James and Joey for being so brilliant, and to Darcy as always for being my bestie.

Finally, thanks to Joe, my husband, for everything he does for me and for always having my back.

ABOUT THE AUTHOR

Portia MacIntosh is the million copy bestselling author of over 20 romantic comedy novels. Whether it's southern Italy or the French alps, Portia's stories are the holiday you're craving, conveniently packed in between the pages. Formerly a journalist, Portia lives with her husband and her dog in Yorkshire.

Sign up to Portia MacIntosh's mailing list for news, competitions and updates on future books.

Visit Portia's website: www.portiamacintosh.com

Follow Portia MacIntosh on social media here:

 facebook.com/portia.macintosh.3

x.com/PortiaMacIntosh

 instagram.com/portiamacintoshauthor

bookbub.com/authors/portia-macintosh

ALSO BY PORTIA MACINTOSH

One Way or Another

If We Ever Meet Again

Bad Bridesmaid

Drive Me Crazy

Truth or Date

It's Not You, It's Them

The Accidental Honeymoon

You Can't Hurry Love

Summer Secrets at the Apple Blossom Deli

Love & Lies at the Village Christmas Shop

The Time of Our Lives

Honeymoon For One

My Great Ex-Scape

Make or Break at the Lighthouse B&B

The Plus One Pact

Stuck On You

Faking It

Life's a Beach

Will They, Won't They?

No Ex Before Marriage

The Meet Cute Method

Single All the Way

Just Date and See

Your Place or Mine?

Better Off Wed

Long Time No Sea

The Faking Game

Trouble in Paradise

Ex in the City

The Suite Life

It's All Sun and Games

You Had Me at Château

Wish You Weren't Here

LOVE NOTES

LOVE IN EVERY CHAPTER

WHERE ALL YOUR ROMANCE
DREAMS COME TRUE!

THE HOME OF BESTSELLING
ROMANCE AND WOMEN'S
FICTION

 WARNING:
MAY CONTAIN SPICE

SIGN UP TO OUR
NEWSLETTER

https://bit.ly/Lovenotesnews

Boldwood

Boldwood Books is an award-winning fiction publishing company seeking out the best stories from around the world.

Find out more at www.boldwoodbooks.com

Join our reader community for brilliant books, competitions and offers!

Follow us
@BoldwoodBooks
@TheBoldBookClub

Sign up to our weekly deals newsletter

https://bit.ly/BoldwoodBNewsletter

Printed in Great Britain
by Amazon

56384826R00165